FALLING IN LOVE IN APPLE VALLEY

"Where I come from, churches are always open to the public," Simon said. "The same is true here in Apple Valley. You can go anytime. Day or night that building will be unlocked."

"Good to know." She settled back against the bench, turned her gaze on Simon. She had the bluest eyes he'd ever seen and the kind of fair complexion he usually associated with redheads. Freckles danced across her cheeks and there was a tiny smear of ice cream at the corner of her lips.

He wiped it away the same way she'd done with Rori, his thumb running along the corner of her mouth. It should have been an innocent gesture, one friend helping out another, the touch there and gone without even a moment of anything else. But something happened when he touched her skin. Not fireworks or sparks. Just . . . heat. The kind he'd tried to avoid the past few years.

Her eyes widened, and he knew she felt it too. Knew he should move his thumb and ease away and pretend things were just the same as they'd been two seconds ago.

Problem was, he'd never been good at pretending . . .

Books by Shirlee McCoy

THE HOUSE ON MAIN STREET

THE COTTAGE ON THE CORNER

THE ORCHARD AT THE EDGE OF TOWN

Published by Kensington Publishing Corporation

THE
ORCHARD AT THE
EDGE OF TOWN

SHIRLEE
McCOY

ZEBRA BOOKS
KENSINGTON PUBLISHING CORP.

http://www.kensingtonbooks.com

ZEBRA BOOKS are published by

Kensington Publishing Corp.
119 West 40th Street
New York, NY 10018

All Kensington titles, imprints and distributed lines are available at special quantity discounts for bulk purchases for sales promotion, premiums, fund-raising, educational or institutional use.

Special book excerpts or customized printings can also be created to fit specific needs. For details, write or phone the office of the Kensington Sales Manager. Attn.: Sales Department. Kensington Publishing Corp., 119 West 40th Street, New York, NY 10018. Phone: 1-800-221-2647.

First Printing: August 2015
ISBN-13: 978-1-4201-3239-7
ISBN-10: 1-4201-3239-3

eISBN-13: 978-1-4201-3240-3
eISBN-10: 1-4201-3240-7

10 9 8 7 6 5 4 3 2 1

Printed in the United States of America

Chapter One

King Henry III gave up the ghost on Monday, September 16th, at 5:55 in the morning. One long puff, one quick choke, a slow roll down a small hill, and he was gone. Just like that.

"Dang it all to Grandma Sapphire's plantation and back!" Apricot Miller dropped her head onto Henry's wrinkled faux leather steering wheel and closed her eyes. She didn't blame the old truck for finally breathing its last. She'd left Los Angeles in a hurry, and she hadn't had time to get the old boy the tune-up he'd needed. To add insult to injury, she'd hooked Henry to the big silver trailer her dad had hauled from Happy Dale, Pennsylvania. A perfect wedding present for his daughter, Hubert had said. There'd been no wedding, but Apricot had taken the gift anyway. She'd needed something to shove all her stuff into, and she'd been in too much of a hurry to rent a moving van.

All Lionel's fault. Two-timing loser that he was.

But she wasn't going to think about that.

Not when Aunt Rose's house was still three miles

down the country road, and not when Apricot was still wearing the giant pink concoction of a wedding dress that she'd spent way too much money on. She'd opposed the dress on principle but had agreed to it in the spirit of harmony.

Harmony?

Ha!

Her almost-mother-in-law didn't have a harmonious bone in her overly Botoxed body.

"What a waste!" She grabbed handfuls of her limp and wrinkled dress and got out of the truck. The road stretched in front and behind. No sign of another vehicle. If she hadn't tossed her cell phone out Henry's window, she'd have been able to call a tow truck. Since she had, she was stuck with the consequences of her decision. Her mother would probably find that amusing. Apricot did not.

She should be a married woman by now. Honeymooning in Aruba, lying on a white-sand beach in the tiny little bikini she'd starved herself to fit into. Instead, she was stuck on the side of a dirt road with nothing but a saggy pink wedding gown and a headache to show for all the months of wedding preparations.

"Stupid!" she hissed, trudging around Henry, her silly stilettos sinking into mud. She kicked them off, letting wet earth squish between her toes. It had rained recently, the air cool and just a little crisp with fall. Not the warmth of Aruba, but Apricot couldn't say she minded it. It wouldn't be long before autumn settled in. According to Rose, Apple Valley, Washington, was beautiful in the fall. Apricot wasn't sure how her aunt could speak with any authority on the subject, seeing as how she'd only ever been in Apple

Valley in August. But that was Rose. She knew a little bit about a lot of things, and she liked to pretend she knew even more.

She also had a good heart, and she had a house right outside of a little town that none of Apricot's LA friends had ever heard of.

Score one for Aunt Rose.

Score one for Apricot, because she might have tossed her phone out the window after Lionel's fifteenth call, but she'd also hooked her bike to the trailer before she'd left LA.

She unlocked it and pulled it off the rack, the old 1940s Schwinn as sturdy as any modern bike, its oversized wicker basket roomy enough to carry groceries from the farmers' market she loved to visit on Saturdays.

Used to love to visit.

Now she planned to spend Saturdays closed away in Rose's house until she decided what she wanted to do with the rest of her life. The life that she'd planned to spend with Lionel.

She climbed onto the bike, bunching the dress up around her thighs, the strap of the dainty little blue purse Lionel's mother had loaned her tossed over her shoulder. The key to Rose's house was inside. Otherwise she might have been tempted to throw the purse into the roadside ditch and leave it there.

If only she could do the same with the past thirty-six hours.

Actually, she'd like to do it with the past five years. Toss them into a ditch, let them be covered by dirt and time until the only reminder that they'd ever been there was a tiny little lump of nothing.

Seeing as how she couldn't do that, she started pedaling, her legs pumping, the poufy skirt shredding as it caught under the wheels and in the spokes of the old bike.

All that money down the drain.

All that time.

All that commitment and trust and faith that things would work out.

Gone!

Just like that.

Hot tears burned behind her eyes, but she'd be darned if she was going to let them fall. Lionel didn't deserve them. What he deserved was to be forgotten, and that was exactly what Apricot intended to do. She also planned to down a quarter-pound burger and an entire batch of homemade fries. Two things that she hadn't eaten since Lionel had moved in three years ago. He believed in organic whole foods. Raw.

Apparently he did not believe in fidelity.

"Better to learn that before the vows than after," she told herself. A magpie screamed a response. Rose would have said it was a sign of trouble. Apricot didn't believe in signs and portents. She believed in hard work and integrity. She believed in doing her best and in treating people with respect. She believed in keeping the peace and compromising.

"And look where that got you," she muttered.

This time, the magpie didn't reply.

She pedaled like mad for ten minutes, then coasted down a small hill, her lungs burning, her ribs chafed from the built-in corset. She couldn't wait to tear the dress off, toss it in the burn pile, and set a match to it.

Couldn't wait to send her family over to the condo to kick Lionel's butt out, either.

Although, knowing them, they'd already been there, and he'd already been kicked to the curb.

She still wasn't going back.

Not for a while.

She needed to regroup, make some decisions about what she wanted to do with the rest of her life. She slowed the bike as she neared Rose's place, cool air bathing her hot cheeks, the soft sounds of country life drifting on the air. Dogs barking. A rooster crowing. Farm machinery humming. Up ahead, an old Greek Revival jutted up from the top of a hill, its white clapboard siding tinged gray with time and neglect. Apricot knew the place almost as well as she knew her little condo in LA. The creaky board at the top of the curved stairs, the giant 1930s stove that took up an entire corner of the kitchen, the drafty windows and ornate fireplace mantel. She'd spent two weeks of every summer there from the time she was seven until she'd gone to college. She hadn't been back since. Obviously, the house was a little worse for wear.

Not surprising. Rose didn't believe in staying anywhere for long. She crisscrossed the United States, meandered up into Canada and down into Mexico, searching for herbs that she could use for the tinctures she sold at farmers' markets and county fairs. As a kid, Apricot had gone with her, helping with the tinctures and oils, selling the wares on Saturday and Sunday mornings. A different town every other week, Rose always cheerful and eager for whatever was around the next curve in the road.

Apricot had been eager for stability, for security, for constancy. She'd wanted college like other people wanted chocolate cake, and when Rose had encouraged her to take everything she'd learned and create her own business, Apricot had taken the concept a step further than her aunt, selling her own tinctures, soaps, and candles online. A business that had been a means to help pay her way through college had morphed into a multimillion-dollar company.

Yeah. A Thyme to Heal was doing just great.

Too bad Apricot's personal life wasn't as successful.

She propped the bike against the porch railing and fished the key out of the purse. She'd barely touched the knob when the door swung in, creaking on old hinges and opening into a wide foyer. Apricot had expected the interior to be as run-down as the exterior, but the front hall smelled like floor polish and beeswax, the hand-carved wood railing gleaming.

Sunlight filtered through white sheers that hung from the living room windows, gleaming on a floor that had been shined to a high polish. The couch and love seat had been covered with crisp white sheets, not a speck of dirt or dust on either of them. She walked to the fireplace mantel and swiped her finger over the mahogany. Clean.

Maybe Rose had hired someone to take care of the property when she wasn't in town, but that didn't seem like a Rose kind of thing to do. Apricot loved her aunt, but like the rest of the family, Rose didn't like rules, didn't want restrictions. She enjoyed doing what she wanted to do, the way she wanted to do it. Responsibility didn't figure into that.

Someone had been taking care of the property, though.

The pocket doors that led into the dining room were open, and Apricot could see out the large windows that looked into the backyard and the orchard beyond.

She stepped into the kitchen, her tattered dress swishing on the old black-and-white tile floor. A rotary phone hung on the wall and she grabbed it, the springy chord keeping her close to the wall.

"Please, just work," she muttered, holding the receiver to her ear.

Yes! Dial tone!

Score two for Aunt Rose.

Apricot was in the middle of a conversation with a towing company when a huge green tractor pulled around the side of the house. She couldn't make out the features of the man driving it, but she figured he was the guy Rose rented the back field to. She could just see it through the gnarled orchard trees, tall cornstalks and a field of wheat that spread up the side of a distant hill. The driver didn't seem to be heading to the field, though. As a matter of fact, he seemed to be pulling his tractor right up to the back door.

She said a quick good-bye to the towing company, nearly tossed the receiver back onto the cradle, and ran outside.

No porch or deck. Just three steps to the lawn. She ran down them, because she was sure the guy was about to barrel straight into the back of the house.

"Hey!" she called, holding up a hand as if that could stop the oncoming tractor. "What are you doing?! Stop!"

The tractor stopped, and she was just at the point

of feeling relief when she saw the shotgun. The driver lifted it, aiming somewhere in the region of her heart.

"Don't you take another step, little missy."

"What are you—"

"No talking either," he snapped.

"But—"

"You got cotton in your ears?"

She wasn't sure if she was supposed to answer or not, so she pressed her lips together and took a tiny step back.

"I said, don't move!" He climbed off the tractor, the shotgun never wavering, his bald head shining in the morning light.

About five-ten. Muscular. Maybe 160 pounds. Gray beard and time-worn face. Mean black eyes.

She filed the details away for the police.

If she lived long enough to call them.

She took another step back.

"Sit!" He jabbed the gun toward her, and she dropped onto a step, the poufy, too-expensive dress spreading out around her. It wouldn't look so hot stained with blood. She tried not to think about that, because it would be a total comedic tragedy if she were to be killed in the wedding dress that hadn't even made it down the aisle.

She'd end up being one of those ghost stories. The kind that kids told late at night while they were sitting around campfires. The jilted bride who'd run from the church and straight into the sites of a crazed gunman.

She eyed the gunman, looking for some sign of weakness. Did he have a daughter that she could channel? A wife who would be disappointed if he turned into a cold-blooded killer? He didn't look down on his luck. Not with the fancy tractor he was driving, but maybe he was in this for cash. A drug habit that no one knew about?

"I don't have any money on me, but if—"

"It's pretty dang obvious that you're broke, lady."

"Broke? No. Actually, I'm not. I have money, and I can get you some, but—"

"I don't want your money," he growled.

"What do you want then?" *Stop*, her brain screamed, but her mouth just kept right on moving. "To scare the bejesus out of unsuspecting women?"

"What I want"—he moved so close the gun nearly touched her nose—"is to make sure that squatters don't get too comfortable in Ms. Rose's house."

"Rose is—"

"I told you—no talking!" the man snapped, the barrel of the shotgun bouncing up and then down before settling about a nano-inch from Apricot's temple.

She really didn't want to die in her aunt's backyard, so she shut her mouth and waited. A magpie landed on the rickety white fence that separated the yard from the orchard. She was pretty sure it was the magpie who'd screamed at her while she pedaled her way along the dirt road. Another joined it.

Double trouble, she could almost hear Rose whisper.

"Here they come," the man with the gun said cryptically.

"Who?" she asked, her voice shaking. She sounded like she was going to cry. She felt like she was going to cry. As a matter of fact, tears slipped down her cheeks. She was too afraid to move so she didn't wipe them away, but, man, if she didn't want to! She hated crying. She especially hated it because she wasn't crying about the gun or the man or even the magpies. She was crying because she was supposed to be in Aruba. On the beach. In the bikini she'd starved herself—starved herself!—to fit into.

A tiny little sob escaped and the man frowned.

"The police are coming, that's who, and don't think those tears are going to sway me from my course."

"What course?" she asked through another sob.

"Turning you in for trespassing, that's what course!" He lowered the shotgun, dug into his pocket, and pulled out a snow-white handkerchief.

"Take this!" He thrust it into her hand, the gun sort of forgotten and hanging loosely by his side.

She could have made a run for it, but if the police were on their way, there didn't seem to be any need. They'd corral the crazy guy and cart him off to wherever local crazies needed to go, and she could get back to the business of hiding out in Rose's house. Hopefully she'd managed to grab some useful supplies during her half-hour packing spree. Hard to know since Lionel had been crying and sobbing and apologizing for getting drunk as a skunk and passing out at his best man's house and waking up two hours after the wedding was supposed to begin.

Of course, she knew where he'd really been.

She hadn't cared enough to tell him.

She sniffed. The gunman frowned.

"I gave you a hankie, didn't I?"

She supposed that meant he wanted her to use it.

Since he was the one with the shotgun, she dabbed at her nose and her eyes.

A car door slammed, and the guy perked up, his beady black eyes gleaming with a little too much delight. "Told you they were coming."

She nodded, because she didn't think he expected a response.

He cocked his head to the side, listening, she supposed, to the crunch of feet on grass. Soon, a police officer or two would round the corner of the house and see her sitting in her ripped-up wedding gown, her nose running, her eyes weeping.

She pulled her knees up to her chest and closed her eyes. Maybe if she tried hard enough, she could just disappear.

"Dusty?!" a man called.

"Back here, Simon!" the gunman, whose name was apparently Dusty, responded.

"Who'd you find this time?"

"Some homeless lady. Riding through town on her bike, looking for a free place to stay."

"I am not—" she muttered without opening her eyes.

"How often do homeless people ride through these parts, Dusty?" Feet crunched on grass and the air beside Apricot stirred. "Ma'am? Are you okay?"

"Fine," she mumbled against her dress.

"You sure?"

"Yes." She raised her head, looked into the greenest eyes she'd ever seen. They weren't gray green like Hubert's. They weren't ocean green like her brother Sage's. They were the deep, dark green of the Pennsylvania forest she'd grown up in.

"So," he said with a smile, "you're Rosa's niece?"

"It's Rose, and yes. I'm Anna Miller." She scrambled to her feet, brushing pieces of grass from her dress. As if that were going to help. "How did you know?"

"Rumor spreads fast in Apple Valley." He offered a hand. "Rose called the electric company to make sure everything was turned on when you arrived. Said something to Agnes Anderson about a pretty brunette in an ugly pink dress."

"This dress is not ugly." She swiped at a smudge of grease that must have been from the bike spokes. "Not much, anyway."

He laughed. "Well, it was probably pretty enough before you rolled around in the dirt. Is the electricity on in the house?"

"Yes," she responded, relieved that he didn't seem to be in a hurry to cart her off to jail. The past twenty-four hours had been sucky enough without adding that into it.

"Good. Hopefully the old boiler is working too. It's going to be cold tonight, and I don't think the fire-places have been cleaned out since old man Shaffer passed away."

"Old man Shaffer?" Dusty frowned. "Is that any way to refer to the deceased?"

"I guess that depends on how the deceased was referred to in life. Seeing as how everyone in town calls him old man Shaffer, I just assumed that's what he went by." The officer kept his tone light and friendly, but his gaze dropped to Dusty's shotgun. "I'm not too happy that you brought that over here, Dusty. How about you keep it at home next time? Otherwise, I might have to run you in."

"Run me in for what?" Dusty demanded. "It's not even loaded."

"This isn't your property, and you haven't been given the task of overseeing it. Until you have, you don't have the legal right to—"

"Bah!" Dusty spat. "I'm doing my civic duty protecting my neighbor's property. There's no crime against that."

He stomped to his tractor and drove away, heading toward the distant cornfield.

Deputy Sheriff Simon Baylor watched him go, calculating in his head just how long he had before his boss called. Five minutes? Ten? It shouldn't take longer than that for Dusty to call the sheriff.

"Well, thanks for helping me clear that up," the woman said with a smile that didn't make it to her eyes. She was, as his twin daughters would have been quick to point out, a mess. Mascara smeared under both eyes, hair hanging limp from some sparkly doodad, pink dress a tattered mess of shredded fabric, she looked like she'd been thrown from a horse and dragged through a field.

Since Simon was at the end of his shift, and he had to get home before his sister-in-law left for work, he would have been happy to let the woman head right on into Rose Devereux's house.

Unfortunately, Rose had been very specific when she'd called the electric company. Agnes Anderson took the call, and she'd been thorough when she'd clued Simon's sister-in-law in on what had been said. Daisy, of course, had spent most of the evening speculating about Apricot Miller's reasons for leaving LA dressed in an ugly pink wedding gown.

Apricot.

Not Anna.

The truck that had been abandoned on the side of the road, the one with the silver Airstream hooked to the back, had been registered to Apricot S. Miller.

Simon wouldn't be doing his job if he didn't make sure Anna and Apricot were one and the same.

He followed her into the kitchen, ignoring the frown she shot over her shoulder.

"The lights really are on," she said, flipping the switch on and off to prove it. "I'll check out the boiler later."

"Sounds good." He leaned his hip against the butcher-block counter, waiting for her to ask why he wasn't leaving.

She opened the fridge, then a few of the cupboards. The way she was going, she'd search the entire kitchen before she said another word to him.

Eight years ago, he could have waited all day and probably would have.

Now he had the girls and a life that wasn't completely caught up in work.

"So, Anna," he spoke into the silence, "I'm curious."

"About?" She turned to face him, her gaze direct. If she were hiding anything, she wasn't showing it.

"Rose Devereux didn't mention anything about a woman named Anna coming for a visit."

She sighed. "She wouldn't. Anna isn't my given name. It's my professional name. If I can find my wallet, I've got some business cards."

She started digging through the purse, but the thing was so small, he thought she'd have found the wallet by now if it were there.

He took it from her hand, set it on the counter. "I think we both know this little tiny bag doesn't have a wallet in it. So, how about you just explain what kind of work you do that you need a professional name?"

She blinked, a smile slowly curving the edges of

her mouth. A real smile this time, it made her eyes sparkle and showed off a dimple in her right cheek. "Good grief! You don't think I'm a . . ." She snorted and shook her head. "I own a nursery in LA. I got tired of explaining my given name to every Tom, Dick, and Harry who met me, so I decided to go by Anna."

"And your given name is?"

"Apricot. Just like Aunt Rose said. If you want the whole legal mess, it's Apricot Sunshine Devereux-Miller."

He did not laugh, but God! He wanted to.

"Apricot Sunshine, huh? Your parents—"

"Were hippies, are hippies, will always *be* hippies. I lived in a commune for the first sixteen years of my life." She smiled again. "And having to give that explanation thousands of times is exactly why I go by Anna. Now, if I could just find my wallet, I could prove my identity, and you could be on your way, Officer . . . ?"

"Deputy Simon Baylor." He offered his hand, and she gave it a firm, quick shake. No nonsense. That was the impression she was giving off.

Her big pink dress was giving off another impression altogether. It was saying froufrou and fluffy, a little flighty and scattered.

"Right. Deputy Baylor. I do have an ID and I do have business cards. They're probably in my truck. I'd volunteer to go get them, but I'm sure you have better things to do with your time than wait for me to do that."

He did have things to do. Daisy worked at the library, and if he knew one thing about his sister-in-law, it was that she liked to be the first in every morning.

When he worked graveyard, she spent the night with the twins so he wouldn't have to hire a babysitter, but she was always dressed and ready for work when he arrived home. He tried to be respectful of her time, leave work as soon as the shift was over, get home well before she actually needed to be at work, but right then, he really was curious about Apricot Sunshine Devereux-Miller, and he wasn't in all that much of a hurry to leave. "I've got time."

"Perfect," she responded. "I'll just hop back on my bike—"

"The Schwinn that's sitting on the porch?" *The one that looks like it should be ridden by Dorothy or by the Wicked Witch of the West?*

"That would be the one," she responded. "Unless you want to offer me a ride. In which case, I could avoid the humiliation of pedaling a 1940s Schwinn in this 1980s monstrosity of a dress."

"I'll drive you to your truck." The girls wouldn't be awake for another twenty minutes, and Daisy didn't have to be at the library until eight thirty. He could give Apricot a ride, check her ID, make sure everything she said was kosher. Give himself a little more to smile about, because he *was* smiling. The pink dress, the tumbling-over hair, the image of Apricot pedaling along the dirt road was probably the most amusement he'd had in a good long while.

The fact was, life had been one long day of routine after another for so many years that he'd forgotten what it was like to live any other way. Breakfast with the girls, walks to the bus stop, drives to the school and the doctor and dance. He didn't mind it, but there were moments lately when he'd felt an itch to go back to what life had been before Megan. Back to his job with Houston PD. Back to city living.

Of course, then he'd look at the girls scrambling to get off the bus at the end of the day and he'd realize exactly what he'd gotten in exchange for what he'd given up.

It was a good trade. Just not the one that he'd expected to make.

That was the thing about life, though. It was never what was expected or planned. Never what was imagined during the teenage years when every possibility seemed there for the taking. It had taken Simon a heck of a long time to accept that. He finally had, and he wasn't going to screw it all up by heading back to Houston with the twins.

But, man! Sometimes he wanted to.

"A ride would be great. If you're sure that I'm not putting you out," Anna, aka Apricot Sunshine, murmured, but she'd already grabbed her little blue purse and was bustling toward the door, her torn-up skirt brushing along the floor, her dark brown hair flopping halfway down her back.

She'd probably looked cute in the dress a dozen hours and a thousand miles ago. She looked pretty damn cute now.

The fact that he was noticing meant that she was trouble, and Simon had had just about enough of that to last him a lifetime. Megan had been a great lady—funny, smart, even a little intoxicating. He'd fallen hard and fast for her, and he didn't regret it. What he regretted was that he hadn't seen the truth, hadn't realized that there'd been a boatload of crap hidden under her easy smiles. Maybe if he'd taken the time to look, he'd have realized that, before it was too late. Maybe if he'd paid more attention to the always-filled prescription bottle on the windowsill, he could have saved her from herself.

He lived with that guilt every day.

He didn't need more of it.

So, he did his job, he took care of the girls, avoided any relationship that might lead him deeper than he wanted to go.

Yeah. Apricot Sunshine was trouble, and the best thing a guy like him could do with trouble was walk away.

That's exactly what he planned to do. He'd give her a ride to the truck, give her a ride back, and be on his way.

Assuming she really *was* Apricot Miller.

If she wasn't, all bets were off. He'd cart her butt to jail and let the sheriff deal with the rest.

Chapter Two

Apricot found the wallet under Henry's bucket seat.

Her ID wasn't in it. Of course.

Because she'd shoved it in the carry-on case she'd planned to take to Aruba. The pretty flowered one that her mother had lent her because she hadn't thought Apricot's plain black one was fancy enough for a honeymoon.

Poor Lilac. She'd been devastated when Apricot had finally walked out of the church. Two hours and fifteen minutes after the ceremony was supposed to begin, five minutes after Lionel arrived, his hair mussed, a dozen excuses on his lips, Lilac had followed Apricot out the side door of the church, begging her to reconsider.

Men cheat, she'd said. *Every last one of them, so why let that be the reason to end a beautiful relationship?*

Because it wasn't really all that beautiful.

That's what Apricot had wanted to say, because her relationship with Lionel *hadn't* been beautiful or even all that compelling.

It had been nice, easy. Convenient.

A lot like the comforter Grandma Sapphire had made for Apricot's fifth birthday. Nothing fancy. Nothing that people would ooh and aah over, but it had kept her warm in the winter, and she'd always reached for it on chilly nights.

She didn't suppose that was the best way to describe a relationship, but it was what it was, and she was sure Lionel had felt the same way. If he hadn't, he'd have been at the church instead of lying in bed with Apricot's personal assistant.

Lilac might have been able to forgive that, but Apricot couldn't. She didn't want to be with a man who didn't want to be with her more than he wanted to be with someone else.

She wasn't her mother, her aunt, her sister Plum. She was herself, and she liked rules and order. She liked commitment, constancy, and, yes, she liked monogamy. Was that a crime? Was it too much to ask of a relationship?

She backed out of Henry, nearly bumping the good-looking deputy who'd been watching her like a hawk. "It's in my carry-on case. In the trailer."

"Is that so?" he asked, a hint of a Southern drawl in his voice. He hadn't grown up in Apple Valley. She'd have been willing to lay odds on that.

"Yes," she responded, grabbing fistfuls of organza and marching to the back of the Airstream. Sixty years old, it looked brand-new. Hubert took a lot of pride in keeping his vehicles that way. He wasn't quite as good at keeping up on the house. Good thing he'd married Jasmine. His third wife was young, energetic, and willing to take on the jobs Hubert wouldn't.

She'd told Apricot all about it at the rehearsal dinner Friday night. Lionel had managed to be there. He'd managed to make nice with her family, act interested in her. He'd told her how beautiful she looked in the candlelight. Only the candlelight had been as fake as his affection, the tiny little electric lights his mother's idea of ambience.

Apricot would have preferred the real deal. Candle- and relationship-wise.

"Taking a plane trip somewhere?" Deputy Baylor stood beside her as she dragged the carry-on case from the trailer. He smelled like the outdoors. Clean and fresh with just a hint of something darkly masculine. She might have been intrigued if she weren't completely done with men.

"Was going to take a plane trip." She unzipped the front compartment.

"To?"

"Aruba." She pulled out her passport and driver's license. Thank God. She really didn't want to spend time in the local jail. She especially didn't want to have to call her family to come bail her out. She loved every one of them, but they were bigger than life.

At least, bigger than *her* life.

She might own a multimillion-dollar business, but she enjoyed peace and quiet. She liked fireplaces and good books, hot chocolate and strolls at midnight.

She did not like chaos and noise and . . . well . . . everything her family stood for—free love, self-expression above personal responsibility, pursuit of happiness rather than financial stability.

"Is that your license?" Deputy Baylor prodded, and she realized she'd been standing there in that blasted dress, staring at her driver's license like it could reveal the secret to self-actualization.

"Yes. Here you are." She held it out to him, blinking as she looked into those forest-green eyes. He had long, black lashes that any woman would have coveted, but somehow they didn't add any femininity to his craggy face.

No. Not craggy.

Lived-in. Fine lines near the corners of his eyes. Deep creases on either side of his mouth. He didn't look much older than her. Maybe thirty-five, but he looked like he'd lived through some tough times.

Deputy Baylor glanced at her license. He didn't mention that she'd been a bleached blonde when the photo was taken. Lionel's stupid idea. Now that she was thinking about it, he'd had a lot of stupid ideas.

"No-good, two-timing son of a chimney sweep," she muttered under her breath.

The deputy looked up, a puzzled smile easing the hard lines of his face. "Did you just call me a two-timing son of a chimney sweep?"

"Not you. My ex. He arrived at the wedding late. Not a good beginning to forever."

"You were married?"

"Almost." She lifted the poufy skirt of her dress. "Isn't that obvious?"

"I'm not much in the know about women's wedding fashion," he responded, that hint of the Deep South even more pronounced. "I'm not much in the know about women's fashion in general."

"You're not from around here," she said. It sounded like a pickup line, and she wanted to pull the dang words right back into her mouth as soon as she said them.

"Neither are you," he replied, without even a hint of flirtation in his voice. That was exactly how she wanted it, but for some reason her cheeks were hot and she couldn't quite meet his eyes as he handed the license back. "You're all set, Apricot. You've got a tow truck coming for this beast?" He patted the side of the Airstream.

"It should be here any minute."

"Who'd you call?"

"Apple Valley Towing."

"Willie is pretty quick, but if Stanley got sent on the call, it might be a while."

"I don't mind waiting." She had nowhere to go, nothing to do. She'd planned for a two-week honeymoon. The nursery managers were taking care of things in LA. Her online business was run by a couple dozen employees. She wasn't needed, and that should have felt good.

It seemed a little sad, though. Like maybe it would have been nice to be needed, to know that she had to stick around town to keep things going the way they were supposed to. She'd spent twelve years building A Thyme to Heal into what it was. Her hands-on approach to the business had changed as the company had grown. Now she spent more time going over accounts than she did creating new products. The whole thing just kind of floated on its own, the products as good today as they'd been over a decade ago. Probably even better, because the market for holistic health products had expanded.

Yep. She was free and clear of obligations and responsibilities for the next fourteen days. That gave her plenty of time to think about the direction she wanted the business to take. The direction she wanted her life to take.

Sans Lionel.

Sans the kids they'd planned to have, the house they'd planned to buy, the yard, the herb garden, and the vegetable garden. The dog.

She blinked back hot tears.

She hated crying almost as much as she hated failing, and she'd failed big-time when it came to relationships.

"I'll give you a ride back to Rose's place." Deputy Baylor touched her shoulder. He could probably see the tears in her eyes, but she didn't want his pity or sympathy. She just wanted to lock herself in Rose's house for a few days. Alone.

Because alone was where she'd spent most of her childhood, hiding out at the little schoolhouse her parents had built for the community, because it was the one place none of her siblings ever seemed to want to be. "It's okay. I can walk back."

"I'm sure you can, but should you? We're talking three miles, and you're in bare feet."

"I spent the first sixteen years of my life barefoot. I think I'll survive."

"I'll walk with you. Just to make sure you do." He stepped into place beside her. He had a confident air, an easy smile. The kind of looks that took a second glance to really appreciate. She didn't plan on giving him a second glance, because she was done with men. Forever.

"Fine. You can give me a ride," she said because she didn't want him to have to walk her to the house and then return for his car. She also didn't want to spend a whole lot of time with him or any other man.

Heck, she didn't want to spend time with anyone!

"Relax, Apricot. It's just a ride to Rose's house. Not a ride to jail, and the only one who lives close enough to see you in my car is Dusty. Since he's out in the fields, I think your reputation is safe." He opened the cruiser door, and she slid into the passenger seat. Obviously, he thought she was worried about being seen in a police car. She'd been seen in a lot worse places, but she didn't think he needed to know about that.

"It's Anna," she told him as he slid into the driver seat. "Not Apricot."

"Your friends call you Anna?"

Only her LA friends. Her Pennsylvania friends called her Apricot. But then, they were the people she'd grown up with, and they'd only ever known her as Apricot.

"Most of them." She answered truthfully, but the truth wasn't quite as easy as she wanted it to be. Life had gotten busy, she'd gotten caught up in her work, in the need to create a successful, structured life. She'd gotten caught up in Lionel too. He'd been handsome and charming, and when she'd been with him, it hadn't seemed like she'd needed anyone else. Obviously she had, because here she was, sitting in a police cruiser, in a town she barely knew. Alone, because she'd spent the past five years being part of a couple that spent most of its time with Lionel's friends. She'd made some time for her friends—the ones from college and work—but obviously not enough time. Seeing as how the only one who'd tried to call her during her twenty-four-hour drive from LA had been Lionel.

"Bastard," she whispered.

Simon heard Apricot clear as day, and he found himself smiling again.

"I see we've moved up in our insults," he remarked as he pulled up to the old Shaffer place. It needed painting, the old clapboard siding dingy gray rather than the bright white it had been when he'd moved to town six years ago. Not surprising. Rose visited the property once a year, stayed for a couple of weeks and then took off. As far as he could tell, she didn't put any time or attention into the property. He'd heard murmurs about irresponsibility and selfishness. The place was, according to the town historical society, one of the oldest in Apple Valley, and it needed to be cared for and cherished.

Seeing as how Rose owned the property, paid her taxes on time, and didn't cause any kind of trouble, it was her choice whether or not she put money into the old house. That was Sheriff Cade Cunningham's official comment when townsfolk filed complaints. Simon knew his boss felt differently. He'd heard him discussing the Shaffer place with his grandmother. Ida Cunningham was president of the town historical society, mayor of Apple Valley for more years than Simon had been in town. She knew every home, every family, every juicy piece of gossip. She also knew how to keep her mouth shut. She had the town's heart for good reason. And Simon's too, because she'd taken his family under her wing when they'd arrived in town—two toddlers and an exhausted, widowed Houston police officer.

"Sorry," Apricot murmured as she opened the car door and stumbled out, pink gauzy material fluttering in the late summer breeze. "He's becoming more a loser with every passing minute."

"He stood you up at the altar?" he asked, even though he was pretty sure he should keep his nose out of it.

"He was *late* to the altar, and I decided I didn't need to spend my life waiting for his sorry behind to show up at important functions," she responded. "There's more, of course. I'm sure Rose has told someone who will tell someone who will tell you, so I'll just leave the rest for rumor-mill. Thanks for the ride, Deputy."

She slammed the car door and flounced away. At least, that's what it looked like she was doing, her skirts bouncing, her hair bouncing, her nose straight up in the air. She might have been dumped or betrayed or stood up, but she wasn't going to let it get her down.

At least not when anyone was looking.

Simon's sister-in-law, Daisy, could learn a little from Apricot. She'd spent the past six months alternating between silent bitterness and loud wailing. At first, Simon had tried to be sympathetic. After a while, though, he'd wanted to give her a little shake and tell her to get over it and move on. Then again, as far as he was concerned, Dennis walking out on Daisy was the best thing that had ever happened to his sister-in-law.

And probably the worst thing that had happened to Simon since he'd moved to town. Without Dennis to take up her time and attention, Daisy seemed to be spending more time over at Simon's place, finding excuses to stay the night, to stay for breakfast, to have lunch with him when he had the day off.

He frowned as Apricot walked up the porch steps.

Yeah. Maybe it wouldn't be such a bad thing if he was a few minutes late getting home. Daisy would feel compelled to leave and . . .

Apricot paused, her gaze jumping to some point beyond Simon's car. She cocked her head to the side, tucked a strand of hair behind her ear. Tried to fix the not-even-close-to-fixable skirt of her dress.

Right about that time, he heard the car chugging up behind him. He glanced in his rearview mirror, every muscle in his body going tight as he saw Daisy's brand-new Ford barreling up the driveway. She stopped behind the cruiser, jumped out of the car, her long jean skirt a little tight in the hips, her brown sweater decorated with fall leaves. Unlike her sister, she didn't carry herself with confidence. She moved apologetically, as if she were constantly afraid of reprimand. That had only gotten worse since the "incident." That's what the blue-haired lady at the diner called it. Daisy called it an unfortunate lapse in judgment.

As for Simon, he'd kept quiet on the issue. Gossip spread like wildfire in Apple Valley, and if he'd said one word about his sister-in-law's . . . lapse in sanity, she'd have known about it before the sun set. Known about it and been bitterly silent about his betrayal.

Because that was how Daisy responded to every slight.

In his opinion, she needed to start opening her

mouth and telling people what she really thought. Then maybe she wouldn't have to stoop to breaking and entering to get the things she wanted in life.

"Hey, Daisy," he said, climbing out of the car and greeting her with a smile he didn't feel. He appreciated everything she did for him, appreciated that she loved the girls like they were her own, that she stayed late at night when he had to work and was there early in the morning if he couldn't be.

But, Daisy? She was difficult.

"What's up?" he asked as she approached, her hair scraped so tightly away from her face that her skin stretched taut over her cheekbones and her eyes seemed elongated.

He wanted to tell her to loosen up, let her hair down, relax a little. As much as he thought her ex was a bastard for dumping her and eloping with a woman he'd met online, Simon couldn't imagine any man wanting to spend his life with an overly uptight and way-too-sensitive woman like Daisy.

"What is up, Simon," she responded, her gaze skittering to Apricot and then darting back to him, "is the time. I have to be at the library—"

"At eight thirty. You have an hour and forty minutes."

"An hour and twenty-seven," she corrected him in typical Daisy fashion. "But I like to be there an hour before then. You know that." She scowled, her mud-brown eyes and mousy-brown hair so different from Megan's dark chocolate eyes and soft golden hair that he sometimes wondered if they were actually related at all.

"Yeah. I do." He glanced in the backseat of Daisy's Ford. No tousled blond heads, so she hadn't brought

the twins along. He wasn't worried about that. Daisy
was a little nuts and a lot emotional, but she was
cautious to the point of being overprotective with the
girls. "Where are the twins?"

"Still sleeping. I called next door and asked Mrs.
Jordan to stay with them. I normally wouldn't bother
her, but I heard the call about a trespasser on the
scanner." She leveled a hard gaze on Apricot, who still
stood on the porch.

"My aunt owns the house. I'm here for a visit," she
offered with a smile.

Daisy stared at her.

"What I'm saying," Apricot continued, "is that I'm
not trespassing. I have permission to be here."

"I know what you're saying. I may live in a small
town, but I'm not a country bumpkin," Daisy snapped.

"I don't believe I said you were," Apricot responded.
She didn't seem ruffled by Daisy's abrasiveness. Simon,
on the other hand, was losing patience.

"Daisy," he cut in. "I've told you before, you can't
respond to the scene every time you hear something
on the police scanner."

"I didn't come because of the scanner. I came because I wanted to tell you that I was heading to work."
She scuffed her high-heeled foot on the—

High heel?

Simon took another look.

Yes. Definitely heels. Black, shiny ones with little
bows on the front.

Maybe she had another guy on the horizon.

Dear God, he hoped so!

"I thought you'd want to know," she continued,
meeting his eyes. Her lashes looked darker than usual,

a little thicker, and he was pretty sure there were little specks of black on one of her eyelids.

Mascara?

Another good sign, and he could feel the "Hallelujah Chorus" welling up from somewhere deep inside.

"I appreciate that, but I know what time you have to be at work, Daisy, and I know what time you leave the house," he responded gently, because as much as Daisy drove him crazy, he really didn't want to hurt her feelings.

"But—"

"You know what you need?" Apricot interrupted, crossing the distance between them, her dress swishing along the ground. She took Daisy's hand, completely ignoring her frown. "You need a nice strong cup of chamomile tea. It's very soothing."

"Tea? I like coffee," Daisy protested.

"I'm sure you do, but it's not the thing. Not with your temperament."

"What's that supposed to mean?" Daisy huffed.

"Nothing that should ruffle your feathers. Just that we all have certain natural tendencies. We need to feed our bodies according to those. Not according to our preferences. Take me, for example. I love a good cup of coffee, but I drink one cup and I can't sleep, because I already have a tendency toward insomnia. People who worry usually do."

"What does that have to do—"

"Chamomile soothes the nervous system," Apricot continued as if Daisy hadn't spoken. "And you and I both need that. Not the stimulant that coffee provides. Plus, it's also good for the complexion," Apricot continued.

"It is?" Daisy patted her cheek as Apricot hauled her toward the house.

Simon was pretty sure he'd been completely forgotten by both women. He could have gotten in his car and driven away, but there was something fascinating about the way Apricot was weaseling her way into Daisy's good graces. Thirty seconds ago, he'd have said it couldn't be done.

Now they looked like best buddies, holding hands as they walked up the porch stairs.

"It is. Drink a couple of cups a day, and your dewy fresh complexion is going to be the talk of the town. And with that light brown hair and those big brown eyes . . ." She shook her head and whistled softy. "Well, let's just say you're going to have men drooling and women begging for your secret."

"I don't think that will—"

"Mark my words, sister. It works. And, fortunately, I always pack a few bags of organic chamomile tea in my purse. I've got some inside. You have time before work, don't you?"

"Well, I . . ." Daisy touched her cheek again. "I suppose I do."

"Wonderful. In we go." Apricot opened the front door, gesturing for Daisy to walk in ahead of her. To Simon's surprise, his sister-in-law went. Since she tended toward superstition, and the Schaffer house was reportedly haunted by old man Schaffer's irritated ghost, he wouldn't have thought she had the guts to cross the threshold.

But there she went, right into the house, heading for whatever herbal tea concoction she was about to be served.

Apricot glanced his way, winked, and disappeared inside.

Simon stood right where he was, looking at the closed door and the old house. The place had been empty for most of the time he'd been in town, but the blue-haired ladies talked about better times. Times when Schaffer's wife, Abigail, hung flower baskets from the front porch and planted a garden in the backyard. The way Simon heard it, her tomatoes were the best in town, and the pickles she made from her cucumbers won a blue ribbon at the county fair every year for six years running.

He wasn't sure how much of the legend of Abigail Shaffer was true, but rumors of old man Shaffer's grumpier personality seemed to be. Even Cade Cunningham, sheriff of the town and Simon's boss, talked about the guy. He'd kept his house and land pristine, had the best apple orchard in eastern Washington, and had shipped and sold those apples all over the inland Northwest. He'd made a boatload of money in his lifetime, but no one knew what he'd done with it. Aside from keeping up on the property, he'd lived a miserly kind of life. After Abigail's death, he'd become even more frugal. He'd died alone in his house one day in September. His body had been discovered when Dusty called the sheriff and asked for a well-check. He hadn't seen Shaffer for a couple of days, and the body was . . . as Cade had put it . . . noticeably decayed.

Of course, that was before Cade's time as sheriff, and he admitted the rumors could have been exaggerated. One way or another, those rumors had set the stage for every ghost story told around every campfire built by every teen in Apple Valley.

Which reminded Simon—he had a workday planned with the local boys' club for later in the week. He had to coral the teens and get them to clean the fairgrounds.

Or, at least, what Apple Valley called fairgrounds.

Really, it was nothing more than a huge dirt parking lot and several acres of grass. In another couple of weeks, it would look like a lot more— apple-pie booths, apple-cobbler booths, apple crafts, apple everything. The girls were looking forward to it, but Simon found the whole thing a little sickeningly sweet for his taste.

He was more the rodeo type.

But there weren't any of those to be had in Apple Valley.

He climbed into the cruiser, glancing at the Shaffer house one last time as he backed around Daisy's car.

Yeah. The place looked neglected, but he had a feeling it wouldn't look that way for long. Not if Apricot had anything to do with it.

Dusty wasn't going to be pleased. But then, he never was.

As for the rest of Apple Valley, Simon thought the good citizens of the little town were about to be turned on their heads by a woman with a butt-ugly pink wedding dress and a quirky name.

Chapter Three

Apricot knew she had one last bag of chamomile tea in her almost-mother-in-law's purse. She also had three ginseng tea bags and a small bottle of Forget the Sheep—an herbal sleep aid made with valerian and hops flowers. She thought that Daisy could use a couple of drops in her tea, but she'd refrain from slipping them into it. It wasn't cool to give someone medicine without full consent. Even if the medicine was herbal and absolutely necessary.

She glanced at Daisy.

The woman had hair scraped back so hard that her eyes were tearing, little bits of mascara dotting her lids and starting to smudge in the dark circles under her eyes.

Poor thing.

She really did need to relax.

Apricot couldn't find a teapot, so she used an old pot someone had stored inside the oven.

"What are you doing?" Daisy asked suspiciously as Apricot ran water into the pot.

"Boiling some water. You can't have tea without it."

"Most people use a microwave."

"Not where I come from." She set the pot on the stove, found some matches in a little tin on the windowsill above the sink. It didn't take long for her to turn on the gas, get the pilot lit, and start the pot boiling. From the look on Daisy's face, it had taken just about an eon. "Why don't you sit down for a few minutes, Daisy? You look like you could use some rest."

Actually, she looked like she could use some fun, but far be it from Apricot to point that out. Especially when she was standing in her wrecked wedding gown, dirty bare feet leaving marks all over the kitchen floor. Obviously, she wasn't having all that much fun either.

"Rest? I have to be at the library in—" Daisy glanced around the room as if looking for a clock. Apricot could have told her she was searching in vain. Rose didn't believe in clocks, deadlines, or sticking to a schedule.

Daisy must have figured it out herself. She dragged a cell phone from a pocket in her oversized sweater and glanced at it. "In a half hour. It's a seven-minute drive from here."

"You timed it?"

"Of course I did," Daisy snapped. "I needed to know how much time I could spend helping Simon if he needed it."

"Does he usually need your help?" Apricot was just curious enough to ask.

"I help him all the time," Daisy responded, dropping into a rickety white chair that had been there the first time Apricot visited with her aunt and would probably be there long after both of them were gone. "I watch his girls. Evangeline and Aurora. They're eight."

"Their mother can't—"

"My sister is deceased. She passed away very unexpectedly a year after the girls were born." Daisy sniffed and used the edge of her sweater to dab at her eyes.

"I'm sorry for your loss." Apricot wasn't sure if she should pat Daisy's hunched shoulders or keep her distance.

She kept her distance.

Grandma Sapphire had always warned the kids in the commune to stay away from rabid animals and to stay even farther away from rabid people. She'd never explained what that meant, but Apricot had had plenty of time to learn.

"Yes. Well, she is missed, but the girls keep me busy," Daisy murmured.

"Glad to hear it," Apricot responded, her gaze on the pot of water.

Please, hurry and boil.

Please.

Because Daisy wasn't the kind of person Apricot liked spending time with. As a matter of fact, she reminded her of Lionel's mother. Mary embodied the meaning of her name—bitter. Apricot had spent five years trying to impress the woman.

It hadn't happened.

It probably never would have happened.

Even if she and Lionel had made it down the aisle and produced the grandkids Mary wanted—one boy, one girl, and maybe a spare—Apricot would never have been more to her than that woman Lionel married.

She opened a couple of cupboards and finally found the small stash of mugs Rose always left there. Two blue. One yellow. All three chipped and well loved.

Apricot opened the purse and took out the tea bags and the tincture. All of them were A Thyme to Heal products, the little thyme-leaf emblem on the bottle and on the tea bags designed by her sister Plum.

"What do you have there?" Daisy suddenly asked, jumping up from her seat, her muddy-brown eyes wide. "Some kind of drugs?"

"Herbs. They're as good as drugs, though. Lots of people are using them to heal all kinds of ailments." She dropped the last bag of chamomile into a mug and poured hot water over it. The sweet, fruity aroma drifted into the air, and she smiled. Nothing like good quality German chamomile. The scent was as soothing as the tea.

"Well, I don't have any ailments." Daisy huffed, turning her pert nose up in the air.

"That's okay. Herbs are good for lots of things. Anxiety. Nerves. And, like I said, chamomile is great for the skin. I have a wonderful lotion that I'd be glad to—"

"I'm not even sure I want to drink the tea!" Daisy frowned, but she took the mug that Apricot offered. The yellow one, of course, because Daisy needed a little color in her life.

She sniffed, wrinkled her nose. "It smells . . ."

"Good?"

"Different." She took a tiny little sip, frowned again. "It's not half-bad."

"I thought you'd like it," Apricot responded, figuring that not half-bad was Daisy's equivalent of fantastic. "If I had honey, I'd put a dollop in there for you. That really adds to the floral notes."

"It's tea. Not some fancy wine," Daisy muttered, staring into the light brown brew.

Apricot bit her lip to keep from commenting.

The fact was, none of her teas were *just* teas. She'd spent years finding just the right leaves, just the right herbs, just the right combinations to create teas that could soothe, excite, relax, invigorate. She'd traveled the world tasting and sampling. She'd trained as a tea sommelier, worked with some of the finest in the world.

Yeah. No. Her tea was not *just* tea!

"It's very good tea," she said lightly. No sense throwing pearls to swine, but she wasn't going to pretend the tea wasn't something special.

"Excellent tea," Daisy conceded, taking a long swallow. "I appreciate you brewing me a cup. Last night was long. I love staying with the girls, but they're at that age." She sighed, plopping into the rickety chair again.

Dang-it!

Apricot hadn't given her tea so they could sit and socialize; she'd given it to her because she'd owed Deputy Baylor for the ride, and he'd looked like he'd had about all he could take of his taciturn sister-in-law.

No good deed goes unpunished, Grandma Sapphire seemed to whisper in her ear.

Obviously, she was right!

Apricot grabbed a ginseng tea bag, plopped it into a mug and poured water over it. She needed energy, lots of it, if she were going to deal with this Daisy.

"It's not that I mind being a mother to those poor little things," Daisy continued. "It's what Megan would have wanted."

"Megan was your sister?"

"My older sister. By nearly seven years." Daisy took another long sip of tea. "When the babies were born, I was just starting my job at the library. It's amazing that I've been able to keep it, what with the hours that I spend with the girls."

"Aren't they in school during the day?" she asked.

Big mistake. Daisy scowled, her eyes flashing. "They are when school is in session. Holidays, snow days, summer—who do you think takes care of them then?"

"I'd assume their father. Or a nanny, if he hired one."

"Would you want a stranger raising your children?"

Apricot didn't suppose she would. Since she wasn't going to ever have them, it was a moot point.

"Would you like me to top that tea off with some hot water?" She'd sidestepped the question, and Daisy frowned, pulling out her cell phone and checking the time again.

"I need to get going. I wouldn't want to be late."

"No." That would be a travesty. "Would you like to take my sleep tincture with you?" She grabbed the bottle, but Daisy shook her head.

"No. Thanks. I sleep just fine." She stood, her jean

skirt completely at odds with her fancy heels, the oversized fall sweater even more discordant.

Not that Apricot was judging. She was, after all, wearing a wedding dress that she was convinced had been someone's prom gown in the eighties. "If you change your mind, let me know. I have plenty in my trailer. I've also got plenty of chamomile tea."

"I'll keep that in—" The floorboards above their heads gave a loud, old-house groan, and Daisy's eyes widened, her face losing every bit of color it had. "What was that?"

"The house settling."

"Since when do houses settle that loudly?"

"Since forever, I'd guess," Apricot replied. She'd grown up in a house that was falling down more than standing, and she'd heard much louder sounds.

"I don't think that's what it was," Daisy whispered, grabbing Apricot's arm and dragging her out of the room, through the living room and straight out the front door. "It's him," Daisy hissed as soon as they stepped onto the porch. "He's in there."

"Who?" Apricot glanced through the open doorway. The curved staircase was empty. So was the landing at the top of it.

"Malachi Shaffer," Daisy said, glancing into the house and then away. "He's in that room upstairs."

"What room?"

"The room where he died." Daisy moaned.

Apricot laughed.

She couldn't help herself.

There were a lot of things to fear in the world. A ghost wasn't one of them.

"It's not funny!" Daisy cried. "He died in this house, and he's stayed in this house. People have seen him!"

"What people?"

"I . . ." She scowled. "*People.* Okay? There've been stories about this place for years!"

"And you believe them?"

"You heard the floor creak!"

"I heard the house set—"

"I don't have time to discuss it. If you're interested in the history of the property, we have several books at the library. Once you read them, you'll realize that I'm right." Daisy hurried down the porch stairs. She probably would have run if not for the fact that her heels kept sticking in the mud.

She peeled out of the driveway in a sporty black Ford SUV, the tires spewing dirt and gravel. Apricot watched her go, offering a wave she knew Daisy didn't see.

Maybe she *would* visit the library. Not because she worried about Malachi Shaffer's ghost, though. She'd always wondered about the history of the property. The first time she'd visited with her aunt, she'd been fascinated with the old house and all the things that had been left behind in it.

She hadn't had time to explore the closets that had still been filled with clothes or to study beautiful old furniture that was still in every room. She'd been too busy learning herbs and teas and tinctures. Too busy making soaps and candles that smelled like everything wonderful that nature had to offer. She'd learned a lot during her summers with Rose, but she'd never learned anything about any of the houses her aunt owned.

Now she had some free time. Plenty of it, and she thought that is exactly what she'd do. She'd go to the library and the historical society. She'd find books and journals and old pictures. She'd figure out everything there was to know about Malachi Shaffer and his orchard.

Because that was so much easier than figuring out everything she needed to know about herself and about where she wanted her life to go after she went back to LA.

She walked inside, closing the front door against the late September chill and standing still in the foyer, listening to the soft creaks of the old house, the quiet groans of settling wood. It didn't sound scary to her. It sounded like home and family, and something warm and wonderful that she'd been missing out on for a lot longer than she wanted to admit.

Sometimes life punched you in the face, knocked you off your feet, and dared you to hop back up again.

That's what Grandma Sapphire always said.

Apricot had been sucker punched and knocked off her feet. Eventually, she'd hop back up and make something great out of the mess she was in.

For now, she'd just go back in the kitchen, sip her tea, and wait for the tow truck to come.

"You're in big trouble, Baylor," Emma Baily said as Simon walked into the sheriff's department.

"And that's news?" he asked, grabbing a cookie from the plate on her desk.

"Well, no," she responded with a smile. "But I thought you'd like to know."

"I guess Dusty called?" he asked, biting into the cookie and glancing at his watch. If the lecture he was about to get from his boss lasted less than twenty minutes, he could still get his report written and be home before the girls got on the school bus. Otherwise, he wouldn't see them until after school.

He hated those kinds of days.

"He called about fifteen times. Cade got sick of it after the third time and called a meeting."

"With?"

"Max. He thought it was vitally important that they discuss security at the Apple Valley Fall Festival."

"Since when is there organized security at the festival?" Usually deputies volunteered to provide help with parking and crowd control. Other than that, the Apple Valley Sheriff's Department simply enjoyed the festival like the rest of the town.

"Since Dusty called fifteen times, and Cade wanted an excuse to not take his calls," Emma said drily.

"Sounds like a good plan to me."

"A good plan except that Dusty is mad as a hornet." She swiped back a strand of golden-blond hair and tucked it behind her ear. Her gray eyes were deeply shadowed, her skin pale. She'd spent the last couple of years caring for her widower father, and her life seemed to consist of work and that. No dates. No movies. No girls' nights out.

"Isn't Dusty always mad as a hornet?" he asked, snagging another cookie.

"He's usually more like a bumblebee, kind of buzzing around without much malicious intent. Of course, he's always willing to sting if someone swats at him."

"Kind of hard to swat a bee if it doesn't leave the hive." As far as Simon knew, Dusty rarely came to town.

"When his wife was around, he was happy enough and came to town all the time."

"That lasted . . . what? A couple of weeks?" Simon had heard the story plenty of times—poor Dusty marrying a woman who'd left him to pursue her dream of becoming a movie star.

"Your guess is as good as mine. I was about three when all that went down, so I've just heard that Dusty used to smile. I've never seen it."

"Maybe he'll return to his old habits if Rose Devereux agrees to marry him and live in Apple Valley permanently. If that happens, it should be enough of a distraction to stop him from calling here every day with a dozen complaints," he suggested because he thought it would make her smile.

She laughed and shook her head. "There you go! The answer to all of Dusty's problems and most of mine."

"How are yours going?" he asked.

"You mean Dad? Same as always. He's grumpy. I'm tired." She rubbed the back of her neck and looked way more exhausted than a woman her age should ever be. "Alzheimer's is a vicious taskmaster, I can tell you that for sure."

He resisted the urge to ask if he could help. She wasn't the kind of person who wanted to look weak or who enjoyed the pity of others. She'd muddle through until she couldn't anymore, and then Simon and Cade would find a way to help without letting her know that's what they were doing.

Like the meals that had been provided for the past couple of months. Ostensibly from the Apple Valley Community Church ladies' auxiliary, the meals had been the product of a late-night brainstorming session between Cade, Max, and Simon. Emma had no idea, and she never would if anyone involved in the covert operation had anything to do with it.

Help from the church her mother had once attended was something Emma couldn't refuse.

Help from her coworkers?

No way would she take that.

He snagged a third cookie, knowing it would annoy her and take her mind off her father.

"Hey!" she said, slapping at his hand just like he'd known she would. "Those are for the customers."

"Customers? The ones having a spa day in our rooms without a view?"

She laughed again, waving her hand toward the back of the building. "Go!"

He went, because time was ticking away and the girls were probably hunched over their cereal bowls complaining that they had to eat puffed rice instead of the sugary flakes Daisy usually bought for them. He'd snuck three boxes of those into Riley Park and fed the ducks and fish with them. He'd figured they'd needed a little extra sustenance before winter arrived. As for the girls, with the amount of sugar Daisy was constantly pumping into them, he didn't think they'd be missing out.

He walked down the hallway that led to Cade Cunningham's office, the cream-colored paint barely covering old brickwork. It was a cool building, probably built sometime at the turn of the last century. He hadn't actually intended to work there. It had just kind of happened.

Megan had wanted to be buried near her parents. She'd told him that while she was pregnant with the twins, because she'd been sure that giving birth to them would kill her. By that time, she'd spent three years struggling with chronic back pain from a car accident that had chipped a vertebra and broken her pelvis. She'd been terrified that carrying twins, giving birth to them, would make the pain intolerable. Simon had been scared too, but he'd watched her bloom during her pregnancy, listened to her talk about the twins and all her dreams and hopes for them, and he'd thought that the pain had diminished, that she was physically healthier than she'd been in years.

She'd seemed so happy after the birth, so content, Simon had allowed himself to believe that the pain she'd been dealing with had been forgotten.

He'd been wrong.

She'd been becoming more and more reliant on prescription drugs to dull her pain and get her through the day. That addiction had cost Megan her life, the bottle that he'd assumed was always full because she wasn't using it, refilled by constant supplies of painkillers prescribed by a half-dozen different doctors. She'd lied to them and to him. More than once, he'd asked her why she didn't just toss the old bottle of medication. Each time she'd told him she wanted to keep it—just in case. He wasn't sure he'd forgiven her for that.

He sure as hell hadn't forgiven himself for not realizing how many lies she'd told.

He'd done what she'd wanted, though. Buried her near her parents' graves in the cemetery at Apple Valley Community Church. He'd planned to go back to Houston after that, raise his girls there, but Apple Valley had an almost magical appeal, the quiet a balm to his soul. He'd spent a week there, then two, staying with Daisy because there wasn't a hotel nearby. She'd made meals for him and for the girls, showed them around town, told him how much help she could be to him if only he'd move to Apple Valley.

His home had been in Houston, and he'd told her that.

She'd planted a seed, though, and it had grown when he'd returned to the house he'd shared with Megan. He'd hired a nanny, tried to fill the girls' life with love and security, but he hadn't been able to shake the feeling that they'd be better off living close to their aunt in a community where everyone had known and loved their mother.

It hadn't been long before he'd made the decision to move.

He'd been in Apple Valley ever since.

Megan would have liked that. She'd have enjoyed knowing that the girls were growing up in the same little town she had.

He knocked on Cade's door, stepped into the small office. Max Stanford was still there, perfectly pressed uniform and overly shined shoes a little out of place in the functional room.

"Speak of the devil," Max drawled sardonically, his blue eyes flashing with amusement. "And he appears."

"I was thinking the same thing when *you* walked in my office, Stanford," Cade Cunningham said with a smile. Unlike Stanford, he had an easygoing, approachable personality. He might be sheriff, but he treated all his deputies like peers, seldom exerting his authority over anyone.

Of course, with a force the size of Apple Valley's, it was seldom necessary.

"I heard Dusty called," Simon said. No sense beating

around the bush. Especially when he was under a time crunch.

"You heard right," Cade responded, tapping a pen on his desk. "He said you didn't take his trespassing call seriously."

"I took it seriously enough to follow protocol," Simon responded.

"I know, but I needed to mention the complaint before I filed it." He lifted a sheet of paper from his desk, slid it into a folder, and opened a file cabinet. "Which I am now going to do." He dropped the folder into the cabinet and closed the door. "So, how is Apricot doing? I haven't seen her in years."

"Aside from the fact that Dusty held her at gunpoint until I arrived, I'd say she was doing pretty well." .

"She want to file a complaint?" Cade asked.

"Not that she mentioned."

"If she does, let's try to talk a little neighborly grace into her. I don't know how long she plans to stick around town, but I'd be really happy if she and Dusty could get along while she does." Cade rubbed the bridge of his nose and frowned. "We have the apple festival coming up. You know how that goes."

"Lots of drama and gossip. Arguments over who has the best spot at the fair. Whispers about whether or not Ms. Janet stole Mrs. Perkins's apple fritter recipe. It's my favorite time of year," Max grumbled.

"Better watch it, Max. You're talking about your adopted hometown," Cade responded lightly. "Anyone hears you griping about the apple festival, and you might lose your job as pie-contest judge."

"If that happens, Charlotte will take pity on me and make me a dozen pies," he responded with just a touch of smugness. Charlotte was, without a doubt, the best cook in town. She was also Max's fiancée.

"Don't know if she'll have time for that what with all the wedding plans," Simon said, stirring the pot a little because he could, and because he enjoyed seeing Max squirm. The guy had dated just about every woman in Apple Valley before Charlotte came along, and had a reputation for being a die-hard bachelor. All that had changed when his ex-girlfriend had dropped a three-year-old off at his place and told Max the kid was his.

"Don't mention the wedding," Max barked. "It's all I've heard about for the past five months."

"Because it's just about the only thing anyone in town is talking about. Which reminds me," Cade said. "Tessa managed to find a few more of the vases Charlotte wants for the reception. You want to stop by our place and pick them up later?"

Max grumbled something unintelligible and scowled. "You're not going to try to get me into one of those old tuxedos, are you? Because if that's the reason your wife really wants me to stop by your place—"

Cade raised a hand and shook his head. "Hey! As far as I know it's just about the vases. If there's any more to it than that, you'll have to bring it up with Charlotte. The old tux was her idea. Not Tessa's."

At the mention of his fiancée, Max softened.

He might like to grumble about it, but there was no doubt he loved Charlotte and he was looking forward to marrying her.

Simon remembered what that was like.

The heady feeling that life was stretching out in

front of you, the only person you wanted to spend it with right there by your side.

He also knew how easily the person you thought you knew could turn into someone you didn't know at all.

No need to tell Max that. If he didn't already know it, he'd figure it out.

"If we're finished discussing Dusty's complaint," he broke in, "I'm going to write up my report and head out."

"We have a meeting in the morning to discuss the apple festival. Seven o'clock," Cade reminded him as he stepped out of the room.

Seven wasn't a good time, but Simon kept the thought to himself. He didn't like to play the single-dad card too often, and he'd had to take a couple of hours off the previous week to bring Aurora in for a strep test. Negative, of course. The girls were healthy as horses, but Daisy had been convinced Aurora had strep. She'd also been convinced Evangeline had a broken leg. Seeing as how the kid had been dancing around the living room and jumping off haystacks in the field behind their house, Simon had decided not to take her to urgent care for an X-ray.

Saturdays the girls had ballet class at nine thirty. Hopefully the seven o'clock meeting would be over before then. Asking Daisy to take them was out of the question. They'd gone together once as a family, because Daisy had thought it would be good for the girls. Daisy had stood with her face pressed against the observation window, yelling for Aurora to stand up straighter and Evangeline to pay attention. She hadn't impressed the other parents, and she hadn't impressed the teachers. She hadn't impressed the twins either. They'd both approached him in different ways, begging him to keep her away from the studio. Evie had been bold-faced about it, but that was the way she was. Rori had written a note and tucked it into his coat pocket. He'd promised to try his best to never bring Daisy to dance again.

So far, he'd been able to avoid it.

He hoped he'd be able to continue that for a while, because he didn't feel like dealing with the drama that Daisy caused. Not with the girls' birthday looming and all those memories hovering right near the surface of his mind. Megan had died the day before their first birthday, a cocktail of prescription pills stopping her heart just a few months short of her twenty-eighth birthday. An accident, that's what the coroner had said. An unintentional overdose, a sad end to a vibrant life.

He pushed the thought aside.

It didn't do any good to dwell on it.

He couldn't change what had happened, couldn't go back to the day before she died, the month before, the year before, and ask the questions that might have kept her alive.

He'd get through September, get through the birthday at the end of it, and then he'd move on. Just like he did every year.

He'd be fine.

The twins would be fine.

After all, the only memories they had of their mother were from stories he'd told and photos he'd shown them. It was Daisy who always needed cheering. Daisy who spent the twins' birthday mourning what the girls didn't have.

Daisy . . .

With her no-good boyfriend out of her life, she was becoming a problem.

He'd have to deal with her eventually.

For now, he just needed to write the dang report and get home.

Chapter Four

Someone was crying.

Or some*thing*.

The sound jerked Apricot out of the half sleep she'd fallen into, and she came up off the couch so fast, she nearly tumbled right back onto it again. Bright sunlight streamed in through the living room window and splashed on the nicked wood floor. Dust motes danced on the air, and the cries kept coming, soft and steady. A newborn?

She tried to run to the front door, but her feet caught in her blasted skirts. Again. She wanted to rip the dress off, toss it into the fireplace and set a match to it, but the tow truck hadn't brought Henry or the Airstream, and she wasn't in the mood for another barefoot bike ride. She had nothing else to wear but the vintage clothes she'd found in upstairs closets, and she hadn't wanted to greet the tow truck driver wearing borrowed clothes.

No more fuel for the gossip fire.

She opened the front door, followed the sound of

the cries to a box that someone had placed on a porch step and covered with a blanket.

"Please don't let this be a baby," she muttered as she ripped the blanket off.

Four kittens looked up at her. Three fuzzy black-and-white babies and a scrawny gray tabby that looked like it had come from another litter. He was the one making all the noise, his mouth opened wide as he mewled pitifully.

"Okay. Okay," she said, lifting the kitten and cuddling him close. He thanked her by digging his claws into her chest and dislodging a few of the gaudy beads that had been hand-sewn to the fabric. She tried to dislodge his claws, and he climbed up to her shoulder, burrowed under her hair, and meowed into her ear.

"All right. I get it. You're hungry." She snagged him by the scruff and plopped him back into the box.

She'd have to feed all four of them, and then she'd have to take them to an animal shelter, because she couldn't keep them. She'd given up the idea of having pets right around the time she'd given up life at Happy Dale. No more chickens. No more cats. No more dogs, goats, skunks, raccoons, or squirrels. She liked her house free of animals and mess.

She had to admit, though, the kittens were cute.

Except for the gray one. He was homely, but as long as he didn't know that, she figured he'd be just fine.

"Let's go, guys." She lifted the box, pausing as the sound of a car engine broke the afternoon stillness.

A white tow truck chugged toward her, Henry hooked up behind it. No Airstream, but that was okay. That was fine. As long as she had Henry, she could fix him up and go back for the Airstream and whatever she and her family had managed to toss inside of it.

She wasn't sure who she expected to jump out of the tow truck. A guy named Willie? Someone with a beard and a bandanna, wearing coveralls and work boots? The woman who got out of the truck was wearing coveralls and work boots. No bandanna, though. No beard, either. Which was probably for the best.

The driver offered a quick wave as she jogged to the back of the truck and released Henry.

Next thing Apricot knew, the woman was climbing back in the truck again.

"Hold on!" Apricot called, the ugly gray kitten calling along with her. "I need to pay you!"

"I'm going back for the Airstream," the woman responded. "You can pay up once I finish the job. You're getting a good discount on the service, too. We're running behind, and we want to thank you for your patience."

"No discount necessary," Apricot said as she jogged toward the truck. "And I can get the Airstream once I get Henry working again."

"Henry?" The woman had one foot in the tow truck, her dark, curly hair pulled back from an austere face. A name tag sewn to her coveralls had the name *Willie* stitched in bright green thread.

"The truck. He has a name."

"He should. He's a good-looking vehicle." She swiped a hand on her coveralls and offered it. "I'm Willetta Pothier. Willie to my friends. And just about everyone else in town." She smiled, and it made her look young. Maybe twenty-two or -three.

"Anna Miller."

"Good to meet you, Anna. I'd ask what you're doing in town, but it's not my business, and I'm already running a couple hours behind."

"How much—"

"I told you I'm getting the Airstream. It's on the order, and I've got to do my job or Stanley will have a hissy fit."

"Stanley?"

"My father. He owns Apple Valley Towing. He was supposed to get your rigs, but he got caught up in a rousing game of chess. You got kittens in there?" She gestured to the box, and Apricot nodded.

"I found them on my porch stairs."

"Yeah." Willie peered into the box. "That's not surprising."

"It's not?" In all her years of life, Apricot hadn't found a box of kittens sitting anywhere. Let alone on her steps.

"The local shelter closed about five years ago. Lack of funding. A new one opened in the next town over. Only about twenty miles from here, but it's not a no-kill shelter, so some people don't want to bring strays there."

"What does that have to do with me finding kittens on my porch?"

"Rose feeds stray cats when she's in town. She takes them to the vet, gets them the shots they need, has them fixed. Then she offers them to people as barn cats. If no one wants them, she takes them with her and finds them homes somewhere else. Once people got wind of that, they started dropping off unwanted litters."

"Rose isn't in town," Apricot pointed out reasonably, hoping against hope that Willie would spread the word.

The last thing she wanted was an endless supply of kittens to rehome.

"*You* are," Willie said just as reasonably. "That's good enough for anyone who has a few unwanted critters. Want me to take them to the shelter for you? Once I'm finished here, I'm done for the day."

"The kill shelter?" she asked, eyeing the kittens. The gray one eyed her right back, his flea-bitten ears just a little too big for his head.

"It's the only one around. I'm sure they'll be fine, though. People love kittens. Someone will take them."

"Thanks, but I think I'll just . . . feed them first." She was going to regret this. She knew she was, but Apricot was not letting the kittens go off to a shelter where they might be killed.

"Suit yourself. I'll have the Airstream back in a few."

Willie hopped into the truck and took off.

Hopefully, she'd be back as quickly as she'd said, because Apricot's day had suddenly gotten busier. Maybe it was for the best. Napping and moping weren't things she'd ever been any good at.

She carried the kittens into the house and put the box on the sofa. She didn't have food for them, but she could at least give them some water. She grabbed a small plastic bowl from the cupboard, walked back into the living room, and saw the gray kitten tumbling out of the box.

"You're going to be trouble, aren't you?" She sighed, depositing him back in the box, watching as the kittens lapped at the water. They looked healthy enough, but that didn't mean she wanted them around. She needed to take them all to the vet, get their shots and get them out of her hair, because she had other things to do with her time.

Like . . .

What?

It was a good question. Two weeks in Aruba had been the plan. Then back to Los Angeles to build a married life with Lionel. First, a move from their condo into something bigger. A house with a yard. They'd put the condo on the market, had been house hunting for a couple of months. Lionel had even put earnest money down on their dream home. Hopefully, he could get a refund. She knew how much he valued dollars when they were his.

Hers he wasn't so worried about.

She'd paid for their luxury condo and all the up-graded finishes. She'd paid for the boat that they'd used exactly twice. She'd even paid for the honeymoon that they weren't taking.

But why be bitter?

She'd accept the offer her Realtor had gotten on the condo, and she'd take the cash and put it into something more practical. Something more her style. Maybe a pretty little bungalow or a cabin in the middle of the woods. Maybe somewhere in Montana or Vermont. New Hampshire?

Wherever it was, she'd make sure she couldn't be found.

Not until she wanted to be, and right at that moment, she didn't think that would ever happen.

The phone rang, but she ignored it.

She knew it was Rose or Lilac. Or maybe Plum. Not Lionel. No one in her family would have given him the number to the house. None of her friends knew it. None of them even knew where she was. She really *did* have to get a new cell phone. Just in case there was an emergency at work.

Which there wouldn't be.

She had great employees.

"Yay, me," she muttered, opening the front door and walking out onto the porch. The sun hung overhead, a golden orb against a pristine sky. Any other day, and she'd have enjoyed the sunshine, the heat that was building as the day wore on.

Why not enjoy it today?

So what if she'd been betrayed?

So what if all her dreams were dead as doornails?

So what if everything she'd thought she was going to have wasn't going to happen?

She lifted her face to the sky, but it just wasn't the same as lying under an umbrella on a sandy beach.

Willie's truck appeared at the end of the driveway, the Airstream behind it. Apricot waved the truck to the edge of the driveway, helped unhook the Airstream, and tried to pretend she didn't notice Willie noticing her dress and bare feet.

"Bad day, huh?" Willie said as they finished.

"Bad five years," she responded. No sense trying to hide things. No doubt Dusty had already contacted everyone in Apple Valley to let them know a squatter had taken up residence in Rose's place. If he hadn't spread the news about her arrival, Daisy probably had.

"That sucks," Willie responded. "I did that. Lived

with a guy for two years. He walked out while I was in the hospital and didn't even bother leaving a note."

"Nice."

"Yeah. Nice. Maybe you and I should get together for drinks sometime. We probably have a lot in common." She didn't wait for Apricot's reply. Just climbed in the truck and took off.

No, thanks, is what Apricot would have said.

She really didn't want to be part of some women-only club. The kind where men were bashed over bowls of melting ice cream or glasses of lukewarm beer. Pity parties weren't her thing. Besides, she liked men. She even loved a few. Her brothers. Her dad. Just not Lionel. Not anymore. Maybe not ever. Which was something she'd have to think about when she was in the mood for it.

Something snagged the back of her dress as she opened the Airstream, and she yanked at the material, heard the loud unhappy cry of the gray kitten.

"What in the world!" She turned and scooped him up. "How did you get out here?"

The front door was still closed.

She walked inside. One corner of the blanket had lifted off the box. The other kittens were huddled together, sound asleep. Food. That's what they needed. Then the vet. Then new homes. If she kept focused on that, she wouldn't have to think about the rest. Like calling her family. Checking in with friends. Explaining in detail how she felt about Lionel, the canceled wedding, the nonexistent honeymoon.

She could do it easily in two very succinct words.

It sucked.

"So, how *did* you escape?" she asked the cat. He purred and closed his eyes. She put him on the floor, hoping he'd run to his escape route. He flopped onto his back and lay there, watching her through slitted eyes.

Useless.

And butt ugly.

Poor thing. Unlike his fluffy little mates, he had thin fur and a ratlike tail. He was also huge. Not the cute little kittens that people oohed and aahed over, he was more likely to strike fear into the hearts of young children and disgust the local cat ladies.

It would be really hard to find a home for him. "I'll give it my best shot, Handsome, but if I can't find someone who will take you, you're going to the shel—"

Bang!

Something slammed against a wall or floor.

Apricot shrieked, the kitten jumped, clawing its way up her dress and under her hair as she ran to the front door. She paused there. First, she hadn't gotten Henry working yet. Second, she couldn't just leave the house with a trespasser in it. Third, she'd never been the overly fearful type, and she wasn't going to start now. If someone was in the house, she was going to boot him or her out.

She marched back into the living room, lifted a small end table. Just in case she needed a weapon.

Bang!

Whoever it was, wasn't being quiet about it.

Bang, bang, bang!

She followed the sound into the kitchen.

Bang!

Something hit the back of the house, and she dragged the door open, barreled outside into bright sunlight, the end table gripped in one hand, the kitten digging its claws into the back of her neck.

A kid stood a few yards away from the house, mouth gaping open, a basketball in his hands. About six-foot with shaggy red hair and dark brown eyes, he had gauges in his ears and a ring through his brow. He eyed the table and the corner of his mouth twitched. It looked like a smile rather than a smirk, so she set her makeshift weapon down.

"What are you doing?" she asked, even though what he was doing was obvious. Paint from the old wood siding had chipped off from the force of his basketball throws and one of the wooden shingles had cracked, half of it falling to the ground.

"I—" He glanced at the ball, his cheeks flushing. "Didn't know anyone lived here."

"Someone does," she pointed out, and his flush deepened. "But even if the property was abandoned, throwing a ball at it wouldn't be cool."

"Sorry," he mumbled. "I was just . . . sorry."

She lifted the broken piece of shingle and frowned. The house desperately needed repainting, but that was only the tip of the iceberg. The shingle felt spongy and malleable from too many years of exposure. Not good.

Rose really needed to take better care of the property.

She'd have told her aunt that, but it would require actually talking to someone who'd been at the church, waiting in the bride's room, patting Apricot on the shoulder and telling her men weren't worth the tears.

Rose and Lilac had been right about that.

Men *weren't*, and Apricot had vowed then and there

to never, ever cry over a man again. She crumbled a little piece of the wood, letting the sawdust fall to the ground. "It was in pretty bad shape before. Looks like you've just added to an already existing problem."

"I can fix it for you," he said earnestly, poking his finger through what had been left hanging on the house. Dust dropped onto the ground.

"It's going to take more than one piece of siding to fix the problem. I bet half the shingles are rotten," she responded.

"More than half. The place needs all-new siding," he agreed. He ran his hand over a few other shingles as if he were some sort of connoisseur rather than a teenage kid carrying a basketball and wandering around throwing it at random houses. "I could get it done before the first frost."

"Get what done?"

"The siding?" He poked his finger into another shingle, and more dust drifted onto the ground. "If you don't fix the problem, you're going to have a bigger one."

He said exactly what she'd been thinking, but she didn't want to hire a fifteen-year-old to do the job. "I'm sure there are some local companies—"

"They'll cost you an arm and a leg," he said, cutting her off, his focus on the house. He took a few steps back, used his hand to block the sun as he glanced at the roof. "The roof looks like it's in good shape. That's probably been replaced in the past ten years, but the siding has to go. You also need new framing on your windows. Take a look at the second floor and the attic. See how warped the wood is?"

Now that he mentioned it, she did.

"Bet you've got mold inside your house. I can fix that, too."

"I think your time would be better spent in school."

He finally looked at her, his dark gaze serious and direct. "I'm eighteen, ma'am. I graduated high school last year."

"College—"

"Costs money that my grandparents don't have. I'm taking a couple of classes this quarter, but next quarter, I'm out of luck unless I can get some work."

He was blunt.

She liked that.

But that didn't mean he was capable of shingling an old house. "It's probably best if I hire a company. Someone licensed and bonded. Just in case there's an accident or something." She tried to be just as blunt, but she couldn't look the kid in the eyes, because she could feel his desperation and she didn't want to see it.

"Homeowner's insurance covers accidents on your property, and I'd write a letter saying I wouldn't hold you responsible if I cut off my hand or knocked myself senseless. I'd even have it notarized. And in case you think I don't know what I'm doing, I worked for my dad from the time I was able to carry a hammer. He owned a restoration company in Seattle." He dug in his pocket and pulled out a business card. Stained and flimsy, it looked like he'd been carrying it around for a while.

She glanced at the card. "You're Justin Irvin?"

"My dad was Justin. I'm Jet." He held out a hand, and she took it, surprised by the strength in his fingers and the rough callouses on his palms. He worked hard, that much was for sure. Whether or not he could actually re-side a huge old house was another story. She'd taken chances on people before, though, and she wasn't opposed to doing it again.

"I'll tell you what. How about you come back tomorrow with that letter and one of your grandparents? Bring a couple of references. Once I check them out, we can talk about the job."

"I can give you the references now. I do some part-time work at the sheriff's office. Sheriff Cunningham can vouch for me. I've also done some work at Simon Baylor's place. He's a deputy sheriff."

"We've met."

"Great! You know where he lives?"

"No."

"He's just off of Main Street. I replaced all his windows and reshingled the roof. Did it all in three days and for a third of the price another business quoted him. I'll write down his address." He pulled a scrap of paper and a pen from his pocket, jotted the information down, and handed it to her. "I'll be back tomorrow."

He grabbed the basketball, tucked it under his arm. "By the way, you have a kitten under your hair."

She disengaged the kitten's claws and held the ugly scrap of fur out. "He needs a good home. Are you interested?"

"He looks like an oversized rat. My grandma would probably take a broom to him."

"He's probably a good mouser," she replied. "Your grandma might appreciate that."

"If you had something cuter, she might go for it, but—"

"Hold on!" She was in the house and back with the

box of kittens so fast, she didn't think he had time to blink. "I have three more. Take your pick."

He looked into the box and frowned. "Will taking one better my chances of getting the job?"

"Only if you take good care of it and I don't find it back on my doorstep tomorrow."

"In that case, which ones are girls?"

She lifted a tiny scrap of black fur. "The runt is."

"So . . ." He took the kitten. "You promise you'll check my references and really consider letting me re-side the house?"

"Yes."

He scowled but held the kitten against his chest. "I'll tell Grandma it's her birthday gift."

"Today is her birthday?"

"Nah, but she doesn't know I know that." He strode away, the basketball tucked under his arm.

One kitten down and three to go, but now she'd have to make good on her promise. She couldn't hire an inexperienced kid to do work that would probably take an entire team of experienced workers a week or more to do. On the other hand, if he knew what he was doing and could do it well, she wouldn't mind giving him the job.

Everyone deserved a chance.

Until they proved that they didn't.

She glanced down at her shredded wedding dress.

Time to move on.

Fifteen minutes later, the dress was off, jeans and a T-shirt were on, and she was ready to start something new, to forget all about the wedding that wasn't.

She tossed the dress into the fireplace as she walked through the living room, stomped it a few times just to get the dust and ashes nicely mixed with the pink fabric. A few beads rolled out, and Handsome chased them across the wood floor, his skinny body sliding under the sofa. He came out with one tiny bead in his mouth, slinked back to the fireplace, and deposited it there.

"Smart cat," she murmured, scratching him behind the ears. "I'm going to fix the truck, and you and your friends are staying in here. Then we're going to the vet and to town. Behave!"

She tossed the command over her shoulder, realized she was talking to a kitten, and sighed. So . . . *this* was where life had led. Definitely not where she'd expected, but she'd make a go of it. If there was one thing Lilac and Hubert had taught her, it was that circumstances didn't make the person. The person made the circumstances. She might not be where she'd planned, doing what she thought she'd be doing, but by God, she'd make things work.

She marched outside with her head high even though there wasn't anyone around to see it, opened Henry's hood, and got to work.

What to make for dinner . . .

That was the question.

The one Simon had no answer to.

He glanced out the front window. The girls were still sitting behind their lemonade stand, hair up in ballet buns, pink tutus pulled on over cut-off shorts. Rori had paired hers with a pale pink tank top. Evie wore a plain white T-shirt. No fuss or muss for that girl. Identical in looks, the girls were as different in personality as night and day.

Both liked chicken nuggets, though, and he thought

he just might take them to Riley Park, let them run off some steam and then treat them to dinner at the diner. No cooking required, and they'd all be happy.

Except for Daisy, who thought home-cooked meals equated to good health and love. Full fat, gobs of butter, more grease than any meal had a right to— that's the way most of the meals she cooked were, but Daisy still thought they were healthier than diner food.

He let her think it because he did most of the cooking, nice well-balanced meals that the girls enjoyed. Fresh veggies, fresh fruit, lean protein. Tonight, though, he was tired. He'd worked an overnight shift, and he didn't care much about anything but getting food into the girls' stomachs and getting them into bed.

He glanced at his watch. Five thirty. Definitely time to close down the lemonade stand. As far as he'd been able to tell, the girls had sold a cup to the neighbor and about five cups to James Finely. He'd been mowing his lawn and apparently felt the need to pay a quarter for a glass of lemonade instead of just drinking the water that was sitting in a glass on his front porch.

James had five kids of his own, and Simon had almost told him not to waste money that he could use for them, but James was a proud guy, and he'd have probably given each of the girls twenty dollars . . . just to prove he could.

Simon had kept his mouth shut.

Rori started waving frantically. Must be a car coming. A new customer and Simon's cue to make an appearance. Sure, Apple Valley had a low crime rate, but that didn't mean there weren't predators roaming the streets.

He stepped outside, saw an old Ford truck easing to a stop near the curb. He knew the truck. Knew the driver. Could have gone right back in the house, but he doubted Apricot Miller had found her way to his place by accident, and he was curious to see what she had to say.

Curious to see her again.

That was the truth, and Simon had made a habit of always being honest with himself. His mind had been wandering back to the Schaffer place for the better part of the day, wandering to a place where he'd allowed himself to think about Apricot and her called-off wedding, her broken-down truck, her disastrous pink dress.

She rounded the truck, her slim legs encased in faded denim, a fitted gray T-shirt clinging to her flat abdomen. She'd brushed her hair into a ponytail, and she looked about a decade younger than she had before.

She smiled at the girls, took a bill from her pocket. "How much for a cup of lemonade?"

The girls fell all over themselves in an effort to answer. Next thing Simon knew, Apricot had a cup of lemonade in each hand and the girls had the money in the glass jar they'd taken from the cupboard.

"We have plenty more where that came from," Evie said, offering up the plastic pitcher as proof.

"Well, I may have to get a refill before I leave, then," Apricot responded. "I need to talk to your dad first, though."

She swallowed down an entire glass of lemonade.

"You know, if you girls wouldn't mind terribly, I'd love to buy a cup of water. I'll pay the same thing I paid for the lemonade."

"You don't like our lemonade?" Rori asked, her chin quivering.

Simon knew what was coming. The kid had the sensitive nature of her mother, and she hated to disappoint anyone.

"Ror—" he started, but Apricot was shaking her head and pulling more money from her purse.

"Are you kidding me? It's the best I've had in years." Apricot took a swig from the other cup, wiped her mouth with the back of her hand. "I need the water for the kittens."

"Kittens?!" Evie shrieked.

"No!" Simon barked as he strode to the lemonade stand. "We don't have time for a kitten."

"I just want to see them, Daddy," Evie insisted with all the earnestness of an eight-year-old girl who loved every animal that existed. "And maybe pet them if the lady says I can."

"That's up to your dad," Apricot responded diplomatically. "I've taken them to the vet. He gave them shots and a clean bill of health," she added, smiling in his direction.

She had a pretty smile. The kind that made her eyes glow, made her soft lips look even softer. The kind that someone might be tempted to fall for. Fortunately, Simon was past the age of being tempted by pretty, and past the point in his life when he had time to pursue anything but work and the twins.

"We can't keep a kitten," he told the girls before they asked. Because they *would* ask. They'd been asking for a kitten since Daisy had gotten a fluffy Persian five months ago.

"Of course you can't. Kittens are a lot of work," Apricot agreed, leaning into the cab of the truck and grabbing a box covered with a blanket. "I'm not here to pawn kittens off on you. I'm here about a young man named Jet Irvin."

Jet. Yeah. The kid had had some tough times, but he was trying to make good with his life. "What about him?"

"He said he did some work for you?" She carried the box to the front porch, sat cross-legged with it on her lap. The girls moved in close, Evie nearly vibrating with excitement, Rori hanging just a little behind her sister.

"That's right."

"I'm thinking of hiring him, but I wanted to get a few references first." She pulled the blanket off the box, revealing two little black-and-white kittens and a big ugly gray one.

"They are so cute!" Evie squealed. "Aren't they cute, Rori?!"

Rori nodded. "Yes," she whispered. Which was more than she usually did when strangers were present. One of her teachers had suggested she suffered from social anxiety and told Simon that the then six-year-old needed medication and therapy.

Simon had suggested the woman get a life.

That hadn't gone over very well.

"Can I pet them, Daddy?" Evie begged. "Please?"

"Why don't you both go get them some water first?" he suggested.

The girls bounced into the house, slamming the door behind them. Of course.

"Cute kids," Apricot said as she nudged the gray kitten into the box. It jumped out and clawed its way up her arm, perching in the little hollow near her ear.

"I think so." He lifted one of the little black-and-white puffballs from the box and eyed it. "But I'm not going to let them talk me into one of these."

"Of course you aren't," she agreed. Again.

"You're not going to win this with reverse psychology, Apricot."

She didn't correct him on the name, just smiled that pretty smile of hers. "Like I said, I'm here about Jet. He wants to replace the siding on Rose's house. I'm trying to decide if he's the guy for the job. He gave me your name and the sheriff's as references. I've already spoken with Cade. He seemed really enthusiastic about Jet's work."

"I'm not surprised. Jet is a great kid. I'd recommend him to anyone."

"Being a great kid is nice, Simon, but I'm more interested in the kind of work he does. I can give him some odd jobs that don't require a high level of skill or I can let him hang new siding and replace the gingerbread trim on the porch. It just depends on the work he's done here." She'd gone from sweet smile to all business, and he wouldn't have been surprised if she'd taken an iPad out of her purse and started taking notes.

"He replaced my roof two months ago. Replaced and reframed my windows. So far, no leaks," he offered. "Took him about four days, and he cleaned up his mess when he finished. I'd say it would take longer to side the Shaffer place."

She nodded. "I'd say so. He hasn't given me a time frame, and I didn't ask, but if he works alone, we're probably talking a few weeks."

"He does most of the work alone, but he did have a guy helping with the roof. An older guy who works for a company in Spokane and does freelance work when he has time."

"Hmm. I guess that means paying two for the job?"

"No. I paid a set fee and Jet paid his friend. No fuss or muss. No trouble. No complaints from the freelancer. If you hire Jet, you're going to have to buy the supplies. He doesn't have cash in hand to do that." That hadn't bothered Simon. He'd already purchased everything he needed to do the job. He just hadn't had time to do it. With fall closing in and winter right around the corner, he'd needed to get the work done. Even if he'd been willing to wait, his hundred-year-old home hadn't been.

"That's not a problem. As long as he's able to tell me what I need."

"He gave me an itemized list along with reasonable prices for supplies. Want to take a look at the work he did?"

"Sure." She stood, box in hand. "As long as I can bring the kittens in. Handsome keeps escaping the box, and I don't want him to get run over."

"Handsome?" He opened the screen door, touched her shoulder to urge her in ahead of him. Got a quick swat from the ugly gray kitten as a thank-you.

"This guy." She dragged the gray kitten off her shoulder and set him in the box. "He's trouble."

"You think you're going to find him a home?"

"Someone will feel sorry for him and take him in. I hope."

"Hope is nothing to hang your hat on," he responded, smiling as she laughed.

"I guess you're right about that, but don't worry. I have a plan B."

"Yeah?"

"If no one will take him, I'll bring him to the . . ."

The girls barreled into the foyer, each of them carrying a bowl of water.

"Shelter," Apricot finished.

"No!" Evie shouted. "You're not taking them to the shelter! You can't. Aunt Daisy says they kill animals there."

Apricot met Simon's eyes, mouthed *I'm sorry*. Then smiled at Evie. "Don't worry. I'm sure I'll find them all good homes."

"If you don't, you have to keep them," Evie insisted. "It's the only right thing to do."

"Not if I don't have time for them. That wouldn't be fair to the kittens," Apricot responded. "But, like I said, I'm sure I can find them all good homes."

"But—"

"That's enough, Evangeline," he cut in, knowing his daughter would continue to press her point. At eight, she insisted she wanted to be a veterinarian. Simon was convinced she'd grow up to become an attorney. "How about you girls bring the kittens into the kitchen and give them the water there? I need to show Apricot—"

"Your name is Apricot?" Rori gasped, her dark chocolate eyes wide, some of her natural shyness disappearing in the face of the wonder of Apricot's name.

"Yes, but most of my friends call me Anna."

"But Apricot is such a pretty name. Like a fairy-tale princess name," Rori breathed, and Simon could see all the little-girl dreams in her eyes.

"Rori," he began, wanting to stop his daughter before she got too caught up in the fantasy. "She's not a fairy-tale princess. She's just—"

"Very flattered that you like my name," Apricot broke in with a gentle smile. "I never thought of it as all that special, but I think after today, I will. Give your sister the water, and I'll hand you the kitten box. You'll be careful with them, right?"

"Yes." Rori nodded solemnly. No overflowing enthusiasm, no jumping and squealing. She was the quiet twin, the one Simon worried about most, because her feelings were so close to the surface and so easily hurt.

Too bad he couldn't put her in a bubble and keep her there, safe from all the meanness in the world.

She handed the water to her sister, who took it without protest.

A minor miracle considering the kid always wanted to be in charge.

Like Rori, she seemed to have fallen under Apricot's spell, her big brown eyes wide with wonder as Apricot handed over the kitten box.

"Is your hair real or is it the clip-on stuff that my first-grade teacher wore at her wedding?"

"What kind of question is that?" Simon asked.

"One I want an answer to. I've never seen a grown woman with hair as long as hers." Evie didn't seem at all apologetic. "And are those your real boobs?

Jackson Anderson at school says most women have fake ones. I told him that only women in magazines have them, and he told me I was stupid."

"Enough!" Simon commanded.

What kind of school was he sending his kids to, if that was the kind of conversation they were having?!

"But, Daddy," Evie said. "It's a reasonable question, and I just want a reasonable answer. I'm going to be a woman one day, and I have to know these things."

Apricot laughed, and Simon would have laughed too, if it had been anyone else's daughter making the pronouncement.

"You're eight," he muttered. "You should be worried about bedtime and lunch boxes."

"Jackson says—"

"How about we discuss Jackson and his opinions later?" he cut in. "The kittens are thirsty and they're probably hungry too. Take them into the kitchen and feed them some of that food Aunt Daisy keeps here for Sweetums."

"Sweetums?" Apricot asked as the girls walked away.

"The cat from hell. I think she got him from a breeder who charges an arm and a leg for squash-faced kittens with bad attitudes."

She laughed, following him into the living room, the scent of summer sunshine filling the air as she moved. "I'm getting the impression you're not Sweetums's biggest fan."

"He scratched up my favorite recliner. I had a friend reupholster it, and he clawed it up again."

"Is that the recliner?" She gestured to the chair he'd bought a few months after he and the girls had moved in. The sides of the chair looked like they'd been put through a giant paper shredder.

"How'd you guess?" he asked drily.

"I'm not always as clueless as I was the day I accepted my ex's proposal," she responded with a smile that made her eyes sparkle.

"You've got an awfully good attitude for a woman who was—" He stopped short of saying what had popped into his head. No sense rubbing salt in an open wound.

"Jilted?" She finished for him. "I told you. I wasn't. I was left waiting. For a long time."

"And?"

"I decided I didn't want to wait any longer. He showed up right around the time I was telling my family the wedding was off."

There was probably more to the story, but he didn't ask and she didn't tell. That would be a little too much like getting to know each other, and Simon didn't think either of them wanted to do that.

"Is this one of the windows Jet replaced?" she asked, crouching in front of the double-pane glass and touching the oak framing.

"Yes." He crouched beside her. "He used wood from an old house that had been demolished, and cut molds to match the frames that weren't dry-rotted.

"It's gorgeous," she murmured, running long fingers over the smooth wood. Her nails were unvarnished and short, her face makeup-free, a few long strands of hair escaping her ponytail.

She didn't look high maintenance, but her wedding dress sure had been. If he'd based his assessment of Apricot's nature on that, he'd say she was the kind of woman who liked fine dining and spa treatments, who liked fancy furniture and expensive jewelry. The kind of woman who wouldn't blink an eye at spending thousands of dollars on a dress she was only going to wear one day.

He and Megan had argued about that.

Funny how he was just now remembering.

Two weeks after they'd gotten engaged, Megan had told him her grandparents had put aside five thousand dollars for the dress. He'd suggested she spend half that and they could use the rest for a down payment on a house. She hadn't liked the idea. She hadn't even liked that he'd had it. It had been their first big argument, and he thought it had surprised both of them. In the end, she'd had her fancy dress, and they'd lived in an apartment for the first two years they were married. He hadn't minded all that much. He'd loved Megan, would have lived in a hovel with her if that's what they'd had to do to be together.

"How many windows and frames did he put in?" Apricot asked, pulling him from the memory.

"All the windows were replaced. He rebuilt the frames in here and in the kitchen." He glanced toward the dining room. The girls were being very, very quiet. "I can take you in there."

"If they look as good as these, there's no need." She brushed the stray hair off her face, tucked it back into the ponytail holder, the gesture unconsciously feminine and much more appealing than Simon wanted it to be.

Time to get her out of the house, because his mind was heading places it shouldn't be going unless he wanted to get himself involved in something that would take way more time than he had.

He straightened, holding out a hand to help her to her feet. "In that case, I'll walk you to the door."

"Am I being kicked to the curb, Simon?" she asked with a grin that made him notice the deep blue of her eyes and the freckles on her cheeks.

"Just out the front door," he responded. "I have to feed the girls dinner."

"Much as I'd like to allow myself to be kicked out *without* the kittens, leaving them with you seems like the wrong thing to do."

The kittens. Right. He'd almost forgotten. Something about looking in her eyes was messing with his brain!

"Girls!" he called. "Apricot has to leave."

They came running into the room, the box wrapped in a bright pink blanket and cradled between them.

"Quiet, Daddy," Evie said solemnly. "They're sound asleep."

"Must be their full tummies getting the best of them," Apricot whispered, taking the box from the girls. "Thank you for taking good care of them."

The girls followed her onto the porch and watched wide-eyed as she put the box in the passenger seat of her old truck and took off.

"Is she a princess, Daddy?" Rori asked, tugging at his hand and pulling his attention away from the retreating truck.

"Of course not," he responded, bending so they were eye to eye. "You know that princesses are only for fairy tales."

"That isn't true, Daddy," Evie argued. "There are princesses in Europe and in Africa and—"

"How about we get dressed and go get chicken nuggets at the diner?" he said, cutting into what was destined to be a very long debate with his daughter. "We can discuss princesses there."

"The diner!" the girls squealed in unison. "Yay!"

"First we have to get water. We're thirsty. Aren't we thirsty, Rori?" Evie asked, grabbing her sister's hand and tugging her inside. He followed more slowly, glancing over his shoulder and calling himself every sort of fool because what he was looking for, what he was hoping to see, was one last glimpse of Apricot's truck as she drove away.

Chapter Five

Two of the kittens were missing.

Apricot discovered the horrifying fact a few seconds after she walked into Rose's house. She glared at the lone kitten—Handsome, of course—and lifted him from the box. "Where are your siblings?" she asked.

He yawned.

"Never mind. I already know," she muttered, placing Handsome on the floor and watching as he chased his ratlike tail. "You need some toys, big boy."

And she needed to call Simon and let him know what his daughters had done. She didn't have his home number, and that was as good an excuse as any to put the inevitable off for a while longer.

The phone rang, and she answered it, figuring it was either Simon or one of her family members. "Hello?"

"Babe?" Lionel's voice was as unwelcome as a viper in a spring garden. She almost hung up. *Almost.*

"How did you get this number?"

"I had a friend pull up property records for your aunt. I figured you'd probably be at one of her places.

Her number is in the directory in Apple Orchards, so I gave it a shot."

"Apple Valley," she corrected, because there was really nothing to say. No reason to even be having a conversation with Lionel except to put some closure on what they'd had for five years.

"Right. Whatever. When are you coming home? Someone changed the lock on the door and—"

"Really?" Not surprising. Her family didn't waste time.

"Yes. Really," he responded in his am-I-speaking-to-a-toddler tone.

She'd always hated it, but she'd ignored it because she'd loved Lionel. At least, she'd thought she loved him. She didn't feel nearly as heartbroken as she thought she should. Not about the wedding being called off, not about him calling because he couldn't get into the condo, not even about him sleeping with her assistant the night before their wedding. All she felt was . . . tired.

"And all my stuff was piled up at the curb. My clothes were on the ground, and a dozen homeless people were picking through them when I got home from work," he continued, every word he said all about him. Why hadn't she ever noticed that before?

"That's a shame, Lionel."

"I'm glad you think so. Now, what are you going to do about it?"

"About what?"

"About your family locking me out of our place and dumping my stuff," he growled. She could picture the scowl on his face, see it as clearly as she could see Handsome scurrying under the sofa and chasing a dust bunny out.

"How do you know it was my family?"

"Don't be obtuse, Anna. Who else has access to our condo? Who else—"

"It's not *our* condo, Lionel. It's mine. I bought it. My name is on the deed. I paid it off last year."

"I lived in it for five years. By law—"

"By law, if your stuff isn't in it and your name isn't on the title, you don't belong there. So, how about you find another place for you and Diane to sleep?"

"I'm not with Diane," he protested. "I made a mistake, and I regret it, but it was one night. It didn't mean anything."

"Not to you, but it means a heck of a lot to me." She hung up, because she was done with Lionel and his excuses.

When the phone rang she ignored it.

When it rang again, she walked out back.

Dusk shrouded the yard in deep purple and gray, turning old trees into giants and thick bushes into gnomes. She walked across the yard and into the orchard beyond. The air held a hint of apple and the ripe, thick scent of rotting fruit. At one time, the trees had been pruned and tended, but years of neglect had taken their toll. Still, with a little elbow grease and some initiative, the orchard could produce again. After years of working with herbs and leaves, she might just be ready for something new. She snagged an apple that hung from a gnarled branch. Small and tough, it had been overcrowded and had grown accordingly.

"I can fix this," she said to the evening sky and the cool, crisp breeze that was blowing through the trees. The leaves rustled, and she figured that was more of a reply than she'd have gotten if Lionel had been standing beside her.

"Idiot," she muttered, and she wasn't sure if she was talking about herself or Lionel.

Somewhere a rooster called a warning, and a bird flew from the tree beside her. She'd spent most of her childhood walking the woods of Happy Dale. Mostly alone. Lots of times at night when her overwhelming family had been too loud and boisterous and she'd wanted nothing more than to escape the little house and all the crazy people in it. She knew night sounds and nocturnal animals. She knew the difference between a deer stepping gingerly through a thicket and a man sliding through trees.

Right at that moment, she was sure she heard footsteps.

She glanced over her shoulder. Rose's house jutted up from the yard, light spilling out of the kitchen window and splashing gold across well-trimmed grass. A shadow moved near the corner of the house, undulating with the branches of an old pine tree that stood near the edge of the yard.

"Hello?" she called, moving toward it.

Something lunged from the shadows, and she screamed, backed up so fast she fell on her butt. She lay there for a moment, stunned, staring up at the dusky sky.

Get up, her mind screamed. *You're about to be attacked, and you're just lying here like a sack of potatoes!*

She was almost on her feet when something landed on her back. Not a heavy weight. Light and purring.

"Handsome?" She gasped, so relieved she sat down again, dragging the kitten off her back and into her lap. His purr sounded like an old-man's snore, his claws digging into her thighs as he tried to make himself comfortable.

"Ouch. Cool it!"

"Cool what?" a masculine voice asked, and she screamed so loudly, Handsome jumped off her lap and ran for cover.

"Sorry. Didn't mean to scare the living daylights out of you."

She knew the Southern drawl, the broad shoulders backlit by the kitchen light. Simon.

Relieved, she accepted the hand he held out, allowed herself to be pulled to her feet.

"What are you doing here?" she asked, his hand still wrapped around hers, all warm and calloused and nice.

"Do you even need to ask?"

"Yes. No," she blabbered, her heart beating way faster than it should have been, her cheeks flushed. "The kittens, right?"

"I heard them crying while I was helping the girls with their homework. I guess they weren't happy about being in a box under Evie's bed." He released her hand, and she had to admit she was just a little sorry about it. Simon was one of those guys her family liked to laugh at—straitlaced, kind, uncomplicated, drama-free.

Dependable was the word Rose would have used, and she'd have spit it out like it was dirtier than any four-letter curse she'd ever uttered.

"They're all waiting on the front porch," he continued, heading around the side of the house. "The girls are probably ringing the doorbell sixty-five thousand times."

"Doorbells are fun when you're eight," she replied, her insides all kinds of soft and mushy as she watched him scoop Handsome out of a bush that pressed up against the house.

"Here's the other one. I guess the girls didn't think he was worthy of stealing." He sounded disgusted and just a little tired.

"They weren't stealing. They were giving the kittens a home."

"Let's not play the semantic card, okay?" He sighed. "They took things that weren't theirs, hid them in their room, and didn't plan to say a word to me about it."

"You're really angry about a childish mistake."

"A mistake is when you drop a glass or knock over a cup of water," he grumbled, stalking up the porch steps.

The twins were there. One had tears streaming down her face. The other looked fit to be tied, her eyes flashing with frustration, her lips pressed together.

"I see my missing kittens have returned. I was wondering where they'd wandered off to," Apricot said, hoping to lighten the mood. There'd been very few rules when she was a kid, so she had no idea what it felt like to be on the receiving end of a parent's ire, but she had a feeling the twins had already found out.

"They didn't go missing, Apricot," the sobbing twin managed to gasp. "We took them, because we love them."

"And Daddy said we had to apologize," the scowling twin added. Had to be Evie. She seemed to be the feisty one out of the pair. "Even though we didn't do anything wrong."

"You took someone's cats, Evangeline," Simon said, and he sounded like he was at the last edge of his patience.

"How about we all go inside for a minute?" Apricot suggested. "We can sort it out there."

"Into the haunted house?" Rori breathed. "What if the ghosts get us?"

"There are no ghosts." Simon rubbed the bridge of his nose, and Apricot had the absurd urge to knead the tense muscles in his neck. She clenched her fists to keep from giving in to it.

"Aunt Daisy says—"

"Your aunt has a wonderful imagination." Apricot cut off whatever Evie planned to say. She didn't think Simon could handle it. "But she's wrong about the house. I spent every summer here when I was a kid, and I can tell you there's not a ghost to be found."

She opened the door and the girls followed her inside, Simon right behind them, holding Handsome close to his chest. His very broad, very muscular chest.

She should not be noticing that.

But she was, so she looked away, her cheeks hot.

"Are you sure there aren't any ghosts in here?" Evie asked suspiciously, her gaze darting around the living room. Apricot hadn't uncovered the furniture yet, and even she had to admit the cavernous room with its shrouded white furniture looked unlived-in and just a little creepy.

"Positive."

"How can you know?" Rori asked quietly, tears drying on her cheeks. "Aunt Daisy says that ghosts only show themselves when it's nighttime, but they're even around during the day. She says—"

"Aurora," Simon said gently, "your aunt needs to

stop filling your head with silly stories, and you need to stop believing them."

"They're not silly." Rori didn't stamp her foot, but Apricot thought she wanted to.

"They are too silly," Evie interrupted. "And I knew all along there were no ghosts in this house. Just sheets on sofas." She plopped down onto the couch, her blond hair a wild mess of fine strands. She needed a comb and something to keep her mind occupied.

That would be Apricot's assessment, but then, she didn't know a whole heck of a lot about kids. She'd been just young enough to avoid being a nanny to the younger children in Happy Dale. By the time she'd been old enough to do her stint as babysitter, Aunt Rose had already taken her under her wing. While her sisters had been shepherding little ones, she'd been learning the difference between mint and clover. While they'd been helping a dozen or more children with homework and chores, she'd been building greenhouses and making candles to sell at farmers' markets.

She eyed Evie.

"You have a kitten in your pocket," she finally said, because the little girl actually did have a kitten in her jacket pocket, its little white-and-black face peeking out.

"Because Daddy wouldn't even give me one second to find a box for her. He said we had to get these dog-gone cats out of the house before he blew a casket."

"Gasket," Simon corrected.

"That's what you said," Evie wailed. "And it really hurt my feelings a lot, because Sassafras is not a doggone cat."

"Neither is Princess!" Apparently, Rori didn't want her sister's grief to outshine hers. She started wailing too. Handsome joined them, yowling with so much passion, Simon set him on the couch and took a step away.

"What a mess," he muttered.

"The cat or the kids?" she asked.

"All three of them." He ran a hand down his jaw, shook his head as he eyed his crying daughters. "You know, Apricot," he said, "I had a feeling you were trouble. It looks like I was right."

"Me?"

"Yeah. You."

"All I did was ask you for a reference," she protested.

"And bring kittens into my house. The one thing the girls want above all else."

"It's not like I knew that, and it's not like I offered the kittens to the girls. They took them."

"We're sorry," the girls cried in unison, and if it hadn't been so sad, she probably would have laughed at the picture they made—two little towheads with tiny kittens in their jacket pockets, crying as if the world were about to end.

"It's okay," Apricot said.

"No, it's not," Rori cried.

Things had gotten out of hand.

Simon wasn't quite sure how.

He'd planned to bring the kittens back, get the girls in the car, and drive away. Instead, he was standing in Rose's living room listening to various howls and sobs.

Enough was enough.

He had a meeting in the morning and plenty to do before the girls went to bed. "Okay, girls. Give Apricot the kittens. It's time to say good-bye."

Tears poured down the girls' faces, but they carefully removed the kittens from their pockets, smoothed fuzzy fur, murmured good-byes that Simon could only partially hear.

Maybe he wasn't doing the right thing making the girls give up the kittens. Maybe ten years from now, they'd be rebellious young women, living lives of crime and citing this one moment as the thing that had turned them into criminals.

Apricot sidled up beside him, her hand settling on his shoulder as she stood on tiptoe and whispered in his ear. "You know, Simon, having pets teaches children wonderful things about responsibility and love."

"No," he replied without looking at her, because he had this odd feeling that if he did, she'd see the doubt in his eyes, sense his weakness and move in for the kill.

"Studies have shown that children who have pets have better social skills and are more successful as adults," she continued, her lips brushing his hair, her breath whispering against his cheek.

"Liar," he responded, but his mind was only partially on the cats and the kids. The rest of it was on Apricot and her warm hand on his shoulder.

"Maybe, but they do look cute together, and you can't deny that pets teach responsibility." She stepped back, scooped the ugly gray cat from the floor, scratched it behind the ears. "Besides, sometimes the punishment needs to fit the crime, and what better punishment for kitten rustlers than to clean out litter boxes and be woken three or four times a night by crying babies? They don't have to keep the kittens, but babysitting them for a couple of days wouldn't hurt," she added blithely.

"No," he repeated, but she had a point.

The girls were going to give the kittens back, but they weren't going to understand exactly why he'd been refusing to allow pets in the home.

"Fine." Apricot's hand slipped away. "Let me just get a box to put the kittens in. You and the girls can say good-bye."

She walked from the room, and he looked at the girls and the kittens and all the tears, and he had one stark moment of realization that he was making a huge mistake before he opened his mouth and made it.

"I've been thinking—" *Don't,* his brain shouted. *Whatever you do, do* not *think about this.* "You stole the kittens, and you thought it would be a great idea to try to take care of them yourselves. Instead of leaving them here tonight, we're going to take them home."

"Ya—" The girls started to shout in excitement, but he held up a hand and cut them off.

"I didn't say we're keeping them. I said you're going to take care of them. Then you're going to help me find them a good home."

The wails commenced again, and he was sure he heard Apricot's laughter from somewhere deep inside the old house.

When she brought the box a few minutes later, there wasn't even a hint of a smirk on her face. He was sure, though, that he saw the amusement in her eyes as he put the kittens in the box and carried them out into the cool September evening.

Insomnia sucked.

It especially sucked in a strange house with no television, no radio, and nothing but the darkness pressing against the windows to keep her company.

And Handsome.

Who'd been howling pretty much nonstop since midnight.

It was three in the morning.

He was still going strong.

"Hush." She fished the kitten out from under the daybed she'd been lying on. He started purring immediately.

If Simon was having as much trouble with the kittens the girls were babysitting, she was probably going to hear about it.

Really, though, he only had himself to blame.

It wasn't like she'd forced him to bring the kittens home. She'd simply planted the seed. Of course, as Rose often said, seeds grow what's planted.

Rose.

Yeah. She should probably call her. Let her know that things were fine and that she appreciated her getting the lights and gas turned on.

Tomorrow.

Or the next day.

No doubt Rose had a lot to say about Lionel. Lots that she hadn't already said after the wedding. Apricot wasn't in the mood to hear it.

She set the kitten on the daybed and went to the

kitchen, pulling dry herbs out of one of the boxes that she'd found in the Airstream. Rose must have packed it. She believed that there was nothing in life that couldn't be cured by the right combination of herbs or tea leaves. Even a broken heart.

Not that Apricot's heart was broken.

It was just a little bruised, and she was just a little at loose ends, a little off-kilter. That was to be expected. She'd spent a lot of years with Lionel. She'd invested time and emotion into their relationship, and she had every right to be disappointed that it hadn't worked out.

The thing to do was focus on something else, get herself involved in a project that would take up time and leave her too tired to worry about the fact that she was nearly thirty, all her plans and dreams for the next few years dead.

She brewed a cup of chamomile tea and walked outside. The moon had already dropped below distant mountains, the sweet scent of mown grass hanging on the night-cool air. She'd forgotten how dark early mornings at Rose's were. She'd forgotten the velvety feel of fresh air, the heavy comfort of country quiet.

"It's been too long," she said to herself and to whatever nocturnal creatures were bedding down. Something rustled in the trees at the edge of the yard. A deer, maybe. Or a coyote. She and Rose had seen several during their summer stays.

The thought didn't scare her. Whatever creature was lurking in the trees would leave soon enough. In the meantime, she dropped onto the step Dusty had made her sit on, pulling her knees to her chest, her faded cotton pajamas cool against her skin. Thank goodness all the sexy lingerie she'd bought for the honeymoon had been removed from her bags. Probably one of her sisters' doing.

A bird called from the gnarled orchard, the sound a sweet good morning that made Apricot smile. Insomnia sucked, but sleeping in meant missing a lot of beauty. In Los Angeles, she'd always been up at the crack of dawn, working from her home office before the nursery opened. There'd been smog, of course. Noise. Lots of people, and she'd loved every minute of it, but somewhere deep inside, she must have missed country living, because being at Rose's house felt like returning home after being away for much too long.

She stood, the tea in her hand, her mind humming with something odd, something a little surprising given her circumstances. It felt like hope. Like excitement.

She headed toward the orchard, cold grass under her bare feet. She needed something to keep her mind occupied, and the neglected apple trees were begging for some attention. She'd spend the next few days doing some trimming. If the orchard could be saved, she'd hire a few locals to help her do it. In a few years, the land would be producing again. Then her aunt could sell more than tinctures, soaps, and candles at the local apple fair. She could sell apple cider, apple butter, apple pies.

She stepped into the thick copse of trees, her hair snagging on branches. The trees weren't the only things that needed trimming! She'd been growing her hair out for three years because Lionel liked it long, and she'd been idiot enough to want to please him.

Come first light, she was going to find a salon and get every inch of it cut off.

A twig snapped behind her, the sound reverberating through the quiet morning.

"Is anyone out here?" she called.

"Yes," a man replied.

She jumped, whirling to face the speaker.

He stood at the edge of the tree line. Tall. Broad shoulders. Face hidden in shadows. She wanted to get a good look at him. Just in case she needed a description for the police.

That would involve moving closer, and she had no intention of doing that.

"I have a gun," she lied, taking a step back. She'd have gone farther, but her hair snagged another branch.

"I doubt it." He laughed, his voice vaguely familiar. "But if you do, please don't use it."

"Who are you?"

"Cade Cunningham."

Not a serial killer.

Thank God!

"Dusty wasn't complaining about me again, was he?" She yanked her hair from the tree branch. "Because I haven't done anything for him to complain about."

"No. I was driving by on patrol and saw your lights."

"So you stopped in for a visit?"

"Not quite. I heard you own A Thyme to Heal."

"That's right."

"Daisy said your chamomile tea is fantastic."

"I'm glad she liked it."

"My wife is thirty-five weeks' pregnant—"

"Is she still suffering from morning sickness?"

"No. She—"

"Sleep issues, then?"

"My wife is fine," he responded. "It's her aunt who is having issues. Gertrude has been pacing the house like a caged tiger, and she's driving everyone in it crazy. I thought maybe some of that chamomile tea would help."

"Is she a tea drinker?" she asked as she led him inside.

"Not even close, but I'm getting desperate. My wife needs some sleep, and I need some peace. If we don't get Gertrude to calm down, we may have to move out until the baby is born."

"That bad, huh?"

"Worse." He ran a hand over dark brown hair, rubbed the back of his neck. She'd known him when they were kids; not well, but enough that she wasn't surprised that he'd become sheriff or that he cared enough about his wife's health to stop for help in the wee hours of the morning.

"Chamomile might help some, but you may want to get her involved in some physical activity." She grabbed a box of chamomile from the cupboard and handed it to him. "Steep this in hot water. Not boiling."

"Got it."

"And take her on long walks."

"She's not a dog." He tugged at his uniform tie. "And she can't be convinced to do something that she doesn't want to do. There is no way Gertrude is going to want to participate in any kind of exercise."

"You could tell her she needs to be healthy for the baby's sake," she suggested, wondering what it would be like to have a man like Cade in her life. One who would go out of his way for her rather than expecting that she would always go out of her way for him.

"We told her that to get her to quit smoking. She's still bitter."

"When'd she quit?"

"A few months ago."

"No wonder she's pacing the house and driving you all crazy." She grabbed the sleep tincture from the windowsill and handed it to him. "She can take a couple of drops of this before bed."

"I can tell you for sure, she won't. Gertrude is stubborn as a mule." He set the bottle on the counter.

"I guess we're back to getting her to exercise."

"Right." He sighed.

"Don't sound so defeated, Cade. Eventually your wife will have that baby and Gertrude will have something else to focus her attention on."

"Right. I'll try to keep that in mind," he responded, glancing around at the kitchen, running his palm over the butcher-block counter. "How are things going for you?"

"It's three in the morning, and I'm awake. Do you really need to ask?"

He laughed, shook his head. "I don't suppose I do. I know you're not asking for my advice, and you probably don't want it. But I feel the need to give it anyway. Don't waste your time mourning the guy you dumped. You deserve better. Being here and away from him? It's the best thing that could have happened to you. Now, I'd better get back to work. Thanks again for the tea."

"No problem." She followed him outside, waited on the porch as he drove away, the cold air seeping through her pajamas reminding her of childhood evenings, cold wind, hot fires, people who loved her.

She blinked back tears.

There was no need for them.

Cade was right.

Being here and away from Lionel was the best thing that had happened to her in a very long time.

So why did she feel like crap?

She settled onto the porch step, hugged her knees to her chest, let the silence and the darkness drift around her as she waited for the first golden rays of sun to crest the distant mountains.

Chapter Six

Things were happening at the old Shaffer place.

That's what the blue-haired ladies at the diner were talking about when Simon brought the girls there for lunch. The kittens had been in residence for three days, and the girls had tucked them into their box before they'd left, kissed them good-bye, acted like they might be separated forever.

Now Rori and Evie were giggling, their purses slung over their shoulders and clutched tight to their sides, every bit of their hard-earned allowance money tucked away inside. They'd planned out the whole day for Simon. First, they were making a stop at a dance store to buy some frilly little tutu Evie had been eyeing. Then they were going to the pet store to spend the rest of what they had on toys for the kittens. He hadn't had the heart to remind them that the kittens weren't staying for much longer.

The fact was, the girls had taken to their new responsibilities with an ease and cheerfulness that surprised him. They'd fed the kittens, kept the water bowl filled, cleaned the litter box. Not one complaint and no fights about who was going to do what.

He took a bite of his quarter-pound hamburger and watched the girls divvy up the fries and chicken strips he'd ordered them.

"Need a refill on those sodas?" Maura Cline asked as she sashayed past their table. She'd been waiting tables at the diner for longer than Simon had been alive. It's what she loved, she'd tell anyone who asked. Simon thought it was more likely that she was waiting for Mr. Right to come rolling through town, hoping that he might stop in for a bite to eat and take her away from Apple Valley. Fiftysomething and still clinging to her twenties, she had bleached blond hair, blue eyes, and enough makeup on her face to sink a battleship. "Free for the kids. Just like always."

"No. Thanks, Maura."

"But I'm still thirsty, Daddy," Evie complained.

"Then you can have water. It's healthier."

"Your dad is right, sweet cheeks." Maura snagged a pitcher of water from behind the counter and poured some into a glass.

"This stuff?" She set the glass down in front of Evie. "It'll keep your figure nice and youthful. A girl needs to think about such things."

"Not when she's eight." Evie pouted, her eyes flashing with frustration. She looked so much like Megan, Simon's heart clenched, that old guilt, that old feeling of failure welling up in him.

"Don't be rude, Evie," he snapped, his voice much harder than he'd intended it to be.

"I'm not being rude." She sniffed. "I'm just being honest. Isn't that what you always tell me to do?"

Maura let out a bark of laughter. "You got a smart

kid, Simon. You'd better be careful or she'll have you running in circles trying to keep up with her."

"She already does," he replied, and Maura laughed again. She glanced around the nearly empty diner, leaned in close. "You hear anything about what's going on at the old Shaffer place?"

"Just what the blu—just what the women in the booth behind me were discussing."

"I heard them. Bunch of busybodies, if you ask me. Of course, no one is asking me, so I'll just keep that opinion to myself."

"Thanks," he said drily. If she caught his sarcasm, she didn't let on.

"The way I hear things, that woman who moved into the Shaffer place is tearing the old house down and building one of those newfangled modern homes. All glass walls. No privacy. Guess a fancy city lady like herself doesn't think she needs any." Maura huffed.

"She's not tearing the place down," he responded. He'd have believed a lot of things but not that. A woman with an ancient Ford truck and a 1950s Airstream knew the value of old things.

"I'm telling you right now that she is. I heard it from Caroline Randall, who heard it from Jasper Guthrey. He got the information from Tim Wyatt. Tim's the one helping Jet with the project."

"Building a house is a mighty big project, Maura. Do you really think Jet is up to it?"

She shrugged, her breasts heaving under a T-shirt that was three sizes too small. "He'll give it a try. I suppose if he can't do it, she'll just hand the job over to a big company. She's got the money for it. I can tell you that for a fact."

The diner door opened and the woman they were discussing walked in. Apricot was like a breath of fresh air after a long day working in an office. Like sunshine after a long, hard winter. She brightened the room, her smile offered to everyone.

"It's her!" Evie squealed. "Princess Apricot."

"Apricot?!" Maura scoffed. "Her name is Anna."

"No, it's not," Rori said more quietly than her sister. "It's Apricot. She was over at our house one day, so we know her name perfectly well."

"Over at your house?" Maura met Simon's eyes, raised one very narrow brow. "Is that so?"

"She wanted a reference. For Jet," he explained, because he knew if he didn't, rumors of his engagement would spread like wildfire. No matter how much he denied it, he'd never be able to undo the damage.

"Sure she did." Maura's eyes glittered as she waved at Apricot. "Annie! Over here!"

"Apricot!" Evie shouted, and Simon should have been way too busy shushing her to notice Apricot's shorn hair or the way her body seemed to glide beneath a long blue skirt and bright white tank top. She wore a tiny little sweater over the tank. It didn't do anything to hide her curves.

"Hello, everyone!" she said as she sidled up next to Maura. Something in the big bag she had flung over her shoulder moved, but Maura didn't seem to notice, and Simon decided not to call attention to it. "I'm just in for one of the diner's famous club sandwiches, Maura, and a glass of water to go. If you don't mind."

"Business is business," Maura responded, jotting

something on her order pad even though she never used the thing.

She stalked away, muttering under her breath as she went, and returned seconds later with a carryout cup. She slammed it down on the table. "Sandwich will be ready in ten. Better pay at the register before you walk out," she said loudly enough for everyone in the diner to hear.

Apricot sipped water through the straw and smiled. "I will. Thank you, Maura."

"Humph!" Maura replied and stalked away again.

"I get the distinct impression that woman doesn't like me," Apricot said, taking a seat next to Evie. "Mind if I rest here for a spell while she gets my sandwich?"

"For a spell?" Rori repeated. "Are you going to make a spell while you sit?"

"It means for a while. It's just a different way of saying it," Apricot explained. The bag moved again, and she patted it. "I rode my bike into town, and I'm tired."

"Is that why you cut all your hair off? Because it was too heavy for your tired head?" Evie asked, her eyes wide as she studied Apricot. Simon had the feeling his daughters wouldn't find the short pixie-ish cut nearly as beautiful as they'd found Apricot's long hair. Of course, in their minds, princesses always had long flowing locks of silky hair. Daisy made sure to keep them informed of such things.

"My hair—" Apricot touched her head and frowned. "It's a long story."

"I love stories," Rori said.

"In that case, I don't mind telling you this one. I went to this place in Apple Valley to get it cut, and

I said I wanted it to here." She touched her shoulder. "I ended up with it here." She pointed to a spot right below her ears. "And out to here." She held her hands out a foot on either side of her head. Both girls giggled.

"Could you fit through a door with it that big?" Rori wanted to know.

"Just barely," Apricot said, meeting Simon's eyes and smiling. "It was so difficult to get into my house, I decided I'd better drive to Spokane and have another hair dresser fix it. This very short cut was the only way they could do that."

"I think it's pretty!" Evie claimed. "I think I should get my hair just like that, Daddy."

"It would be kind of hard to get it into a ballet bun," he reminded her. Not that he cared much about the length of the girls' hair. It was Daisy who insisted they keep it long. Daisy who'd signed them up for ballet. Daisy who insisted that they wear dresses a few times a week. He'd stepped back plenty regarding those things, because it hadn't mattered all that much. Although, when she'd tried to dress the girls for picture day in outfits that looked like Laura Ingalls Wilder might have worn them, he'd put his foot down.

"He's right," Rori said quietly. "Plus, Aunt Daisy wouldn't like it. She doesn't like short hair." She glanced at Apricot. "I think it's pretty, though. It makes your eyes look bluer."

She was right. Apricot's eyes did look very blue, and her skin was flawless, a few freckles sprinkled across cheeks that were flushed pink with exertion or embarrassment. Simon wasn't sure which, but he thought it was time to change the subject. Since her bag seemed to be crawling across the bench seat, he figured that was as good a subject as any.

"Did you bring someone with you?" he asked, and her flush deepened.

"Shhhh!" She grabbed the bag and dropped it into her lap. It meowed and both girls giggled.

"You have more kittens," they squealed in unison, and Apricot sighed.

"Not kittens. Kitten. Just one. Handsome is more trouble than he's worth. I can't leave him home, because he escapes from the house and goes on Dusty's property. Yesterday he found a way into Dusty's house and managed to break a vase and shred a chair. Dusty said that if he ever sees Handsome on his property again . . ." She looked at the girls and pressed her lips together.

"I get the point," Simon cut in. Dusty wasn't known for his patience. Not with people. Not with animals. "But I don't think Maura will be any more understanding than Dusty is. If she finds out you have a kitten in here, she'll ban you for life."

"I know." She smiled. "I was planning to wait outside, but it's hot as Hades. I really thought it would be cooler around here this time of year." She stood and stretched, the tank riding up along smooth, creamy flesh.

She tugged her shirt back into place and grabbed her water, hitching the bag with the errant kitten over her shoulder. "Enjoy the rest of your lunch. I'll see you around."

"We're done." Rori hopped up, her quick movement and loud voice surprising Simon. She was never loud or quick.

"Aren't we done, Evie?" she prodded her sister.

"We are! We'll wait outside with you, Apricot. Daddy can bring out your sandwich when it's ready. I'll give him the money." She dug in her purse.

"You do that and you won't have enough money for that tutu we're supposed to get this afternoon or for the toys you want to buy the kittens," he reminded her.

In true Evie fashion, she sighed dramatically. "Some things are just more important than tutus."

He was surprised that she realized it. She'd been talking nonstop about the blue tutu she'd seen at Empire Dance Shop. She'd scrimped and saved and even done extra chores so she could afford the glittery, gauzy thing.

"You're right about that. There are plenty of things more important than a tutu. My sandwich isn't one of them, sweet cheeks," Apricot responded with a laugh. "Besides, I have cash right here." She opened the purse and Handsome popped out, taking off like a flash and dashing under a table.

"Handsome! No!" Apricot cried, running after the kitten.

Nancy Edgar spotted the kitten as it dashed away from Apricot's grasping hands. Ninety years old if she was a day, the woman had the shrillest voice Simon had ever had the displeasure of hearing. She used it to full advantage, shrieking so loudly, Simon's water glass vibrated.

"A rat!" she screamed. "This place has rats!"

Next thing Simon knew, all hell broke loose.

The cook ran out of the kitchen, broom in hand, Maura chasing along after him. The few customers who were there jumped onto chairs. Except for

Campy Sampson. He reached for the pistol Simon knew he had concealed beneath his jacket.

"Freeze!" Simon shouted.

Nancy froze. Maura and the cook froze. Even Campy froze.

Only Apricot was still moving, skidding under another table, her skirt bunched up around long legs.

"Don't even think about it, Campy," Simon added for good measure, his gaze on Apricot and the ugly gray kitten she was chasing. He would have laughed, but he thought Maura would slap him upside the head with the frying pan she was holding.

Somehow, Apricot managed to snag Handsome by the scruff of his neck. She murmured something about the ruckus and sprinted from the diner.

Apricot didn't get her sandwich and she wasn't happy about it. As a matter of fact, she was fairly pissed off as she pedaled away from the diner. Handsome, on the other hand, was happy as a clam, sitting in the basket of the bicycle, his head to the wind.

"That's it," she shouted at him, not caring that there were half a dozen people walking along Main Street. "I'm bringing you to the shelter! And I'm not going to feel bad about it. At all!"

A car chugged up behind her, but she didn't even pause in her frantic pedaling. Obviously, coming to Apple Valley on a day when she would have been better off staying in bed had been a bad idea. If not for the noisy, boisterous crew of teens Jet had brought to help him haul away old siding, she'd have done what she felt like doing and stayed under her covers until the sun went down.

Her new iPhone rang, and she snagged it one-handed from the depth of the purse she still had on her shoulder. "What is it?" she growled.

"Is that any way to greet the woman who carried you in her womb for nine months? The one who squeezed your big head out of her—"

"Lilac, I am not in the mood for a rehash of the details of my birth."

"Moody some?" Lilac asked.

"I am not moody," Apricot responded as she passed the Apple Valley Sheriff's Department. Across the street, gates opened into Riley Park. Beyond that, a small white church stood atop a hill that looked over the park and the town. Rose had taken her there once. Not to hear the preacher, but to see the historic building, the beautiful stained glass windows, and the cemetery that spread out across lush green lawns.

"Of course you are. How long has it been since you've had—"

"Do not"—Apricot panted as she steered across Main Street and pedaled through the gates—"ask me about my love life."

"I would never!" Lilac proclaimed. A bold-faced lie, but Apricot didn't have the energy to point it out. "I was simply going to ask how long it's been since you've had some soothing chamomile."

"An hour," Apricot ground out. A few kids were loitering on the path, and she had a good mind to hand Handsome to one of them.

"You need more, but that isn't why I called. I'm worried about you, Apricot. You should be in Happy

Dale. With your family. Not in some uptight small town where you don't know anyone."

"Apple Valley isn't uptight, Lilac." Not according to most people's standards. To Lilac, it would have been oppressive.

"We'll see, won't we?"

"What's that supposed to mean?" Apricot pulled over to the side of the path, hot September sun beating down on the back of her neck. It had been a long time since her hair had been short, and she'd forgotten to sunscreen her nape.

"Your father and I are driving out there."

"What?!" she shouted, and an elderly woman sitting on a bench a few feet away scowled, her frizzy orange hair bouncing as she shifted to get a better look at Apricot.

"We're driving out there. You need support and—"

"No. Not just no, but *hell no*!"

"The decision has already been made."

"Unmake it then, because the last thing I need or want are two people who argue over the color of the sky staying with me."

"We won't have to stay with you. I'm sure there is a hotel nearby," Lilac responded. "I won't even mention the fact that Rose's house is so big that Hubert and I wouldn't even have to see each other if we did stay with you."

"It's not that big."

"Five bedrooms, right?"

She hesitated, absolutely sure she was stepping into a trap but not sure how to keep from doing it. "Yes."

"Well, that's perfect then. One for Hubert. One for me. Rose will stay—"

"Rose is coming?"

"Of course. A woman needs family at a time like this."

"Not *this* woman."

"That's because you don't know what's happened. If you did . . ." Her voice trailed off. "I'd better go. We have a lot of packing to do."

"Hold on!" Apricot barked, and the woman with orange hair stood, not making any secret at all of the fact that she was listening. "What happened?"

"Lionel and that floozy of his flew off to Aruba together. Rumor has it, they're eloping."

"And this should bother me, because?" she said, even though her heart shook and her stomach churned and everything inside of her just kind of iced over.

"You're saying it doesn't?"

"That's exactly what I'm saying. Lionel is a loser. What he does doesn't impact me at all."

Lie, her heart whispered, because no matter how much she knew she shouldn't care, she did.

"Well, all right then," Lilac responded in typical Lilac fashion. If she knew that Apricot was lying, she didn't let on. She wouldn't, because Lilac believed in parenting by allowing her kids to figure things out themselves. She didn't believe in the hierarchy of parent-child relationships. For as long as Apricot could remember, she'd been treated like her mother's friend rather than her daughter. "I'll talk to Hubert, and we'll make a decision about whether or not we should still come."

"There is no decision to be made," she said, but Lilac had already hung up. She shoved the phone back in her purse, righted the bike, and would have pedaled away, but the orange-haired woman was suddenly in front of her, blocking the path that led around Riley Lake.

"Family trouble, huh?" she asked, pulling a cigarette from the pocket of fuchsia sweatpants and tapping it against her thigh.

"I—"

"No need to answer. I know all about it," she continued. "Gertrude McKenzie." She shook Apricot's hand. "You know my nephew-in-law, Cade Cunningham."

Apricot nodded. This must be the aunt he'd been talking about. The one who'd been pacing around the house driving everyone crazy. "Apri—"

"I know who you are, doll. Everyone in town does. Heard you got jilted at the altar." She tapped the cigarette against her thigh again and tucked it in her pocket.

"I was the one who did the jilting," she corrected, because she didn't want everyone in town talking about how she'd been left at the altar. Pitiful was not how she wanted the citizens of Apple Valley to view her.

Of course, thanks to Handsome, they were probably more likely to think of her as crazy.

"Really?!" Gertrude cackled in delight. "Perfect. Guy deserved it, didn't he? He cheat on you?"

"I'd rather not discuss it."

"So, he *did* cheat. Bastard! He comes sniffing around here, trying to get you back, you kick him in the balls and tell him—"

"Apricot!" a little girl called.

Thank God!

She turned, glad to have a reason to end the conversation. Rori and Evie were loping toward her, their blond hair gleaming in the sunlight, pigtails bouncing as they ran. Simon was walking just a few yards behind, his stride long and brisk. He'd dressed for a day off—dark jeans that looked like they'd been worn many times before, a light blue T-shirt that clung to his chest and flat abdomen. He winked, and her heart just about flew from her chest.

"So, that's the way things are," Gertrude murmured just loud enough for Apricot to hear.

"We have your sandwich!" Rori called, holding up a Styrofoam carryout container.

"And I even made Maura give you the chips that are supposed to come with it," Evie said, panting as she skidded to a stop beside Apricot's bike. She glanced at Gertrude. "Hello, Ms. Gertrude."

"Hiya, doll. What are you and your twin up to today?"

"We're going to the dance store." Rori opened a little purse that hung from her shoulder and flashed some bills and change.

"Are you? What you going to get there?"

"I'm getting new shoes," Rori said shyly. "I wore a hole right through mine." She handed Apricot the sandwich container and lifted Handsome out of the basket. "Poor Handsome," she crooned. "Did those mean old people scare you?"

Handsome purred in response.

Simon reached the group, tipped his head in Gertrude's direction. "Good afternoon, Ms. Gertrude."

"What's good about it? It's nine thousand degrees out here, and I've been kicked out of the house. For some reason that I can't understand, Tessa says I'm driving her crazy."

"Could it be you're getting antsy about that baby?"

he asked, tracking his daughters as they walked to the pond and called to some ducks that were floating near the shore.

Gertrude snorted. "Hardly. I've been down this road before with my niece Emily. I coached her through her entire pregnancy with Alex, and then I was at her side when she gave birth. I've got no reason to be antsy about this. I'm cool as a cucumber."

She took out the cigarette again, smashed it against her thigh. It didn't seem like the chamomile tea had done her much good. Maybe passionflower would do the trick.

Apricot dug into her purse. She always carried samples of A Thyme to Heal's most popular teas.

"If you're calm, why are you smashing your cigarette?" Simon asked.

Gertrude scowled. "What's it to you? I'm not smoking the damn thing. That should be good enough for everyone."

Apricot finally found the tea. "Are you a tea drinker, Gertrude?" she asked, hoping to distract the woman.

"Well, I'll be honest," Gertrude responded, the scowl still plastered firmly on her face. "I usually drink coffee. My mother? She loved tea."

"It might be nice to revisit your mother's habits. Tea is very soothing. This"—she handed Gertrude the two tea bags—"is passionflower tea. It's wonderful and smooth."

"I got to admit, I liked the chamomile you sent home with Cade. I don't suppose it'll hurt to try this. Now if you don't mind, I'm getting out of here." She tossed her bright orange hair. "I'm going to the diner to get some lunch. Tess doesn't want me at home, I don't need to be at home."

She walked away without another word, shoulders bowed, head bent. She didn't look angry. She looked weighted down and worried.

"Poor Gertrude," Simon commented as she disappeared from view. "She's got herself tied into all kinds of knots about the baby."

"Do they think there's going to be a problem with the delivery?"

"Far as I know, the doctor has given mom and baby a clean bill of health." He shrugged, his focus on the girls. Rori still had Handsome, and Evie was dancing close to the water's edge. "Watch it, Evangeline! You fall in, and we'll have to go home and change. We have to do that, and our trip to the dance store isn't going to happen."

"Okay, Daddy!" Evie sang, her blond pigtails swinging straight out to either side of her head as she whirled and twirled.

A few other families were taking advantage of the sunny afternoon. Kids on bikes and skateboards, couples holding hands as they walked along the path, all them enjoying the beautiful day.

Somewhere in the far recesses of her mind, Apricot had always thought of Apple Valley as the perfect place to raise a family. She'd spent a lot of time traveling when she was a kid. She'd gone from town to town and city to city, but she'd never found a place quite like this one.

"You okay?" Simon asked quietly.

She'd been staring a little too long, she guessed. Looking at all those families and all that happiness and wondering why she hadn't found it yet. "Fine.

Thanks for bringing me the sandwich. I'm surprised Maura let you take it." She dug ten dollars from her purse.

"She was pissed, but Maura is more interested in money than grudges. She did say that if you ever bring that rat-cat back in the diner, she'll feed it to you for dinner."

"Nice," she responded, handing him the money.

"Actually," he said as he tucked it back in her purse, "the girls paid for it, and they don't want to be paid back."

"I can't let the girls buy my lunch," she protested.

"Would you rather disappoint them? They're trying to do something nice, and I applaud that."

She looked at the girls, thought about herself at that age. Even then, she'd loved herbs and plants. She'd had a garden and sold the produce on the side of the road. Every cent she'd earned had been used to buy the things her family needed. Shoes for the youngers, schoolbooks for the olders, pencils, paper. "Of course not," she replied. "But what about the tutu Evie planned to buy?"

"She'll get it another time."

"Or maybe a friend could buy it? As a thank-you."

"For a sandwich?" He smiled.

"As a thank-you for taking the kittens off my hands and for babysitting Handsome. That cat is a pain in the butt."

"Really, Apricot, it's fine. The girls were happy to buy your lunch. Girls!" he called. "We've got to go!"

Both hurried over, Rori handing Handsome over with a shy smile that made Apricot's heart ache. She'd always thought she'd have kids one day. Now? She thought she'd probably end up with Handsome.

Chapter Seven

Anger did funny things to people.

It made them do what they normally wouldn't.

For example, there was no way on God's green earth that Apricot would ever have considered following a good-looking guy and his twin daughters into a city she didn't know if she weren't pissed out of her mind. There she was, though, pulling into a parking lot behind a small brick building somewhere in the bowels of Spokane. Empire Dance Shop. She checked the directions she'd pulled up on her phone. Yep. She was in the right spot.

"It's not like I really followed him," she said as she got out of Henry III. "I just kind of showed up at the place he was going."

Handsome meowed from his box on the passenger seat.

"What?" she asked, scooping him up and depositing him none too gently into her purse. If it weren't so hot, she'd have left him in the truck, but it was. Handsome might be a pain in the butt, but she didn't want to cook the poor thing. "The guys are still making a racket at the house, and I needed to get out for a while longer. This is as good a place as any to go."

Handsome meowed again.

She ignored him as she walked around the side of the building. She knew she should have just stayed home. She didn't know the girls well, and Simon had made it very clear that he didn't want her to pay for the tutu.

Five years of her life . . . *five years!* she'd wasted on Lionel.

Five years of loyalty, of monogamy, of explaining to friends and family that Lionel was a great guy even if he did stand her up on dates a time or two and go out with his buddies on a few too many occasions.

Tears burned the back of her eyes, but she'd be danged if she let them fall. Lionel wasn't worth it.

She yanked open the door and walked into the store. The Baylors were there. The girls sitting in chairs in the center of the store, Simon standing nearby, hands in his pockets, a frown line etched in his forehead. He didn't look all that happy to see Apricot. She smiled anyway, glancing around the store, trying to take in details through the tears she wasn't going to shed.

A rainbow of leotards lined the walls. Pink ballet shoes sat on shelves. Tiny little tutus hung from a rack. A display case and counter stood to the right, a pretty blond woman standing behind it.

"So," Apricot said. "This is the place where girls come to buy blue tutus."

"Among other things," a man said as he walked out of a back room. He had a small shoe box in one hand

and a pink ballet flat in the other. He also had a heavenly accent.

"Are you looking for something in particular?" he asked.

"A blue tutu. And maybe"—she looked at Rori and made a quick guess—"a pink one."

"For you?" The man knelt in front of Rori and slid the pink shoe on her foot.

Rori giggled. "She's not a dancer, Mr. Phillip. She makes potions."

"Does she now?" He checked the fit of the shoe, took another one from the box. "What kind of potions would that be? Princess potions?"

"I'm an herbalist," Apricot explained, moving deeper into the store and studiously avoiding Simon's eyes. "And the tutus are an early birthday present for some young friends who helped me out this morning."

That sounded good, didn't it?

It sounded like a reasonable excuse for buying tutus for girls she didn't know.

"Would they happen to be about this tall?" Phillip held his hand to the twins' height. "With blond hair and pretty brown eyes?"

"That sounds about right," she responded, smiling at the guy because it was a lot easier than looking at Simon. Besides, Phillip wasn't exactly hard on the eyes. She'd have put him in his midforties, his hair touched with just a hint of gray, his body slim and muscular. If she'd had to make a guess, she'd have said he was a dancer.

"I think my wife can help you with that. Sally, can you grab that blue skirt from the back room?" he said, pulling Rori to her feet and eyeing the shoes.

"Sure. There are some pink ballet skirts right behind you." The woman behind the counter pointed Apricot to a rack of multilayered skirts. Most were fairly plain, but one looked like just the thing. Ruffly with tiny pink bows sewn to its hem, it would have been exactly the type of thing Apricot would have worn when she was the twins' age. If she hadn't been stuck with her brother's hand-me-down overalls.

She turned to carry it to the counter and nearly ran into Simon. Or, to be more accurate, Simon's very broad, very muscular chest. It looked good encased in light blue, but she had a feeling it would look good in anything. Or even nothing.

She stepped back, knocked into the rack, sent half a dozen tutus flying.

"Oh, for God's sake!" she muttered, scooping them up and haphazardly rehanging them, her face so hot she thought her skin might spontaneously combust.

"Just deserts." Simon took the pink tutu from her hand.

"For what?"

"Being stubborn."

"I'm not stubborn."

"And yet you're doing exactly what we agreed you wouldn't do."

"We didn't agree to anything." She snatched the tutu back and marched to the counter with it. "You said I shouldn't buy Evie the tutu as a thank-you for the sandwich. I'm not."

"You're buying early birthday presents instead?" He crossed his arms over his chest, his biceps bulging, his forearms tan and muscular. Lionel had been a runner. Lean and almost too thin, he had long, sinewy lines. Nice enough if you were into that sort of thing. Apricot had been more into his mind, which had been quick and bright. It had also been sneaky and full of excuses.

"Sure. Why not?" She shrugged, tapping her fingers on the counter and trying not to look into those beautiful green eyes of Simon's.

"You don't even know when their birthday is."

"Sometime in the future," she responded as Sally returned with a pretty blue skirt that looked a lot like the pink one.

"Here you are," Sally said with a smile. "I'm sure the girls will enjoy them. Do you need anything else?"

A new life? New dreams? A concussion that knocked every memory of Lionel from her head?

She glanced around the shop, spotted colorful hairnets in a little display box on the counter. She chose one pink and one blue and set them next to the skirts. "These too."

"Apricot," Simon warned.

She ignored him as she paid. Forty dollars down . . . thousands more of the money she'd saved for married life to go. Maybe once she spent it all, the hollow feeling in her gut would be gone.

"Here." She thrust the bag into his hands and rushed outside, because she really thought she might start crying. Not so much because of Lionel, but because she had everything anyone could ever want, and she felt like she had nothing at all.

Which sucked, because she wasn't the kind of person who liked playing the self-pity game. As a matter of fact, she'd only been wallowing for forty minutes, and she was already sick of herself.

Sunlight glinted off the pavement as she walked

back to the truck. It drilled itself straight into her head, bringing on what promised to be a raging migraine if she wasn't careful. She put on sunglasses, realized they were the expensive designer pair that Lionel had felt she needed, and threw them onto the ground, smashing them under her heel without even a moment of hesitation.

Wasteful. That's what Grandma Sapphire would have said if she'd been around.

She'd have been right, too.

Which should have made Apricot feel even more crappy than she already did. Except that she was already just about as low as anyone could be.

She opened Henry's door and took Handsome out of the bag, fighting off little claws that snagged her skin and ripped open her thumb.

"Apricot!" Simon called as he and the girls jogged around the corner of the building. She had half a mind to ignore them. She was sure her eyes were bloodshot from held-back tears.

The girls looked so happy, their pigtails swinging, their new tutu skirts swishing around their legs. Both wore jean shorts and white T-shirts, and Apricot didn't think they could be cuter if they tried.

"I see you're wearing your birthday presents," she said, closing Henry's door.

"We love them," Evie cried, nearly flying across the space between them and launching herself into Apricot's arms.

Apricot stumbled backward, but managed to keep both of them from tumbling to the ground.

"We really do," Rori added quietly. "Pink is one of my favorite colors."

"I thought it might be." Apricot set Evie down.

"We're going to wear them on our birthday," she gushed. "Daddy said we could even if Aunt Daisy wants us to wear those big ugly dresses. Right, Daddy?"

Simon nodded, his expression neutral. He had something in his hand. It looked suspiciously like the glasses she'd just stomped into the pavement.

"I think," he said, holding them out to her, "you dropped something."

"I guess I did."

"And—" He held them up by a bent earpiece. One lens was completely missing. The other had a few broken pieces still attached to the frame. "It looks like you might have stepped on them after you dropped them."

"It's possible," she conceded.

"I guess you had a reason for that?"

"I guess I did."

"I don't suppose you'd like to explain it over ice cream? I told the girls we'd stop for some on the way home."

Would she?

Probably not, but ice cream sounded better than going back to Rose's place.

"Sure," she finally responded, and Simon offered a smile that made her feel all warm and fuzzy inside. It almost did away with the hollow, empty feeling in her stomach.

"Great! Do you know the place on Main Street? Sweet Treats?" he asked.

"I don't think so."

"It's a half mile north of Riley Park. We can grab some cones and go for a walk. That should help you avoid another incident with Handsome. We wouldn't want you to get a reputation as a crazy cat lady."

"I think it's too late for that."

He chuckled, tucking the glasses into her purse. "Everyone has a reputation for something in Apple Valley. That may as well be yours. See you in a few." He chucked her under her chin the way her eldest brother used to, but being around him felt nothing like being around Sky.

She slid into King Henry, shoving Handsome back into his bed and starting the truck. It purred to life thanks to Willie and some old parts she'd claimed had been lying around her father's mechanic shop. Apricot had doubted the parts for the old Ford had just been lying around anywhere. She suspected Willie had ordered them with the express purpose of doing justice to the vintage car. That was fine with Apricot. King Henry had needed a tune-up and Willie had done great work. Now the old boy purred and gleamed. Even the seats were brighter.

A few years ago, she and Lionel had driven King Henry to the Oregon coast. Lionel hadn't been happy about it. He'd been all for trading the truck in for something prettier and fancier. When they'd returned to LA, he'd insisted on visiting dealers and tried to convince her to do a trade-in. King Henry for a beautiful 60k Jeep. She'd agreed to buy the Jeep, but she'd kept King Henry. He'd been her very first vehicle. One she'd bought with money earned on her trips with Rose.

Lionel hadn't been happy.

They'd had a fight about it.

Which she'd kind of forgotten about until just that moment.

She pulled onto Sherman Road, listened to the GPS voice on her phone guide her out of downtown

Spokane. Distant mountains butted up against a pristine summer sky. It wouldn't be long before they were tipped with snow. She could imagine the sun rising above the mountains to the east, setting below the mountains to the west, clouds tinged purple with sunrise or sunset. No smog. No noise from LA traffic. No friends who'd eye her skeptically as she claimed that she was just fine. No clients who'd come to the nursery just to see if she was fading away from a broken heart.

No chance of ever running into Lionel and his new wife.

The thought of that was enough to make her want to puke.

She didn't. Mostly because she didn't want to mess up all the hard work Willie had done on Henry's interior.

Up ahead, Simon merged onto the freeway. Apricot was pretty sure she saw two arms waving frantically from the backseat of his car as she followed.

Sweet Treats was exactly what Simon had envisioned when Charlotte Garrison had talked about opening a storefront on Main Street. Mostly homemade baked goods, the shop also had a few flavors of homemade ice cream. Charlotte made large batches of vanilla and chocolate and added cookie pieces or bits of cake into it. The girls loved Charlotte's ice cream almost as much as they loved her.

He held the door open and ushered the girls into the small shop. Once a soda shop, the place had a 1950s feel, the old booths and tables from a bygone era. Every time he entered it, he thought of Megan.

It was the kind of place she'd loved. A little different, a little quaint, but with great quality items. She'd loved vintage fashion and old books. She'd believed in fairy tales and magic in a way that was both naïve and charming. She'd had problems. More than Simon had realized, but she'd been sweet and tender with a romantic soul that had made Simon want to do everything in his power to protect her.

"Afternoon, Simon! Girls!" Charlotte smiled from behind the old-fashioned soda fountain. A transplant from Billings, Montana, she'd been through a lot, but she'd found a place for herself in Apple Valley. As far as he could tell, the town accepted her, loved her, wanted the best for her. It also wanted her baked goods. Most days, Sweet Treats sold out before its five o'clock closing time.

"Sit yourselves down," Charlotte called. "I'll bring pop and coffee."

"Water for the girls, Charlotte. I'll take the same," he said as the girls scrambled into a booth near the counter.

The girls looked crestfallen, but they didn't dare complain. A trip to Sweet Treats was a rare occurrence. One that he usually saved for special occasions. He'd planned to buy a half gallon of ice cream from the grocery store and give the girls cones at home. He'd changed his mind after seeing Apricot stomp her sunglasses into pieces.

She'd been about to cry.

No doubt about that.

He figured that was something to do with her ex. He also figured the fancy sunglasses she'd smashed to bits might be something to do with the same. He could have left her to cry it out or stomp it out. Or both.

He hadn't, and he wasn't quite ready to admit the reason for that.

"It's a nice day for a walk in the park." Charlotte set water glasses on the table. "Is that what you guys are planning?" She had a pretty smile, porcelain skin, and dark hair that framed her face. Quiet and unassuming, she wasn't the kind of woman Simon would have imagined attracting the attention of someone like Maxwell Stanford, but she'd not only attracted him, she'd managed to turn the guy into a family man.

Or maybe Maxwell's daughter had done that. Having kids had sure changed Simon.

"We're waiting for Apricot!" Evie offered, eyeing the water glass like it was filled with the vilest of poison. The girl knew how to be dramatic. Simon would give her that. "Eden says that drinking too much water can make a kid drown," she commented.

"I take it Eden is one of your friends from school?" Charlotte asked.

"Yes." Evie nodded. "She knows a lot of stuff."

"I don't think she knows about drowning, though," Rori cut in. "Because I don't think you can drown from drinking too much." She eyed her glass suspiciously.

Simon had visions of water boycotts and trips to the ER. "A glass of water isn't going to cause problems. Your sister is just trying to get a soda pop."

"I do want soda, but that's not why I'm saying what I'm saying." Evie took a sip of water. "Ms. Randall says that—"

"How about we stop repeating what other people say and start thinking for ourselves. Okay?" He rubbed the back of his neck and tried to hold on to his patience. He loved Evie more than life itself, but the girl wore him out. While Rori sat with books and little craft kits that Daisy kept her supplied with, Evie bounced off the walls, asking questions about anything and everything that caught her attention.

"Or," Charlotte suggested, "you could think about what kind of treat you're in the mood for. I've got coconut cupcakes today. Butterscotch bars. Pecan praline cookies."

"Ice cream?" Evie asked.

"Now that you mention it, I do have ice cream. Chocolate brownie bit, strawberry cheesecake, and peach cobbler. Interested?"

"I want—"

"We can't order yet," Rori said, looking anxiously at the door. "Apricot isn't here."

"Is that the lady who is staying in the old Shaffer place?" Charlotte stepped behind the counter and opened a chest freezer that stood near the wall. "Max said she's probably not going to be in town long."

"Did he?" Simon wasn't sure where Max had gotten the information. Rumors were flying about Apricot. Simon wasn't much for rumors, so he'd tried not to be pulled in by it. Not an easy thing, seeing as how Daisy had been talking nonstop about Apricot since she'd arrived.

"I guess she's got money and lots of it." Her voice was muffled as she reached into the freezer. "Not that I'm much for what people say, but I've got to admit I'm curious. If she's got that much money, why's she hiding here and not in some fancy resort where she can get massaged and pampered?"

"Her fiancé dumped her," Evie responded before Simon could. "He just up and said, *I don't want to marry you. You're just not pretty enough for me.*"

"Evie! What kind of story is that?" Simon barked.

"The kind that Aunt Daisy said is pit-i-ful. She said that—"

"No more!" He held up a hand. "We are done telling stories about other people. It isn't nice."

"I told her that, Daddy. I told her that when she told everyone on the playground at school all about poor Apricot. It's not Apricot's fault that her boyfriend is a scoundrel," Rori offered, her eyes big and wide and filled with the kind of innocent indignation that only she could manage.

"Good God! How many kids were on the playground?" Simon groaned. He was tempted to bang his head against the wall. He was going to have to talk to Daisy, and he was going to have to do it sooner rather than later. That was a problem for him, because he hated having discussions with Daisy about the girls and what they should not do. Much as he appreciated his sister-in-law's help, he didn't approve of some of her child-rearing methods. Filling the girls' heads with gossip was one of them.

"Just everyone in our class, Daddy. Seventeen kids and Ms. Chandler," Rori said.

"She's our aide," Evie added. "She does stuff Ms. Randall doesn't want to do. Like take us outside when it's really hot. Ms. Randall doesn't like hot weather on account of her hot flashes. She says that's what happens when you're old. You get hot flashes and wrinkles."

Charlotte laughed as she approached the table. "You two girls sure do know how to make a person smile."

"Only if that person is not their father," Simon muttered.

"Cheer up, Simon." She handed the cups to the girls, snagged little plastic spoons from a box on the counter. "They'll grow out of the talking-about-everyone phase and grow into the talking-about-boys phase."

"Is that what I have to look forward to?"

"That and a lot of other things." She handed each girl a spoon. "Probably the best thing to do is just focus on today and face the rest as it comes."

Good advice, but he could never quite shake the worry about the girls. Was he doing things right? Doing them wrong? Making mistakes that would impact the girls for the rest of their lives?

Was he missing something big? Overlooking some tiny detail that meant something huge?

Like that bottle on the windowsill?

Like Megan's deep sleep and the slurred speech that he'd thought were from exhaustion but had really been from drug use?

He was a police officer, for God's sake! He should have known that his wife was an addict, but he'd missed it because he'd loved her, because he'd trusted her and himself and the life that he'd thought they had.

He didn't want to make that mistake with the girls, *couldn't* make that mistake.

The door opened, a tiny bell above it ringing as Apricot walked in. Warm air floated into the shop, filling it with the scent of flowers and fresh mown grass.

"I made it!" she announced, her skin dewy from heat, her cheeks tinged pink from it. Strands of wet hair stuck to the back of her neck and framed her face, a few droplets of sweat glistening in the hollow of her throat. "I thought LA was brutal in the summer. Apple Valley takes the cake! If it doesn't cool off soon, I'm going to have to break down and get a car that has air-conditioning."

"You wouldn't really trade Henry in for a little cool air, would you?" Simon handed her his water glass and she gulped greedily.

"Not in a million years," she said as she swiped moisture from her lips. Not the plumped-up lips of an LA starlet. Just full, soft-looking pink lips that were probably very, very kissable.

Simon's gut tightened at the thought, his gaze dropping for a fraction of a second and landing on the slim column of her throat. Kissable too.

"I just like to threaten him every now and again." She smiled at Charlotte. "You must be Charlotte. Just about everyone I've met has told me I need to come to Sweet Treats. I'm glad I've finally listened. It smells wonderful in here."

"Does it?" Charlotte inhaled deeply. "I think my nose is immune after so many years of baking. Can I get you another glass of water?"

Apricot didn't think water was going to cool the heat that seemed to pour through her blood every time she looked in Simon's eyes.

She shook her head. "No. Thanks. I think we were going to get ice cream. Is that right, girls?" Apricot asked, doing everything she could to avoid Simon's gaze. He was studying her with the kind of steady assessing look that made her feel . . .

Uncomfortable?

No.

More like . . . anxious. Antsy. Just a little unsettled.

"So, what'll it be?" Charlotte asked, and Apricot realized she'd been so focused on avoiding Simon's gaze that she'd missed every word the pretty brunette had said.

"Um . . ." She glanced around the cute little shop. No list of ice-cream flavors. No menu. "What are you girls having?" she finally asked.

Evie spoke up first. "I want the chocolate brownie ice cream. Three scoops."

"One," Simon corrected, his voice gentle.

So, of course, Apricot had to look. She couldn't miss the softness in his eyes, the worry etched into his brow. It had to be a big responsibility raising a couple of kids on his own.

"May I please have the strawberry cheesecake ice cream?" Rori asked.

"Of course, sweetie. And you two?" Charlotte asked, her gaze jumping from Apricot to Simon and back again. No doubt she was wondering what they were to each other. Apricot wanted to let her know in no uncertain terms that they were nothing, but that might seem like protesting too much.

"I'll take the same as Evie," she said instead.

"That sounds good. I'll have the same." Simon smiled into Apricot's eyes, and her mouth went dry, her pulse racing just a little faster than it needed to be.

He was a handsome guy. A mature guy. A guy

with kids and responsibilities. What he wasn't was a rebound relationship waiting to happen.

"One scoop for everyone?" Charlotte asked as she walked behind an old-fashioned counter. The shop had a 1950s vibe, a glass display case offering a view of a couple dozen different baked goods. Pretty white shelves lined one wall, each displaying old-fashioned jars filled with penny candies. One shelf had been painted azure blue, the crystal vase that sat on it containing a pure white feather.

Not a goose feather. Apricot had seen plenty of those in her life. Not a chicken feather. She moved closer, ran a finger along its soft edge.

"Interesting, right?" Simon murmured in her ear, his breath ruffling her cropped hair. "They say that it came from an angel."

"Really?" She tried to laugh, but he was so close she could feel the heat of his chest against her back. It seeped through her tank top, made her insides melt like butter on a hot skillet. *That* was no laughing matter.

"They also say that whoever has it will be blessed with love and happiness."

She did laugh then, because that was the kind of thing Grandma Sapphire would have said. Portents. Signs. Good-luck charms. Those were her specialty.

"You sound like my grandmother," she said as she sidled away from Simon and his all-too-tempting heat.

"Do I?" His eyes crinkled at the corners, his smile easy and inviting. She had no choice but to return it. To touch the feather again and imagine that she could feel just a little of the happiness and love rubbing off on her.

"Sapphire sees signs in the clouds and in the creeks that run through Happy Dale."

"That's where you grew up?"

"Yes. My father bought a hundred acres in the Pennsylvania hills and started a commune there about forty years ago." It wasn't something that she told many people, but the information just kind of slipped out as she looked into Simon's forest-green eyes.

"Must have been an interesting place to grow up."

"That's one way to describe it."

"You didn't like it there?"

"I didn't *not* like it. I just . . ." She shrugged. She'd never even told Lionel why she'd left Happy Dale. Not that he'd ever asked. He'd assumed that she'd been too sophisticated for her family, too smart to stay in a village of free-thinking hippies. In reality, she'd just gotten tired of being a square peg shoved into a circular hole. No matter how much she'd tried to understand her family's chaotic and over-the-top lifestyle, she hadn't. She'd grown up feeling dull in comparison to the brightness of her parents, her aunts, her grandmother, her siblings.

"Needed to figure out who you were when you weren't part of what you had there?" Simon suggested.

"Something like that," she admitted.

He studied her for a moment, his head cocked to the side. "Did you?"

"What?"

"Figure out who you were when you weren't part of your family."

"I'm twenty-nine, Simon. Way past finding myself." She laughed, her throat tight and dry. Of course she knew who she was without her family. She was a businesswoman. A successful one. A friend. A . . .

Lover? Girlfriend? Fiancée?

Those were the words that popped into her head, and just about every one of them had to do with her relationship with Lionel.

The problem was, Lionel wasn't part of the equation anymore. Without him, she'd reduced who she was by three-fifths.

"Twenty-nine." Simon nodded as if that answered the question better than anything else she'd said. "It seems to me, you have a lot of years left to do your figuring out. Maybe being in Apple Valley will help you with that." He touched the feather, running his finger along the outer edge just like she had.

Heat swept over her, mixing with a longing so deep and undeniable that she clenched her fists to keep from touching his cheek, running her hand along the smooth angle of his jaw.

"Cones are ready," Charlotte announced cheerfully, her voice like a bucket of ice water dumped on Apricot's head. Everything came back into perspective. The cute little shop with the heavenly scent of baked goods hanging on the air. The girls bouncing excitedly at the counter. The soft whir of an air conditioner and cool air blasting from a vent in the ceiling. Charlotte smiling as she handed out the cones.

And, of course, Simon.

He looked like any other guy—just a little handsomer, a little kinder, a little more interesting. Which sucked. Apricot needed him to be mean or selfish or boring. She needed him to make snide comments to Charlotte and disparaging comments about people on the street.

You need him to be like Lionel? a voice whispered in her head.

She would have told it to shut up, but Charlotte handed her the cone. "Here you are."

"How much do I owe you?" She opened her purse, nudging Handsome to the side as she reached for the wallet. Thank goodness he'd worn himself out and didn't budge as she pulled a few bills from the soft Italian leather.

"First cone is always on the house," Charlotte responded with a smile.

"I can't—"

"Don't argue with her," Simon interrupted as he handed Charlotte cash. "You won't win. Charlotte might look soft and easygoing, but the woman is stubborn as the old hound dog my grandfather used for hunting. That hound could track just about anything with legs, but I'll tell you what; once he got on the scent, he would never let it go. One year, Mule—"

"I thought you said he was a hound dog," Apricot said, amused by the story and by the rapt look on the girls' faces. She wasn't sure if Simon's tale had put it there or if their ice-cream cones had. Charlotte had given them each a scoop that looked to be three times the size she'd given the adults.

"A hound dog named Mule. Pay attention." He scowled, but his eyes twinkled. "One year, Mule got on the scent of a rabbit. Problem was, that rabbit was my sister's pet. He chased the poor thing all over the house. Mom was screaming fit to be tied and waving a broom like she planned to wallop one of them or me."

"Now, why would your mother wallop you with a broom?" Charlotte took the cash Simon handed her and got change from a register. "I've met your mom; she's as mild-mannered as they come."

"She's mild-mannered until one of her sons lets a hound dog in the house. That's when all bets are off," Simon responded. "So, she's chasing Mule all over the house and he's chasing my sister's rabbit, and I'm trying to avoid the broom. I figured it might be best if they all ran around outside, so I opened the door. Let me tell you something." He whistled softly and shook his head. "That was one of the biggest mistakes I've ever made. The rabbit ran out. Mule ran out. Mom ran out. According to her, Mule chased that rabbit all the way to Dead Man's Creek."

"Dead Man's Creek," Evie breathed, dabs of ice cream on the corners of her mouth. "Is that really what it's called, Daddy?"

"It is." Simon nodded. "One day, I'll take you girls there. It's about ten miles from Pop Pop and Grammy's house. Poor Mom, she ran all the way, shouting loud enough that I swear we could hear her the entire way. I'm pretty dang sure the whole community could, but Mule? He'd have nothing to do with her telling him to stop. He just kept running until he got to the creek."

"What happened then? Did Mule eat the rabbit?" Rori asked, gnawing on her lower lip instead of her ice cream. Unlike her sister, she didn't seem enthralled by the story. She seemed scared.

Simon crouched down in front of her, tucked a strand of golden hair behind her ear. "Sweetie, Mule finally cornered that rabbit at the edge of the creek. Grammy was running up behind them both and Mule picked the rabbit up just as gentle as could be, carried it like he would one of his own puppies, straight back to the house."

"Really?" she asked hopefully, and Apricot's heart ached for how tender she was. Her sister Peach had been that way when she was little—so innocent and sweet and gentle. Now she was a twenty-year-old with gauges in her ears and black lipstick on her mouth. At least, that's how she'd looked the last time Apricot had seen her. She hadn't come for the wedding. She was going through that phase that kids went through, finding herself on the streets of Washington, D.C., playing music in bars on the weekends and going to college during the day.

"Yes, really," Simon responded. "Now let's go for that walk. Daisy is making meat loaf for dinner, and she'll be upset if we don't get back in time for it."

"Meat loaf?! Gross, Daddy! She puts broccoli in it!"

"And, her potatoes always come out of a box, and she puts peas in with them and sometimes, even, corn," Evie added.

"That sounds . . ." *Disgusting* was on the tip of Apricot's tongue. "Interesting."

"It is not interesting at all!" Evie cried. "It's horrible. Like she's trying to poison us or something."

"Don't exaggerate, munchkin," Simon chided mildly as he opened the door. A woman was standing on the sidewalk a few feet from the shop. It took about three seconds for Apricot to recognize her. Dark hair pulled into a bun. Long jean skirt. Sweater despite the heat.

Daisy.

And she didn't look happy.

"Simon!" she said with a smile that looked as brittle as old bones. "I saw your SUV. I thought you and the girls were in Spokane for the afternoon." Her gaze dropped to the girls and she frowned. "And I thought we agreed that if the girls wanted tutus, they had to pay themselves. Did Rori somehow manage to earn enough for one?"

"I don't recall agreeing to anything," he responded, not mentioning that Apricot had been the one who'd paid. "We're going to take a walk in the park. You on lunch break?"

"I—" Her cheeks flushed deep red, her mottled skin a little dry. Apricot didn't think she'd been drinking her medicinal tea, but now wasn't the time to ask. "Yes. We got new inventory today, and I had to shelve it, so lunch is late."

"Do you get light-headed when you eat late?" Apricot asked, because Daisy looked a little anemic. If she had a problem with blood sugar regulation, that could play a part in her anxiety and irritability.

"What's it to you?" Daisy snapped.

"If your blood sugar levels—"

"They're fine, so how about you stop trying to solve my problems and solve your own?"

"What problems would those be?" Apricot asked, bracing herself for a rude comment about her love life or the fact that she was hiding from the world in a little town at the edge of nowhere.

"Jet told Ella Stanley that your house is cursed. He said the doors open and close all by themselves and that he constantly hears something walking around in the attic." Daisy's eyes were blazing with fanatical light.

"That's it?" Apricot snorted, because she knew all about Jet and his friend. Ella believed in ghosts and goblins, and Jet had asked to bring her over one night to watch movies. He thought it might be just the right time to convince her that they should go out. Apparently, he'd been trying to scare her into his arms. Apricot would have to ask him if it had worked.

"It? *It?!* You're in trouble, girlfriend!" Daisy poked her finger toward Apricot, spittle flying from her mouth.

And Apricot couldn't help it. She laughed, because the entire thing was so ludicrous. Next thing she knew, the girls were laughing and Simon's mouth was twitching, and poor Daisy looked like she was ready to spew lava.

"I'm sorry," she tried to say, but Daisy was having none of it.

She turned on her heels and stalked away, her jean skirt swishing and her head bobbing. She should have looked haughty, but she just looked sad.

Chapter Eight

Daisy had issues.

Simon had never had any doubt about that. Lately, though, those issues were making it difficult to justify all the time the girls spent with her. It was one thing to be a little emotional and high-strung. It was another to believe stories of ghosts and goblins, to fill the girls' heads with romantic notions and superstitions.

"This has got to stop," he muttered, eyeing the girls and wondering how in God's name he was going to ease them out of their aunt's overly protective clutches.

"She means well," Apricot responded as if she knew exactly what he was talking about.

"Mercy killers mean well, Apricot, but that doesn't make what they're doing right."

She laughed, the sound spilling out into the quiet afternoon. Even weekends weren't loud in Apple Valley. People meandered along Main Street looking in store windows and sipping lemonade or iced coffee. Most were heading to the park, where baseball diamonds and basketball courts were usually bustling with activity.

"You're laughing, but you're not the one who has daughters whose heads are being filled with fairy tales and superstitions." He was only partially kidding about that. He worried about Daisy's influence on the girls. The nice routine existence he'd carved out in Apple Valley still had the easy rhythm of home and family, but there'd been a discordant note for the past few months. He'd chalked it up to Daisy's rough breakup, but maybe there was more to it than that. The niggling thought had been bothering him more than he wanted it to.

"I'm not much for superstition, but fairy tales are wonderful. Romance and danger and happily-ever-afters, what could possibly be wrong with that?" Apricot bent to swipe ice cream from Evie's chin. Rather than pulling away like she would have if it were her aunt, Evie smiled, a kind of eager longing in her eyes that made Simon's heart ache.

"Plenty," he responded, his tone gruffer than he'd intended. "There are no easy roads in life, and it's best if the girls understand that early."

"Difficult roads are exactly the reason why we should all believe in fairy tales." She licked ice cream from her knuckle, her profile all steep angles and smooth skin. He didn't think she had a bit of makeup on, but somehow she looked flawless. "They give us something to hope for and dream about and work toward. Who doesn't want a happily-ever-after?"

"Is that what you thought you'd have with your ex?"

She shrugged. "I thought I'd at least have a contently-ever-after."

"No offense, but that sounds about as exciting as table tennis."

"Some people love table tennis." She grinned, her eyes sparkling despite the deep shadows beneath them. The girls were a few yards ahead, waiting at the crosswalk, their fluffy skirts billowing out as they twirled.

"Careful near the street!" he called even though there wasn't a car in sight.

"So, what's it like?" Apricot asked. "Raising a couple of girls on your own?"

"You thinking of adding to your family?"

"No!" she laughed. "Handsome is more than enough for me. I'm just curious. I have a few friends who are raising kids alone. Some say it's easy. Others are struggling."

"It would be easier to answer that question if I were actually raising the girls without help, but I've got Daisy and an entire community backing me up."

"Does the community drive you as crazy as your sister-in-law?"

"You ask a lot of questions, Apricot, for someone who doesn't plan to stick around town long."

"Who says I don't?"

"Just about everyone I've run into the past few days. Rumor has it you're getting Rose's place ready to sell."

"Wonder who started that rumor?" She sounded more amused than angry, but there was a hint of sharpness in her gaze, a hardness to her jaw that made Simon think she was more annoyed than she wanted to let on.

"I can't tell you that, but I can tell you certain people aren't happy about it."

"Certain people meaning Maura?"

"Good guess."

"Educated guess," she corrected. "The woman was shooting daggers at me *before* Handsome escaped."

"People around here like things to stay the way they are."

"Even if that means that a beautiful old house falls to ruin?" she asked as they reached the girls.

"Sometimes even then."

"Well, I'm not letting Rose's place fall to ruin, and I'm not selling it." She took Rori's hand, looked both ways, and headed into the street. He followed with Evie, the two of them making quite a picture for anyone who cared to look. He had a feeling plenty of people were looking.

That was the way it was in a small town. People pressing their noses against windows, watching as life played out, then reporting it to anyone and everyone they ran into.

"Not selling, huh?" he asked.

"Of course not. The house belongs to Rose, and she loves the place. The problem with my aunt is that she loves lots of things and lots of people. She can only focus on one of those loves at a time. Whatever is right in front of her is what she puts her energy into."

"Out of sight, out of mind?"

"Something like that." She smoothed her hair, her fingers long, her nails short and unpainted. Megan had been all about lotions and makeup and having her nails done every week. She'd loved pretty things and pretty places. He'd found that amusing and cute when they were dating. During their marriage her obsession with physical perfection had gotten old.

He'd spent too many hours trying to convince her that she was beautiful, that her outfit was just right for the occasion, her hair gorgeous.

And he'd spent too much time thinking about her these past few days.

She'd been gone nearly seven years. He'd made peace with her death even if he hadn't been able to forgive either of them for it. "It isn't your responsibility to fix up your aunt's place. You know that, right?"

"Sure, but I like the house too. I want to see it restored."

"What's your aunt think about it?" he asked as the girls raced through the gates that opened into Riley Park. Just beyond it, a path meandered its way around Riley Pond. A playground stood to the east. Added a few decades before Simon arrived, it had an old swing set, a slide, monkey bars, and several seesaws. The girls ran toward it, their cheerful screams making him smile. He had two days off a week, and he tried to spend every minute of them with the girls. It didn't always work out. They had school and dance and swim lessons that Daisy had insisted on. They also had friends who wanted playdates and trips to the bowling alley. He tried not to be resentful of those things, but the older the girls got, the more he could feel the swift current of time dragging them all along. It made him want to hold on tight to every moment he had with the twins.

"I haven't asked. Rose is pretty laid-back. I'd say she isn't going to care," she responded as she scanned the area. "This is a lovely park. Someone spent a lot of time planning it out."

"The first mayor of Apple Valley commissioned it

after his wife died. Originally it was just gardens, but it's been expanded over the years."

"It's nice. Very natural. It must be stunning in the spring when the foliage blooms." She touched the leaf of a cherry tree. No flowers this time of year, but she was right, in the spring, it came alive with pink buds.

"It is. One of the prettiest places in Apple Valley."

"One of the prettiest? Are there other gardens?" She dropped down on a bench near the playground and took Handsome from her purse. He settled onto her lap, rolling himself into a tight ball of coarse gray fur and purring loudly.

"Private gardens. Some of them are pretty big, but I was thinking about Apple Valley Community Church. It's one of the twins' favorite places. The grounds are nice and there's a cemetery in the back of it. The building is a little older than the park." He sat beside her, his thigh just close enough to hers for their heat to mix. He could have sat farther away, but he didn't want to. He liked Apricot. She amused him, took his mind off of things he'd rather not think about.

There was a little bit of danger in that, sure. He wasn't in the market for a relationship. Wouldn't be in the market for one until the girls were grown and gone. He dated on occasion, but never more than two dates with the same woman. The way he saw things, three dates was the kind of thing a woman could pin hopes on, and he didn't want to disappoint anyone. He had enough guilt on his shoulders for six people. He didn't want to add to it.

"I remember the church. My aunt took me there when I was a kid. I haven't been there in years." Apricot stretched her legs out and crossed them at the ankles, showing off white high-tops and muscular calves. Her skin looked silky and smooth and he had the absurd urge to run his hand up her calf to see if it was. Not a good place for his mind to be going, but he let it go there anyway. Nothing wrong with a little harmless flirtation. He doubted Apricot wanted anything more. Not with what she'd just gotten out of.

"It's not far if you want to visit." He gestured to the building that stood at the top of Riley Bluff. Stark white in the afternoon sun, it belonged on a vintage postcard or in a Norman Rockwell painting.

Or in a town like Apple Valley.

"Is it open to the public?"

That made him laugh, and she scowled, poking him in the upper arm. "That was a legitimate question. In LA, nothing is left unlocked. Not even churches."

"Sorry." He managed to stop the laughter, but his lips were twitching and, no matter how much he tried, he couldn't quite keep the smile off his face.

"No, you're not." She huffed, and he laughed again.

"Maybe not. Where I come from, churches are always open to the public. The same is true here. You can go any time. Day or night that building will be unlocked."

"Good to know." She settled back against the bench, turned her gaze on Simon. She had the bluest eyes he'd ever seen and the kind of fair complexion he usually associated with redheads. Freckles danced across her cheeks and there was a tiny smear of ice cream at the corner of her lips.

He wiped it away the same way she'd done with Evie, his thumb running along the corner of her mouth. It should have been an innocent gesture, one friend helping out another, the touch there and gone without even a moment of anything else. But something happened when he touched her skin. Not fireworks or sparks. Just . . . heat. The kind he'd tried to avoid the past few years. The kind that led a man to do stupid things and a woman to make unwise choices.

Her eyes widened, and he knew she felt it too. Knew he should move his thumb and ease away and pretend things were just the same as they'd been two seconds ago.

Problem was, he'd never been good at pretending.

He didn't do games.

He'd been raised to go into every friendship, every business deal, every partnership, with unbridled honesty.

"This is going to be a problem," he said quietly, his thumb sliding down smooth, silky skin. First her cheek, then her neck. Her pulse fluttered rapidly beneath warm skin, and he imagined pressing his lips to that spot. "A very big problem."

She cleared her throat, scooted away. "I don't see why it should be. We'll just . . . avoid being around each other."

"That's about as practical as a swimsuit in a winter storm."

Her lips twitched and she shook her head. "Stop being charming and funny, Simon. That'll help."

"Charming, huh?" *Nice* was the word most women used. Nice. Helpful. Kind. That was the way he liked it and the way he'd worked hard to keep it.

"Yes. And you know it," she accused. "So don't play innocent. The honey-smooth Southern accent, the gentlemanly manners. It's disgusting." She scooped Handsome up, deposited him in her purse, and stood.

"I'll tell my parents you think so," he offered.

"You know what Grandma Sapphire says about guys like you?" she asked.

"Do I want to?"

"Probably, but I refuse to repeat it." She might have walked away, but he snagged her hand, pulled her back so she was standing between his thighs.

"Now you've got me curious, so give. What's she say?"

"She says that if you find a guy with good old-fashioned Southern manners and good old-fashioned Southern charm, you need to hold on to him. According to her, those kinds only come around once in a lifetime."

"I think I like your grandmother," he said.

"You would." She snorted, tugging her hand from his and placing both fists on her slender hips. "The problem with Sapphire is that she married when she was eighteen."

"A man filled with Southern charm and Southern manners?"

"Of course. They were married fifty years, and she swears they never had one fight worth remembering."

"It could be true," he pointed out.

"It could also be that they fought like cats and dogs, and she forgot that after he died. People do that, you know. Make the past prettier than it was."

"Sometimes they just tell it like it is, Apricot. Maybe the fights she had with her husband weren't important enough to remember. Maybe the joy they had together outweighed everything else. Whatever the case, she found the kind of love most of us want and can only hope to achieve."

She eyed him for a moment, then shook her head. "You really are good, Simon."

"I'm not trying to be good." He stood, their bodies so close their heat combined and made a furnace that Simon knew he'd be wise to move away from. He stayed right where he was, looking into Apricot's eyes and listening to the girls squeal as they took turns on the slide. The sun was hot and bright, the day just perfect enough for the beginning of something wonderful. "I'm trying to be honest. I have a grandmother too, and she says honesty is always the best policy unless you're discussing weight or looks."

She laughed, and he wanted to capture the sound on her lips, savor the taste of her happiness. He might have done it if his cell phone hadn't rung. He still might have if Apricot hadn't stepped away.

"Are you going to answer that?" she asked.

"Sure." He pressed the phone to his ear, his gaze still on Apricot. Her eyes sparkled and her cheeks glowed, her hair brushing against her nape as she turned to watch the girls.

"Simon, here. What's up?" he asked, distracted by the deep red and bold gold streaks in Apricot's hair.

"It's Max. We've got a problem." Stanford's gruff voice was the splash of ice water Simon needed. He turned toward the entrance of the park, watching as a couple walked toward the pond.

"What kind of problem?"

"Daisy has been robbed."

"What?!" His blood ran cold, adrenaline pumping through his veins. "Where and when?"

"Near as we can tell, it happened in that little alley between the bank and the diner. I'm trying to get the details, but Daisy is in hysterics. It might be best if you come to the hospital."

"She's hurt?"

"A torn skirt and maybe a scratch on her arm. Can't really tell on account of the woman is screaming her head off and won't let anyone near her. Cade is here, and he told me to call you. He thought you might be able to calm her down enough that we could get the full story. Until we do, we can't look for a suspect."

"I'll be there in ten." He shoved the phone in his pocket and ran toward the girls. "Girls! Come on! We've got to leave!"

"What's going on?" Apricot asked as he grabbed Rori and lifted her off the slide.

"Daisy—" He looked at the girls, who were watching him with wide-eyed curiosity. "I need to get them home and ask the neighbor to watch them. God! I hope she's home. If she's not—"

"I'll take care of them. You go do what you need to do."

Any other time, any other circumstances, and he would have refused the offer, but as big a pain in the butt as Daisy had become, she was family. If she needed him, he wanted to be there. Now. Not ten minutes from now.

"Are you sure? I could be a while."

"As long as you don't mind me bringing the girls to my place, I'm fine with it. I told Jet that I'd—"

"You're going to need booster seats for the girls," he said, cutting her off. "I don't think your truck has shoulder belts. You take my SUV. I'll take the truck."

She didn't ask questions, just took his keys and

gave him hers. "Henry is fickle. Give him a little grace and don't expect him to accelerate too quickly."

He nodded. "Thanks. Be good, girls!" He dropped a kiss on each girl's head, his heart beating the passing seconds, his stomach hollow with worry and anger. Apple Valley wasn't the kind of place where people were robbed in the middle of the day. The crime rate was so low that most people in town left their doors unlocked. The thought of Daisy being robbed was almost inconceivable. The thought of her being hurt made him want to hunt down the perpetrator and teach him a lesson he wouldn't forget.

He raced toward the park entrance, his heart pounding a million miles an hour. He'd failed Megan, and he'd never forgiven himself for that. There was no way in hell he was going to fail Daisy. Apricot's truck was parked right where she'd left it, the blue paint gleaming in brilliant sunlight. The interior smelled like her—flowers and sunshine with just a hint of summer rain. He filed the information away as he pulled onto Main Street and raced toward the hospital.

"Daddy sure can run fast," Rori commented as Apricot led the girls along the path Simon had taken. "Do you think something horrible happened? Do you think there's a bad guy that he has to catch?"

What she thought was that something had happened to Daisy. She wasn't going to tell the girls that. "Whatever is going on, I'm sure he'll handle it just fine."

"Daddy can handle anything," Evie said with a full

measure of pride in her voice. "He helped a girl have a baby at the grocery store last year."

"Did he?" Apricot responded, her focus only half on the conversation. Whatever had happened to Daisy, it couldn't be good. Simon's expression had said the things he hadn't—he was worried and angry.

"Yep. Andrew Danner's mom was right there when it happened. Eliza Jane is only fifteen years old, and she hadn't even told anyone she was going to have a baby. That's probably why she had it right in the middle of aisle six. Thank goodness Daddy was there. He knew what to do. He helped his dad birth like a million calves and it's almost the same thing."

"Except a baby is a lot smaller than a calf," Rori broke in.

"Doesn't matter," Evie responded. "Andrew said that his mom said Eliza screamed so loud a bottle of pickles shattered into a million pieces. Do you think that's true, Apricot? Do you think having a baby hurts so bad a woman could break a pickle jar from screaming so loud?"

Dear God in heaven! What was she supposed to say to that? "Well—"

"Don't be silly, Evie! Her scream didn't make the jar break. She kicked the shelf with her foot on account of she was basically trying to push a watermelon-sized head out her—"

"It would take some really powerful lungs to break a jar," Apricot cut in, hoping to heaven that the girls would drop the subject.

"Or a big sledgehammer. One time a bunch of kids broke the school windows, and that's what Daddy said they used. Sledgehammers." Evie skipped ahead, her blue tutu swishing around scrawny legs. She had bruises and scratches on her calves and a few bruises on her arms.

"Have you been climbing trees, Evie?" Apricot hurried to catch up, dragging the slower-moving Rori along beside her.

"How'd you know? Magic? Because Andrew says that you're a witch. I told him he was wrong, but it would be kind of cool if you were."

"She's not a witch!" Rori exclaimed, her cheeks pink with indignation. "You're not. Are you?"

"No." Apricot laughed. "I'm an herbalist."

"What's that?" the girls asked in unison. "Jinx!" they both cried.

Silence followed. Blessed, wonderful, joyous silence. Silence that was not filled with questions about childbirth and women's screams or about their father and where he'd gone.

Hopefully there hadn't been an accident. Hopefully Daisy was just fine. Apricot had a bad feeling about things, though, and Sapphire had always said a person couldn't go wrong trusting her gut.

"Say my name," Evie whispered, her lips barely moving.

"Pardon me?"

"My name. You have to say it so that I can talk."

"You're already talking," she pointed out.

"Because she's a cheater," Rori whispered so softly Apricot barely heard her.

"I am not!"

"Are too!"

"Am not!"

"Girls!" She shouted so loudly an older woman across Main Street turned to frown in her direction.

"No bickering," Apricot added more quietly.

"You have to say our names," Evie whispered.

"Right. Okay. Evie and Rori, no bickering."

"You did cheat," Rori said immediately. "And I'm going to tell Daddy. You know what he says about cheaters."

"Well, you cheated too! You talked before she said your name!" Evie shot back, her blond hair shaking with the force of her rage. Apricot hadn't been around kids in more years than she wanted to admit to, but dealing with childish squabbles had been part and parcel of growing up in Happy Dale. She might have been away for a long time, but she hadn't forgotten the skills she'd learned there.

"If you two keep it up," she said quietly, "I'm not going to let you help me paint my living room."

They fell silent, both of them eyeing her with suspicion. "Daisy never lets us help paint," Rori said.

"Maybe Daisy doesn't have a lot of painting that needs to be done. I do. An entire house. Today, I'm starting the living room."

"You could paint it pink," Rori suggested.

"Or blue and pink stripes. That would be really cool. Don't you think it would be cool, Rori?"

"Yes! And you could get pink couches, Apricot. And blue curtains and a blue rug. We could even help you pick them out."

"As nice as that sounds, I can't do it. The house doesn't belong to me. It belongs to my aunt."

"You have an Aunt Daisy?" Evie asked.

"I have an Aunt Rose. She owns the house, and she likes the furniture in it, so I can't change that. Pink and blue walls just won't look right with the furniture she has." Apricot unlocked Simon's SUV and opened the door for the girls.

"It isn't brown furniture, is it?" Evie wrinkled her nose as she climbed in. "Because I think brown would be an ugly color for the wall."

"No brown. I bought a pretty cream."

"Cream is boring. You should pick something else so people don't think you're boring too." Evie buckled herself into a child's booster seat.

"That's not nice," Rori responded. "If she likes boring old cream, she should paint the walls with it. I still won't think she's boring."

"Thanks, sweetie." Apricot chucked her under the chin and closed the door. The girls were cute as could be, precocious and just a little naughty. Which she absolutely loved. But she already had a headache, and their chatter wasn't helping it go away.

She glanced in the review mirror as she pulled onto Main. The girls had settled into silence, both of them looking out the windows, their arms stretched across the emptiness between them, their fingers entwined.

They looked like angels, sweet and innocent as could be, so she kept driving down Main Street and out of town, the afternoon sun shimmering in the cloudless sky as she made her way back to Rose's place.

Chapter Nine

In the six hours she'd had the girls, Apricot had learned several things. First, eight-year-olds couldn't be counted on to keep paint off the floors or the furniture. She'd assumed that before they'd begun the project, but the extent of paint splatter was confounding. She'd spent more time wiping up drips and spatter than she had painting cream over the dingy white walls. Somehow, though, they'd managed to finish the living room with impressive enthusiasm.

The second thing Apricot had learned was the girls didn't like artichoke hearts. They weren't keen on whole grain pasta with fresh pesto, either. She'd discovered that right around the time Rori started gagging on the dinner Apricot had presented to them. Both girls had been polite, but it was obvious neither was going to be able to choke down the food.

She'd finally given in and ordered pizza. Extra cheese for the girls and sausage and mushroom for Jet. He'd worked until the sun had nearly set, then taken the pizza and headed home.

Which had led Apricot to her third discovery—the

girls asked a lot of questions. A *lot* of questions. Most of which she didn't want to answer.

"You know what Andrew said?" Evie asked as Apricot led them into the backyard.

"I'm not sure I want to," she murmured, but Evie didn't seem to hear.

"He said your boyfriend dumped you. He said it was because you spent too much money on fancy wedding stuff and not enough money on your boyfriend."

"That's nice," she responded, because there was no way in the world she was going to discuss Lionel with an eight-year-old.

"No, it's not." Rori grabbed her hand, tugging her down so that they were eye to eye. "It isn't nice at all, and I know it isn't true. You probably spent lots and lots of money on your boyfriend, and he didn't appreciate you."

Evie nodded solemnly. "Just like with Aunt Daisy and Dennis. He didn't know what he had until he lost it."

Apricot held back a chuckle. Barely. "I take it Dennis was your aunt's boyfriend?"

"They were supposed to get married, but he ran off with that no-good hussy from Spokane."

"Evie!" Rori gasped. "You know Daddy said you're not supposed to use that word!"

"I didn't use it. Daisy used it. She said that hussy used her feminine wiles to steal Dennis away. Is that what happened to your boyfriend, Apricot? Did someone steal him away?"

Apricot wasn't sure if she should laugh or cry, so

she took the girls by the hands and walked toward the orchard.

"You made her sad," Rori whispered loudly enough to drive a family of quail from the undergrowth. "She probably thought her boyfriend just got icy feet. Now she thinks a hussy stole him away."

"Cold feet, sweetie," she corrected. "And I was the one who walked out of the church."

"Your feet got cold?" Evie eyed her doubtfully. "Aunt Daisy says it's always the men who get nerves on account of they want to sow wild oats."

"You can't believe everything you hear. Plenty of women get cold feet." She wouldn't touch the sowing wild oats thing with a twenty-foot pole. She didn't want to discuss relationships either. The more she listened, the more she agreed with Simon. The girls were too young to have their heads filled with the kind of stuff Daisy was spouting off.

Speaking of Daisy . . .

Apricot glanced at her watch. She hadn't heard from Simon, and that worried her. In her experience, the longer it took to deal with a crisis, the worse the crisis was. Hopefully that wasn't the case this time, because whatever was going on, it was taking eons.

"Where are we going?" Rori's grip on Apricot's hand tightened, her footsteps slowing as they approached the fence that separated the yard from the orchard.

"To the orchard."

"You mean those creepy old trees?" Rori stopped in her tracks. The descending sun had set fire to the distant sky, painting pink and orange streaks across the horizon. Mountains jutted up against the colorful display, casting deep shadows across the yard and house.

Apricot supposed that from a kid's point of view, the darkness of the orchard might be sinister. "They're apple trees. Farther in, there are pear trees and some cherry trees. They just need a little attention and love and they'll be beautiful."

"I don't think so," Evie said, but she walked to the fence and stood on the lowest cross rail. "What kind of apples do they grow?"

"All different kinds. The ones closest to us are Red Delicious. Three rows in are some Granny Smith."

"Granny Smith?" Evie giggled. "Why do they call them that?"

"I'd say it's because a granny named Smith grew them first, but I don't know for sure. I do know they're green and very crisp. I thought we could pick a few and make them into cobbler for your dad."

She hadn't really been thinking that. The apples weren't quite ripe, and she'd have to add a boatload of honey to her grandmother's cobbler recipe to sweeten them up. What she'd been thinking about was getting the girls outside, letting them run through the trees and explore the orchard while the sun was setting. She'd been hoping to get a few minutes of quiet. Since that obviously wasn't going to happen, they'd make cobbler.

"Charlotte makes the best apple cobbler in the world. We could just buy some from her," Rori offered, her gaze glued to the gnarled trees and the dark shadows beneath them.

"You're scared. She's scared." Evie jumped off the fence and hugged Rori. "She doesn't want to go in the creepy trees, and I don't either."

"You don't want to sit on the bench under the grape arbor and listen to the animals tuck themselves in for the night?" Apricot asked. It was the kind of thing Rose or Lilac would have said, but the words were foreign on Apricot's tongue. She was more a fact kind of gal. She was all about numbers and stats and building things up with good information and realistic goals. It had been a lot of years since she'd thought about hiking through the Pennsylvania woods with her mother, listening as she told stories about the flora and fauna there. Lilac was a born storyteller, and she made a good living off of it, traveling to schools and fairs and even colleges to retell stories she'd learned while traveling through South and Central America. She had a doctorate in anthropology. Not that anyone who met her would ever know it.

"Where's the grape arbor?" Evie asked. "Because I want to hear animals putting themselves to bed. You do too, right, Rori?"

Rori didn't look enthusiastic, but she nodded, her eyes big with worry.

"Let's go then." Apricot took Rori's hand and opened the gate. Evie grabbed her free hand, and they walked into the orchard together.

The girls didn't say a word as Apricot led them through the trees. They didn't speak as she pushed through brambles and into a small clearing she'd found a few days before. A grape arbor stretched several feet across overgrown grass, a wrought-iron bench beneath it. She sat on the cool metal and patted the seat on either side of her.

"We can't sit there," Rori whispered.

"Why not?"

"It's for old man Shaffer's wife. Andrew says he put a bench right in the middle of the orchard so his dead wife could always sit in her favorite spot."

"Let's not worry about what Andrew says."

"But—"

"If Mr. Shaffer put the bench here, it's because his wife loved this spot. I've heard she was a very nice woman, and I think that a very nice woman would want other people to enjoy what she loved so much." She thought the girls must have heard the weariness in her voice, because they plopped down beside her without another sound.

She thought they'd pick up the conversation again, but the quiet evening must have woven its spell. Grape and apple filled the air with the sweet scent of summer growth and a hint of fall harvest. Leaves rustled and a bird called a quiet good-night. Still, the girls didn't say a word.

A small, dark shadow slipped from between the trees, and the girls scooted closer.

"It's just Handsome," Apricot whispered, almost afraid to break the silence. It seemed filled with something lovely and light. Something that defied the darkness and the old gnarled trees that stood watch. Maybe it was the blazing sunset just visible through the canopy of trees. Maybe it was the two girls pressed close to her sides. Maybe it was just that Lionel had moved on, and she had no choice but to move on as well. All the lectures she'd given herself, all the assurances that she would never take him back, that she was better off without him, hadn't eased the sting of waking up alone in the morning and going to bed alone at night.

Handsome jumped into her lap, butting his head against her stomach as he made himself comfortable.

Every morning, she told herself she was going to take him to the animal shelter, and every evening, he was still happily ensconced in her life.

A twig snapped. A branch broke. The girls tensed, but Apricot pulled them closer.

"Shhhh," she breathed. "Just watch."

Seconds later, a doe meandered through the clearing, picking her way through the grass, a fawn following along behind. The girls didn't move. Apricot didn't think they even breathed as the doe and fawn slipped back into the trees and disappeared into the shadowy orchard.

"Where are they going?" Rori asked so quietly Apricot barely heard.

"To find something to eat."

"There's lots of things right here. Apples and grapes and grass."

"They want their privacy."

"Shouldn't the baby be sleeping?"

"She probably already slept."

"Can we follow them?" Evie jumped up. "Maybe we can find lots more deer. Maybe I can get close enough to touch one, and you can take a picture of me on your phone and we can show Daddy."

"Not tonight." Apricot stood and stretched. The quiet was over. No doubt about that. "Let's pick some apples before it gets too dark to see. Then you girls can help me cut and core them and put them in a cobbler."

"I still think we should just buy one from Charlotte," Evie muttered. "Plus, we don't even have a basket or a box or anything to put the apples in."

"We'll just use our shirts to hold them. I'll use my skirt." She set Handsome on the ground. The cat could find his way home, no problem. He'd proven that over and over again the past few days. Right then, he was more interested in pouncing on apples and chasing them when they rolled away.

"These are the ones we want." She pulled one from a tree and handed it to Rori.

Rori lifted it to her nose and inhaled. "It smells like apple and happiness."

"That's silly," Evie scoffed. "You can't smell happiness."

"You can if you're a poet." Apricot picked another apple and handed it to Evie. "Take a sniff and see for yourself."

Evie inhaled deeply, a tiny frown line between her brows. If she didn't smell what her sister had, she didn't let on. "Do you think Daddy will pick us up soon? Tomorrow is church, and we always have to take showers before bed and Aunt Daisy braids our hair so it will be curly."

"I'm sure he will be," she lied. She wasn't sure. She was shocked that she hadn't heard from Simon and concerned about what that might mean. She was trying to play it cool though, trying to pretend that she and the girls did this every Saturday night.

"How can you be sure? Maybe I should call him," Evie insisted. Obviously the excitement of being in a new environment was wearing thin.

"Let's pick our apples and make the cobbler. If he hasn't come for you by then, you can give him a call." She picked another apple, using the hem of her shirt to hold it as she reached for another.

The girls looked at each other.

Were they about to stage a mutiny? Scream their heads off? Run back to the house?

They stepped forward in unison, reaching for a branch filled with apples. It drooped close to the ground with the weight of its fruit, and the girls were able to reach it easily. They snapped underripe apples from the branches, dropping fruit and leaves into shirts held out like nets. It reminded Apricot of fall harvest in Happy Dale, little kids working alongside adults to pick fruit and vegetables that would be canned and stored.

There was something cathartic about the process, something wholly healing about working out in nature. She'd forgotten that, but working beside the girls brought the memories back. She reached for apples higher in the tree, and let the memories wash over her and drive away some of the emptiness that she'd been living with since she'd left LA.

Simon sped along the country road that led to Apricot's house, the darkness outside Henry's windows mocking his urgency. It was already ten. Way past the twins' bedtime. He should have had them home hours ago, tucked in and sleeping soundly. Racing to get them now was like trying to plug a black hole with a cotton ball.

He'd have to apologize to Apricot. He hadn't meant to leave the girls with her for so long. He should have called to let her know what was going on and give her some indication of when he'd be home, but he'd been busy dealing with Daisy. It had taken most of the late afternoon and evening to get her calm enough for coherency. Even then she'd been short on details and long on drama. Once he'd finally gotten as much of the story as she seemed able to give, he'd driven her to his place, asked the neighbor to keep an eye on her while he went to the crime scene. Max and Cade had already been there collecting what little evidence there was. Daisy's purse—empty of her smartphone and wallet. A candy bar wrapper. A cigarette butt. They planned to send the wrapper and cigarette butt to the state forensic team. It was possible they could pull DNA from one or the other.

Possible but doubtful.

He pulled up in front of Rose's house, parked Henry, and jogged to the front door. It swung open before he could ring the bell.

"Finally!" Apricot admonished as she took his arm and dragged him through the doorway. "I've been worried sick."

"Sorry. I meant to call, but I got caught up in things."

"What happened? Was Daisy in an accident? Is she hurt?"

"She was mugged. Someone grabbed her purse and pushed her to the ground."

"Is she okay?" She'd changed into pale blue sweatpants that had seen better days and a tight-fitting white T-shirt. Three colorful barrettes held her hair away from her face. He thought they were probably the girls' doing. Same for the bright purple polish on her nails.

"I'd say more scared than anything. The doctor couldn't find more than a scraped knee."

"Poor Daisy. She doesn't seem like the kind of person who'd handle something like this well." She ran a hand over her hair and rubbed the back of her neck. "Not that it would be easy on anyone." The last few words tumbled out as if she were afraid of offending him.

"Daisy doesn't handle stress well, and she's not handling being mugged at all. One of the reasons I didn't call was because I couldn't get her calmed down enough to get the story out of her."

"It sounds like you could use a cup of tea. The girls are sleeping in the guest room. I don't suppose it would hurt them at all to rest for a little longer."

He hated tea, but her arm slid around his waist and he found himself walking into the kitchen. It smelled like apple and cinnamon with just a hint of the flowery scent that always seemed to cling to Apricot. The place had changed. The walls had been painted a buttery yellow, the old linoleum floor ripped up to reveal thick-planked wood nicked and gouged with time. It had been polished to a dull shine, a few stains near the counter and table so deeply embedded they seemed part of the pattern of the floor. "The place looks good."

"Thanks." She filled a kettle and set it on the stove, her scapula jutting against white cotton, the column of her neck delicate and vulnerable-looking. "It's a labor of love."

"On a house that isn't yours," he pointed out.

She shrugged, opening a cupboard and taking out what looked like a jar of tea leaves. "I spent time here when I was a kid. I feel some obligation to the place." She spooned the leaves into a small metal basket that hooked over the edge of a mug. "Besides, if I let things go the way they are, in a decade the place will be falling apart."

"I doubt Dusty would let that happen. He loves the place."

"It's more likely he loves my aunt," she said with a smile that put a little color in her pale cheeks. "He's stopped by more than once to ask if she's planning a visit."

"Is she?"

"God, I hope not! If she comes, the rest of my wacky family will. I'll have a boatload of hippies camped in trailers on the front yard. Can you imagine what Maura would say then?"

"The girls have been talking, haven't they?" He could imagine every word they'd been saying because he'd heard versions of the gossip all over town.

"By nine, I was trying to find their off switch. Apparently, twin girls don't come with one."

"And there isn't a day that goes by that I don't ask the good Lord why not," he responded drily. He'd have to talk to the girls about spreading gossip. *Again.*

Apricot laughed, snagging the kettle from the stove and pouring hot water over the tea leaves. "This is going to be a very mild cup of tea. I don't want to steep the leaves, just get some of the flavor and health benefits into the water."

"I'm almost afraid to ask what's in those leaves."

"I wouldn't dare poison an officer of the law." She lifted the basket and set it in the sink, then handed him the mug, her smile as warm and inviting as sunrise. He wanted to set the mug down, tug her close, and study that smile, her face, the vivid blue of her eyes. Heck with the tea, he wanted to drink Apricot in.

"Go on," she urged, and for a split-second worth of insanity he actually thought she'd read his mind.

"It's just green tea," she continued. "With a little dandelion root and leaves mixed in. It won't hurt you."

"Dandelion?" The liquid was pale and innocuous-looking, but he was more a steak-and-potatoes kind of guy, and he wasn't sure about eating the weed Daisy spent every spring and summer trying to eradicate from his lawn.

"It's chock-full of vitamins and minerals and promotes good liver function. With all the stress you're under, a boost to your immune system isn't a bad thing."

"I'm healthy as a horse, so I'm not all that worried about immunity boosting." He took a sip of the tea anyway. Grassy with a slightly bitter edge, it had a mild flavor that washed down his throat and warmed his stomach.

"Well?" she demanded. "What do you think?"

"It's better than horrible," he responded.

"I think I'll put that on the package. 'Dandelion green tea—it's better than horrible,'" she said with a soft chuckle that warmed him up a thousand times better than the tea had.

"You sell a lot of that stuff?"

"A boatload of it." She leaned against the counter, the oversized sweats bagging around her ankles, her arms crossed over her chest. "We live in a culture obsessed with good health and excess. People want to drink themselves into a stupor and then flush the toxins from their bodies so they can do it all again the next night. They want to eat fast food every afternoon for lunch and then run off the calories in the gym every night. My products can at least help with detoxing bodies taxed by the chemicals in processed food, the poison in alcohol and cigarettes. I don't promise miracles. I'm not claiming a few sips of my tea will cure cancer or prevent it, but the products I sell are a first step to good health." She ran out of steam, her cheeks flushed.

He couldn't say he was all that interested in herbs and teas and whatever else Apricot sold, but he was sure as heck interested in her.

"Sorry," she muttered, the color in her cheeks deepening. "I get a little nuts when I start talking business."

"Get me started talking about law enforcement or my girls, and all bets are off for how long I can talk before taking a breath, so you've got no need to apologize."

"Lionel always said . . ." She shook her head. "Never mind."

"I think I will mind." He took both her hands, tugged her in close. "So, how about you tell me what good old Lionel had to say about you talking business?"

"It doesn't matter."

"It matters." He slid his hands to her wrists, his fingers curving around slender bones and silky skin. "How about I guess? He said that business was business and you shouldn't let your heart get involved. He said that you let your emotions rule, and that you needed him to keep you on track. He said that without him, the business would go belly up."

"He wasn't that bad," she protested, but he knew there was some truth in what he'd said.

"Which means he wasn't that good either."

"He thought the details of what I sold were boring. He was more a facts-and-figures kind of guy."

"That's a poor excuse for being an asshole," he responded.

Her lips twitched, and he was sure there was a smile in her eyes. "Where have you been all my life, Simon?" she asked.

It was supposed to be a joke. He knew that, and his head was telling him to laugh and walk away. It was hollering loud and clear that he'd better hightail it up the stairs, grab the girls, and get out while the getting was good.

Only problem was, he didn't want to make light of things. He didn't want to walk away.

His hands moved of their own accord, sliding up slender arms and resting on shoulders that were thin and muscular. "Raising a couple of precocious girls and waiting for you to come along."

"You really are full of Southern charm, and I really do need you to cut it out." She didn't step away though. Just looked up into his eyes as if she could find the mysteries of the universe in his gaze.

He wanted to tell her to forget it.

He wanted to say that he didn't have any answers. That he wasn't a hero, a savior, someone who could lift her up and carry her through life.

He wanted to say that he'd already failed once, and he didn't want to fail again, but Apricot levered up on her toes and her lips brushed his cheek. He forgot everything then. Everything but the woman standing in front of him. The one who liked old trucks and ugly cats and who seemed to care about everyone who crossed her path.

He turned his head, captured her lips with his before she could back away. He didn't have a plan. It just happened, a kiss that tasted like apple and sugar

and something so dark and exotic that he forgot he
was standing in Apricot's kitchen, the girls sleeping
upstairs. Forgot that he needed to get home, check
on Daisy, call Cade.

He forgot that he had a hundred reasons why
Apricot wasn't a good idea.

Because, right then? All he wanted was more.

Chapter Ten

"What are they doing?" A little girl's voice drifted through a haze of longing so thick Apricot didn't think she'd ever find her way out of it. She wasn't sure she *wanted* to find her way out! What she wanted was to burrow closer to Simon's warmth, trail her hands along his biceps, slide them around his slim waist.

"They're kissing, silly." A second voice joined the first, and Simon jerked back, one of his hands pressed against Apricot's back, the other cupping her jaw.

The look in his eyes . . .

Yeah. *That* look. As if she were the only woman in the world, and as if he would fight dragons to be with her.

"Wow!" she breathed.

His lips quirked in a crooked smile. "I second that," he said. "But we could both be wrong."

"I—"

"I'd suggest that we try again. Just to make sure, but we have an audience." He kept his hand on her back and shifted so he was facing the kitchen doorway.

The twins were standing on the threshold, their eyes big as saucers.

"Are you two dating?" Evie asked. "Because Andrew says—"

"We're not going to discuss what anyone else says, and we're not going to tell anyone about this," Simon said, cutting her off.

"Why not?" Evie put her hands on her hips and stuck her lower lip out. She looked like a kid who needed to be in bed, and she was acting like one.

"Because what happens between me and Apricot is between us. It's not something the world needs to know."

"It's a secret love affair," Rori gasped. "Like in that show Daisy watches when she's home from the library."

"I think your aunt and I are going to have a chat about her choice of television. There are certain shows I don't approve of you girls watching. I also don't approve of gossip. That's what talking about other people's stuff is."

"It's also fun," Evie commented, and Apricot couldn't help chuckling. As tiring as the girls were, she'd found them to be good company. They were helpful, smart, and respectful. They also had wild imaginations. If they started talking about the simple little kiss she and Simon had shared . . .

Simple? Her brain whispered. *Little? There was nothing simple or little about it.*

"It's not fun if someone is hurt by it, Evie," Simon responded sternly.

"Who's going to get hurt if I say that you and Apricot were—"

"Young lady"—he strode across the room and

crouched in front of her—"I am not happy with your attitude. If you want to keep having it, I may have to take away that tutu you got today."

Evie pressed her lips together and didn't say another word.

Whether or not she'd decide to say one when she returned to school on Monday was another thing altogether.

"We made apple cobbler, Daddy," Rori said, running to the fridge and pulling out the pan of cobbler Apricot had said they could take home. "We picked the apples and peeled them and cored them and everything, all by ourselves."

"It looks fantastic." Simon took the pan from her hands. "We'd better get home. Aunt Daisy . . . had an accident, and she's staying at our place tonight."

The girls both started talking at once, asking questions so quickly, Apricot wasn't sure how Simon managed to hear them. Somehow he did, answering one after another as he herded the girls to the door.

"You don't have any kittens hidden on you, do you?" he asked the girls as he walked out onto the front porch.

"No," they responded in unison.

"You're sure? Because if we get home and Handsome climbs out of one of those skirts, I'm going to bring all three kittens back here. Go get in the car. I'll be right there."

The girls raced to his SUV and climbed into the back.

Which left Apricot and Simon standing on the porch, a pan of apple cobbler between them.

He smiled, and her insides melted. "Thanks for

taking care of the girls, Apricot. And for the apple cobbler."

"Thank me after you try it. I'm not sure how it's going to taste. The apples weren't quite ripe."

"Needed something to keep the girls occupied, huh?"

"Yes," she admitted. "Desperate times called for desperate measures, so I dragged them out into the orchard and made them pick apples."

"Desperate, huh? Sounds like they were a handful."

"They weren't. I'm just not used to kids. My nieces and nephews are all on the East Coast, and I only see them a couple of times a year."

"For someone who doesn't spend a lot of time with kids, you sure have a way with them. You're all my girls talk about." He ran his knuckle along her cheek. "Lately, you're just about all I *think* about."

"I'm sure you have way too much taking up your attention to waste a minute thinking about anything other than your girls and your job," she murmured, her throat tight and hot with emotions she didn't want to feel.

"*I'm* sure you haven't been out of your crappy relationship long enough to consider being in another one, but that doesn't mean either of us has to pretend the kiss we shared didn't happen."

"It wasn't a crappy relationship," she said, sidestepping the comment about their kiss. It had felt like a first kiss and like a last kiss and like every kind of kiss in between. She wasn't sure what to make of that, what to think of it, and she sure as heck wasn't going to try to discuss it.

"No?"

"Of course it wasn't! We loved each other."

"There's all kinds of love, Apricot. There's the kind I had with my wife—the kind that waxes hot and cold as quickly as the tide rises and falls. There's the kind like I have for my daughters—uncomplicated, undemanding, and unconditional. There's friendship love and sibling love."

"I'm twenty-nine, Simon. I know all about the different kinds of love."

"Yeah? Then . . . out of curiosity . . . what kind of love did you and Lionel share? It sure as heck wasn't the kind that sticks, because you're here and he's somewhere else."

With *someone else.*

He didn't say it, but the words seemed to hang on the crisp night air.

She wanted to say something clever and maybe a little sharp, but his expression was soft and open, and she couldn't bring herself to do it. "Lionel and I were together for a long time. It's hard to wrap a long-term relationship into a tidy little package and stick a tag on it."

"What's that got to do with love?"

"Love waxes and wanes. It's friendship and commitment that carry a couple through."

"In other words, you didn't love him and he didn't love you."

"I didn't say that."

"You didn't have to. Here's the thing, Apricot." He moved so close she could feel the heat of his body, smell the spicy scent of his aftershave. If she leaned just a little closer, their bodies would collide and all that wonderful heat of the kiss would come back. "Not every relationship is going to be a good one. The only way we can heal from the bad ones is to admit what they are, wash our hands of them and move on."

"So now you're a counselor?"

"I'm just a guy who is curious about you. Maybe it's time you get a little curious about yourself."

"What in God's name is that supposed to mean?"

"Just that you're really good at diagnosing other people's ailments and treating them, but when it comes to yourself, you like to bury your head in the sand and pretend that everything is fine when it's not."

"I'm not pretending!" she protested.

"Sure you are." He touched her cheek, his fingers cool against her heated skin. "You're throwing all your energy into fixing up a house that isn't yours in a town that isn't yours because you don't want to face what you left behind. You're tending to everyone who comes your way, offering herbs and teas and advice. All the while, you're doing everything you can to avoid thinking about what you no longer have."

He was right. Every single word he said was true.

She wanted to argue anyway, because she didn't like that he could see her so clearly, didn't want to believe that she was so transparent. She'd spent five years with Lionel. Five years when saying she was okay was enough to get him to back off. Five years where she swept things under the carpet because he couldn't deal with them.

Five years of pretending things were okay when they weren't?

God, she hoped not!

His cell phone rang, and he stepped back, the chilly evening air sweeping over Apricot's heated skin.

"Hello?" Simon spoke into the phone, his gaze locked on Apricot. He hadn't shaved and she had the urge to slide her palm along his jaw, feel the roughness of the stubble there. She had it bad. Really bad. And she didn't think there was a thing she could do to change it.

Daisy, Simon mouthed, and she nodded, her fists clenched so hard her nails dug into her palm. She tried to relax, but she was wound up tighter than a turkey on Thanksgiving Day. She hadn't walked out of one relationship to walk right into another one. She'd walked out, and she'd planned to stay out. For good.

"I'm at old man Shaffer's place, getting the girls," Simon said. "The doctor said there was no chance you had a concussion."

He squeezed the bridge of his nose and waited. "Seriously, Daisy, I don't think you're going to fall asleep and wake up dead." He paused, listened, then sighed. "Not one person in the history of the world has woken up dead, that's why."

Apricot nearly choked trying to keep laughter from bubbling out. It wasn't funny. Not really. Daisy had been through a lot. She was traumatized, and that wasn't a laughing matter.

But Apricot really did have the urge to giggle. The look on Simon's face—frustration, amusement, concern, bewilderment—made her want to take the phone from his hand and deal with the problem.

So, maybe he'd been right. Maybe she did try to fix everyone else.

"All right, Daisy," Simon continued. "I'm on my way home, but I'm not taking you to the emergency room, because you aren't dying and you're not going to die."

One more long pause, and she was pretty sure he rolled his eyes heavenward. "We'll talk about it when I get there, okay? See you in a few."

He slid the phone into his pocket, raked a hand through his hair. "I need to get home. Daisy thinks she's got a concussion."

"Was she hit hard?"

"Hit?"

"In the head? You said she thought she had a concussion."

"She didn't hit her head. Wasn't hit in the head, either. As far as I know and as far as the doctor who examined her could see, there's not a thing wrong with her that putting the guy who mugged her in jail won't solve."

"I'd offer some more chamomile tea, but I wouldn't want to be accused of burying my own troubles while I try to fix the problems of others." The words just slipped out, and they sounded just a tad bit bitter.

Simon smiled and shook his head. "You took it all wrong, Apricot. I wasn't saying you shouldn't do what you do. I'm just suggesting that you offer yourself a little bit of the grace you offer other people." He dropped a quick kiss to her forehead. "I'd better go. Otherwise, Daisy will call an ambulance and get herself rushed to the hospital. Sweet dreams." He dropped a second kiss on her lips, the contact soft as spring rain.

She watched him walk to his SUV, waved while

he backed out of the driveway. Seconds later, his taillights disappeared.

The night air had grown chilly, the first touch of fall hanging in the moist air. She let it bathe the heat from her face, tried to tell herself that Simon was just like every other guy she'd ever known, that his kisses meant about as much as a penny in a five-and-dime store.

The problem was, she didn't believe it.

Facts were facts, and the fact was, Simon was one in a million. He was the kind of guy any woman would be happy to have, and once a woman had him, she'd be a dang idiot to let him go.

"Darn you, Sapphire!" she muttered as she walked back inside. "Do you always have to be right?"

If Sapphire hadn't been a continent away, she'd have cackled with glee. She was, though, and the only one around to hear Apricot griping was a giant rat-tailed kitten.

"And I'm thinking *you* don't care much about my problems, do you, Handsome?"

Handsome pounced from his place on the couch, landing squarely on Apricot's thigh.

"Ouch! Let go!" She peeled him off her leg and he scrambled across the floor, slid into her purse. Paused. Then jumped inside, burrowing his way into the bag and appearing a moment later, a long white feather in his mouth. It looked suspiciously like the one that had been at Sweet Treats.

"Where did you get that?" She scooped Handsome into her arms, managed to wrestle the feather from his mouth. It didn't seem damaged, the edges still downy and soft, the shaft unbent. She frowned, holding it up to the light. She'd seen a lot of bird feathers

in her life. She was more familiar than she wanted to
be with chickens, ducks, and geese, and she didn't remember any of them having feathers as large or snow
white as this one.

"Whatever it is, we've got to return it, Handsome.
You can't just snag things from other people. That's
stealing. Although, since you're a cat, I'm not sure
they could try you for it." She set Handsome down
and walked upstairs, the kitten scrambling up the
stairs behind her. The bedrooms were furnished
exactly the way they'd been when old man Shaffer
died. Rose hadn't changed a thing. Even the linens
were exactly the same as they'd been the first time
Apricot had visited.

She walked into the room she'd been using. There
was a thin green vase on the dresser that looked like
it had been handcrafted. The glaze was clunky, the
little flowers that swirled up its side primitive. It was
pretty, though, in an old-fashioned sort of way. Apricot thought that Shaffer's wife might have made it.
She put the feather in the vase and set it on a shelf
that she didn't think Handsome could reach.

"Leave it alone. You hear me? I have to bring it
back to Charlotte, and I don't want it cat-chewed
before then."

Handsome seemed more interested in exploring
the darkness beneath the bed than trying to find a
way to reach the feather. How he'd gotten it in the
first place, Apricot didn't know. It had been in the
vase, plain as could be. Handsome had been con-
fined to her purse the entire time she was in Sweet
Treats.

Hadn't he?

She glanced under the bed. He hadn't magically

disappeared, but the cat did have a way of appearing and disappearing. Still . . .

She'd have noticed if he'd been sneaking his way over Sweet Treats' shelves, trying to pilfer the feather.

"I'll figure it out Monday," she said to no one in particular. That's what happened when you went from part of a couple to lone wolf. You kept speaking things out loud like there was someone around to listen.

It wouldn't be long before she started collecting stray cats. In a few months, she'd be the resident crazy cat lady, wandering up and down the streets of Apple Valley, muttering under her breath and reeking of cat urine.

A few months in Apple Valley?

When had that become part of the plan?

Was it part of the plan?

She walked to the window, pulling back the sheers that had probably been hanging there for half a century. Pretty little swag ties had been wrapped around hooks on either side of the window, the tiny flower print feminine and pretty. Apricot imagined Shaffer's wife using the ties to hold the sheers back during the summer heat.

She opened the window, letting in moist, cool air. Fall was definitely in the air. Apple harvest was just around the corner. This year, there wasn't a lot she could do but pick through the fruit and try to find whatever was salvageable. Next year, the orchard would be lush with ripe fruit, redolent with the scent of healthy, harvestable apples and pears.

A dark shadow darted from the trees across the road and headed straight for her property. Apricot switched off the light, looked outside again. The wind had picked up and the trees swished and swayed.

She'd almost convinced herself that that's what she'd seen. Just trees swaying and leaves moving with the wind. Something moved across her yard, and she jumped back, her heart nearly leaping from her chest. There was someone out there!

Whoever it was skulked across the yard. Not overly tall or overly big. Just . . . there, darting toward the corner of the house. She hadn't locked the back door, so she raced to the kitchen, slid the bolt home and then peered out into the backyard.

There was definitely someone out there.

She could see him moving stealthily along the fence line.

She'd left her cell phone in her purse, and she didn't want to take her eyes off the trespasser long enough to get it. Then again, she didn't want to die.

She crept into the living room, snagged her cell phone and ran back to the window. Nothing. No one. Just the shadowy night and the swaying trees.

Had it been her imagination? Some flight of fancy brought on by fatigue?

She pressed her face against the glass, straining to see into the darkness beyond the window. The yard was empty, nothing moving but the dead leaves that skittered across the yard.

She shivered, sure that a shadow was about to separate itself from the others. She watched for so long her legs ached and her eyes hurt, but whoever had been outside was gone.

"It was probably just Dusty making sure I'm not

causing any damage to Rose's property," she said aloud.

Good thought.

But what if it wasn't?

What if the guy who'd mugged Daisy was out in the orchard waiting for an opportunity to break into the house?

She glanced at her watch. Almost eleven. Dusty wouldn't appreciate getting a phone call this time of night, asking if he was wandering around outside.

Besides, if he was outside, he wouldn't be answering his phone.

She could call the police, but that seemed like overkill. Whoever she'd seen had disappeared, and the best thing she could do was go to bed and forget about it.

She tried. She really did. She lay on the bed that had a hollow in the center from too many years of use. She covered herself with a sheet that was soft with time. She closed her eyes, relaxed every muscle in her body just the way her yoga instructor had taught her. The problem was, her brain wasn't a muscle, and it refused to relax.

Handsome snored beside her, his little body pressed up against her side. At least one of them wasn't having any trouble sleeping. Right at that moment, she wished she were back in LA. At least there, she'd have noise to distract her. She'd forgotten how quiet country nights were. Not a sound from anything but the kitten.

She opened her eyes, stared up at the ceiling. She'd plugged her cell phone into the charger and set it on the bedside table. She could call someone,

chat for a few minutes, maybe try to work out some of
the issues that were causing her sleepless nights. It
was early morning hours in Pennsylvania, but Lilac
never cared about things like that. She was all about
being there when she was needed and stepping back
when she wasn't.

If Apricot called her, all bets were off, though. The
entire family would see it as a cry for help, and they'd
converge on Apple Valley like a pack of rats on a plate
of cheese.

No. She couldn't call Lilac or Rose or Hubert. She
couldn't call any of her siblings, because they'd report
the call to the family.

You could call Simon, a wicked little voice whispered.
He's probably still awake.

And—darn it all!—she was seriously tempted to
do it.

Those eyes!

Those hands!

That smile!

And his kiss . . . It had turned her blood to molten
lava and made her want him more than she'd wanted
her next breath.

God! She was a fool to the fifth degree! Had she
not just spent five years of her life pursuing love and
happiness only to have it all snatched away? Did she
really want to go there again?

No! She did not!

Not even with someone like Simon.

Something moved in her periphery, a bit of white
just seeming to float across the edges of her vision.
She sat up, her heart hammering in her chest, her gaze
darting to the thing that still seemed to be moving.

Only it wasn't.

It was just the feather, sitting in the vase on the shelf. Stark white in the darkness, it seemed to glow with its own inner light. She blinked, looked again. Nope. It was just a white feather in a dark room. Nothing magical about it. No power to give anything. Especially not happiness or luck or love . . . or whatever it was that Charlotte had said.

As much as she'd been raised by a storyteller and a free spirit, Apricot had always had her feet firmly planted on the ground. She didn't believe in myths and magic, didn't put any stock in omens and portents. Hard work and the power of personal initiative—that's what got a person what she wanted.

Except when it didn't.

She scowled.

She had what she wanted. A successful business. A family she loved. A nice condo in LA. Money in the bank to buy a new condo in LA . . . because there was absolutely no way in hell she was going to live in the one she and Lionel had shared.

She had it all. Every single thing anyone could ever want.

Except for romantic love.

And, truth be told, that sucked, because she'd planned to have a family and a house and a white picket fence. She'd even gone to the local animal shelter a few times in the weeks before the wedding, just to see what kind of dogs were up for adoption. Because she'd been going to have that too. The dog. The daily walks around the block to give Fido or Fluffy some exercise. She'd been planning in her head the windowsill herb gardens that she'd plant, the flower baskets hanging from the front porch. She hadn't cared much about the wedding. She'd let her future mother-in-law take over as many details as she'd wanted. And she'd wanted to take over all of them.

What Apricot had wanted was what came after.

She hadn't gotten it.

"It sucks. Big-time," she whispered into the silence.

There was no one around to reply, so she turned on her side, interrupting poor Handsome in the middle of a wall-rattling snore, and stared at the bright white feather until she finally fell asleep.

Chapter Eleven

Someone was banging on the door. Loudly!

Apricot put the pillow over her head and pressed it to her ears. She needed more sleep, and she was going to get it come hell or high water! It would take a force of nature to get her out of bed, and even then, she might just cling to the bed frame and hope for the best.

The doorbell rang.

She moaned. "Go away!"

It rang again.

"Crap and cotton!" she muttered, stumbling out of bed, her baggy pajama pants twisted around her hips.

God! She hoped Dusty wasn't standing on the porch. He'd take one look at her in her pj bottoms and tank top and decide she was a slug for still being in bed at . . . she glanced at her watch. Eight in the morning.

Eight!

There had to be an etiquette rule about things like that. Who wrote the famous column? Libby? Abby?

Adele? Whoever she was, Apricot was confident she'd explained reasonable times for visiting. She was just as confident those times did not include eight in the morning!

She peered out the peephole, saw Jet reaching for the doorbell again.

"Hold on!" she shouted, tugging down the hem of her tank top so it covered her stomach. She opened the door a crack, was about to tell him that it was too early to start working on the house.

"Apricot! You've got to help me!" he began before she could open her mouth. "I'm in trouble."

"What kind of trouble?" She opened the door, concerned and a little alarmed by the frantic edge to his words, the wildness in his eyes. He looked scared, and she was suddenly scared for him.

"Law trouble." His gaze jumped from her face to her head, his eyes widening for a fraction of a second before his gaze dropped to her face again.

"You're going to have to give me more details if you want me to help." She touched her head, felt the short strands sticking out in a hundred different directions. This day was *not* off to a good start!

"That crazy librarian chick is accusing me of robbing her!" he blurted out, his Adam's apple bobbing up and down as he swallowed convulsively.

"Daisy?" She stepped to the side and let Jet rush in. "Why would she do that?"

"I don't know why the hell anyone does anything. I just know that woman is always shushing me and my girlfriend while we're at the library. We'll be there trying to study and discuss our work, and she's hovering around the corner just waiting for an opportunity to tell us to shut up."

"It's kind of her job to keep people quiet."

"Is it her job to accuse an innocent guy of robbing her?"

"Are you sure she's accusing you?"

"The sheriff showed up at my grandparents' place around midnight. He wanted to know where I was yesterday afternoon. Why do *you* think that was, because the librarian said I *didn't* do anything?"

Good question, and her brain was too foggy from sleep to think of an answer. "How about we have some coffee and think this through?"

"I don't need coffee, and there's nothing to think through!" he growled, but he followed her into the kitchen, pacing the floor while she started the coffeemaker.

"This sucks," he muttered. "I'm just getting on my feet, proving myself in town, going to college, and some old—"

"Daisy is younger than me," Apricot pointed out.

"She acts old. And bitter. She's that too. I heard her longtime boyfriend left town to get away from her. Just proves how crazy she is." He slouched in a chair. He looked defeated.

"What do you want me to help with?" Apricot asked as she took the chair across from him.

"I know the sheriff is going to show up here to check on my story. I just need you to verify it."

"You told him you were here?"

"I *was* here." He nearly spit the words. "I worked twelve hours yesterday."

"You don't have to tell me that, Jet. I was here, remember?"

"Except when Daisy the dingbat was robbed, remember?" His eyes flashed, but Apricot thought there was more hurt in his gaze than anger. "The sheriff is going to ask you if I was here yesterday, and I need you to tell him that I was. If he asks—"

"Hold on." She held up her hand. She didn't want to hear him ask her to lie. That would put a bad taste in her mouth and make her wonder why he needed her to do it. "I'm not going to tell him I was here when Daisy got robbed."

"I wasn't going to ask you to. I was going to ask you to tell him how much work I got done while you were gone." He scowled and crossed his arms over his chest.

She'd offended him.

If his scowl hadn't told her that, the daggers he was shooting from his eyes would have. "Okay. I can do that."

"Yeah, but can you be specific?"

"About?"

He sighed, ran his hand over his hair like he was too old and too tired to deal with her. "You do know what I got done while you were out, right?"

Of course she knew. He'd provided her with a schedule and an itemized list of supplies that he'd need each day. Tomorrow, if she remembered correctly, he was going to paint the front porch. "You fixed the stairs on the back stoop and you painted the east side of the house."

"That's a lot of work," he said as if he were trying to convince both of them of the fact.

"A ton," she confirmed. "And it looks fantastic."

"Wish fantastic could keep me out of jail," he responded morosely.

"You're not going to—"

The doorbell rang.

Jet nearly jumped out of his chair, wild fear in his eyes. "I bet that's them!" he cried. "Coming to cart me off to the slammer!"

"You've been watching too many cop shows." She headed for the front door, calling over her shoulder, "Just stay there while I see who it is. Then we can decide what to do about Daisy's accusations."

She yanked the door open, blinked twice as she met Simon's eyes. He was in full deputy sheriff's uniform. Crisp shirt and slacks, polished shoes, hat. Sheriff Cade Cunningham stood beside him, his uniform just as pressed, his expression grim. "Good morning, Apricot. Mind if we come in for a few minutes?" he asked.

"Of course not." She smoothed her hair, realized that Simon was watching, a half smile curving his to-die-for lips, and let her hand drop away. "I have a pot of coffee on, if either of you are interested."

"I wouldn't mind a cup." Simon took off his hat, his smile broadening as he scanned her from head to toe. "Looks like we got you out of bed."

For some reason that made her blush. "I was up. Jet—"

"Jet's here?" Cade asked with a slight frown. Apricot didn't know much about him, but her first impression was that he was fair and thoughtful. She didn't think he'd arrest someone for no reason.

"In the kitchen."

"I think I have a few more questions to ask him. Simon has a few to ask you, if you have time to answer." He acted as if she had a choice, but Apricot didn't think she did.

"That's fine," she responded, but he was already

down the hall and disappearing into the kitchen. "Jet isn't going to be happy," she murmured.

"I'm not exactly thrilled either," Simon replied, cupping her elbow and leading her into the living room. She knew he was about to interview her, but all she could think about was the heat that coursed through her every time they touched. "My girls are heading off to church with Daisy."

"So, she didn't wake up dead?"

He smiled and lifted her hand, pressing a kiss to her palm. He folded her fingers over it. "That's payment for giving me my first real smile of the day."

"Should you be kissing a witness's hand?"

"Only if the witness is you." He motioned for her to sit. "Let's get down to business. Seeing as how Jet is here, I'm sure you've heard that Daisy thinks he may be the person who robbed her."

"I heard, and I can tell you that he didn't have anything to do with what happened to Daisy," she said definitively. "He spent all day here working on the house."

"You weren't here when Daisy was robbed," he pointed out. "It would have been easy enough for Jet to leave and come back before you returned."

"He didn't do it, Simon."

"Was anyone here with him?"

"There were a couple of guys working with him in the morning, but they were gone when I got back."

"I don't suppose you have their names?"

She'd been introduced, but she only remembered first names and faces. "There was a short redheaded guy named Damian. He looked like he was in his twenties. There was also an older man. Probably in his midfifties with gray hair and brown eyes. His name—"

"Samuel Morris?"

"Sammy is how Jet introduced him."

"That's him. Sammy retired from rail work a few years back. His wife likes him to take on odd jobs to keep him out of her hair."

"That's terrible!"

"Not really. He likes to be busy, and she's always happy when he comes home. It's a win-win situation," he responded absently as he jotted something into a notebook. "What time did you get home yesterday?"

"Three thirty?"

"You're not sure?"

"It was around that time." Dang! Her cheeks were getting hot again. Just because she was thinking about the park *and* about what happened after their trip to the park.

And, actually, about how much she might like to do it again.

"Did you stop anywhere after you left the park?"

"No. I brought the girls here right after you got the call about Daisy. Jet was painting the east side of the house." That sounded good. It sounded knowledgeable. It did not sound like the words of a woman who was so busy thinking about the dark rim around Simon's forest-green eyes that she couldn't quite focus on the conversation.

"How did he seem when you got here?" He looked up from the pad and every thought in her head just kind of flew away. "Apricot?" he prodded, and she glanced away, focusing her attention on a splash of sunlight on the wall.

"He seemed fine."

"Would you like to elaborate on that?"

"Well . . ." She forced herself to think back to the moment she'd arrived home. She'd been distracted, getting the girls out of the SUV and worrying about what had caused Simon to leave them with her. Jet had come around the side of the house, and . . . "He was red-faced and really hot. Sweating a lot, and I was worried he was going to have a heatstroke. I made him come inside and drink a glass of water. It looked like he'd been outside for hours without a break." There! *That* was important information.

"Did he drive here yesterday?"

"His car was in the shop, so he walked. Sammy brought the paint and supplies in his truck." Another important piece of information. She was beginning to feel more than a little accomplished!

"So, Jet would have had to hitch a ride with a friend or he would have had to walk to town, right?"

"Right."

Simon nodded, still scribbling in his notebook. "That gives me a lot to go on, Apricot. Thanks." He stood, and she realized that the interview was over and that he was walking away.

She figured she'd better follow him into the kitchen, just in case Jet needed her to defend him, but the doorbell rang. Again.

"It's like Grand Central Station around here," she muttered.

She opened the door, got a face full of kitten fur.

"I told you to keep this critter away from my property," Dusty snarled as he stepped inside.

She hadn't invited him, but since he hadn't taken

his shotgun to poor Handsome, she wasn't going to point it out.

"I'm really sorry, Dusty. I don't know how he's getting outside."

"That's what you keep saying, and I keep telling you to figure it out!" He yanked his suit jacket into place and straightened his tie. "Good thing I'm heading to church. If I weren't, I'd have gotten my shotgun and put a bullet right in that rat-cat's—"

"That's okay." She cut him off, setting Handsome down and shooing him away. "I don't really need the details."

"Well, maybe if you have them, you'll do a better job of keeping that thing locked up." He craned his neck, looked like he was trying to see into her living and dining rooms.

"Are you looking for something?" she asked.

His skin flushed bright red. "Just wanted to do the neighborly thing and make sure everything was okay over here."

"Why wouldn't it be?"

"You got two police cars parked in your driveway, girl. Do I have to spell things out for you?"

"There was a crime in town yesterday. The police are questioning everyone." She left it at that. She didn't want him to know that the police were specifically asking about Jet. Of course, knowing Daisy, she'd probably already told the world. Or, at least, her little part of it.

"I heard 'bout that. That librarian got robbed, right? Wonder if the police will be coming to my place. Maybe I should stay home from church." He sounded almost gleeful. More than likely this was the most exciting thing that had happened to him in years.

"No need to skip church, Dusty," Simon called out from the kitchen.

He'd been listening, but he didn't come out.

He might have been busy, or he might have wanted to avoid being asked a hundred questions. Which is what would probably happen if he and Dusty ended up in the same room.

"You sure, Simon?" Dusty brushed past her and made a beeline for the kitchen.

"Dusty! Hold on!" She tried to stop him.

He just kept going, booking it like a New Yorker, head to the wind and moving forward like his life depended on it.

Great. Perfect.

Cade was in the kitchen. Simon was in the kitchen. Poor Jet was in the kitchen. At the rate things were going, rumors of an arrest and conviction would be all over town by sunset.

Apricot raced after him, made it as far as the threshold of the kitchen when the doorbell rang again.

"Dang it all to Grandma Sapphire's plantation and back!" She spun on her heels and ran to the door, the sound of Simon's warm laughter ringing in her ears and causing a slow heat to build in her stomach. God! She wanted to be back in his arms. She wanted to snuggle up close and forget that she had a kitchen filled with people and a handyman who was being accused of a crime. She wanted to forget that she'd been betrayed by a guy she'd spent three years living with, a guy who was supposed to be her best friend and confidant but who'd really been a no-good, cheating son of a mangy mongrel. She wanted to put the whole blasted twenty-four hours behind her and pretend it hadn't happened.

Heck with that! She'd like to put the past six months of stress behind her and pretend they hadn't happened. All the wedding planning that Lionel's mother had forced her into. Picking linens and place settings and food that Apricot wasn't interested in. *She*'d wanted a simple wedding. Outside. With just a few close friends and family. Instead, Lionel had urged her to go with the flow, enjoy the extravagance, get behind the insanity.

She had. Look at the result. It sucked.

Things can only get better from here on in, she told herself, because she didn't want to imagine that they could get worse. Seriously. What would be next? Finding out that Lionel's paramour was already six months' pregnant with his child? The child Apricot had wanted. The one they'd planned to start trying for on the wedding night, because, in Lionel's words— *You're not getting any younger, darling. Those ovaries are going to shrivel up and die a thousand deaths if we don't get them working.*

"Bastard," she growled, wrenching open the front door.

"What's that, dear?" Aunt Rose said, her amber eyes fully lined with kohl, her lips pink with the rose petal–colored lip balm she made. All natural and completely and utterly gorgeous, she held a large fuchsia bag in one hand and her pet guinea pig, Elvis, in the other. Coming up the porch steps behind her, looking like they'd just fought the Thousand Year War, were Lilac and Hubert.

Dear God in heaven!

She'd been wrong.

Things couldn't only get better, because they had just gotten a whole heck of a lot worse!

Simon was escorting Dusty out of the kitchen when the doorbell rang and the commotion began. It sounded like a thousand people had descended on the house. For about three seconds, he had visions of a modern-day lynch mob coming for poor Jet.

And that's exactly how Simon thought of the kid.

Poor Jet.

Daisy's accusations aside, the kid seemed legitimately upset by the accusations lobbed against him. He'd begged to take a lie detector test and had sworn up one side and down the other that he hadn't left the Shaffer place all day. He'd agreed to let Cade search his room at his grandparents' house, begged him to check the broken-down junk car he used for transportation.

As far as Simon could tell, Jet was being honest. He hadn't robbed Daisy. Of course, there was room for error in human judgment, and it was possible the kid was just a good liar. So far, he didn't have a criminal record, hadn't been in any kind of trouble in school. Up until his parents' death, he'd been living in obscurity, doing whatever things teens did nowadays.

"What's all the ruckus? It's too early in the morning for that kind of noise," Dusty groused as they walked to the foyer. The guy was pissed because he wasn't being allowed in on the investigation. Dressed in his Sunday best, he looked ready for church and for a little bit of information dissemination. Too bad there was nothing to disseminate.

"You think she's having some kind of pot party? Probably planned it before we all showed up to stop it," he continued.

Simon didn't respond. He was too busy taking in the small group standing in the foyer with Apricot. Two women. One man. The women wore ankle-length skirts and loose tops. One had her hair in a long, black braid, flowers woven through the strands. She carried a huge bag and what looked like an over-sized guinea pig.

Simon recognized her immediately. Rose spent a couple of weeks every summer in Apple Valley. He'd figured she wouldn't show for another couple of weeks, seeing as how the apple festival where she sold her wares didn't begin until then.

"Rose!" Dusty gasped and tripped all over himself trying to get to her and take the bag from her hand. "I wasn't expecting you until the end of next week."

"Yes." She smiled, and Simon was sure Dusty just about dropped dead with the force of it. "That is when I planned to arrive, but my niece needed me, so I decided to come early."

"You should have let me know. I would have made that curried cauliflower you love so much," Dusty said gently, taking Rose's arm and leading her into the living room.

He didn't give the couple that was left standing in the foyer the time of day.

"Simon, these are my parents," Apricot said, the words gritty and a little tight. If her folks noticed, they didn't let on.

The woman smiled, offering a hand, a ring on every finger, a bunch of bracelets rattling on her wrist. "Lilac Miller."

"Nice to meet you, Ms.—"

"*Doctor* Miller!" Apricot's father spat. "And don't you forget it, because she sure as heck never does."

"Why should I?" Lilac asked, fluffing her curls, her bracelets jangling even louder. "That's Hubert. He's bitter."

"I'm not bitter. You're a bi—"

"Hubert! Lilac!" Apricot snapped. "Enough! Wasn't a continent's worth of fighting enough?"

"Of course not," Lilac responded. She looked to be in her early forties. Either she'd had kids really young or she'd aged well. "Do you know the tale of—"

Apricot cut her off. "Not the time, Lilac."

"There is always time for a story, Apricot," Lilac chided. "Stories teach us important lessons. They are living truths passed from one generation to another." She shifted her gaze to Simon and smiled sweetly. "Don't you agree, Simon?"

"I suppose that depends on what the story is, ma'am."

"*Ma'am?*" Rose called from the living room. "Did I hear a Southern gentleman out there? Stop keeping him to yourself, Lilac. Bring him in here!" she demanded.

"We'll come when we're ready. Won't we, Simon?" Lilac purred.

He wasn't quite sure what to make of that, but he had a feeling that Hubert's bright red face and flashing eyes might have been part of her motivation.

"Stop it! Your season for making Hubert jealous ended about ten years ago." Apricot tugged her away, gave her a gentle push toward the living room. "Besides, Simon has work to do. He can't entertain the two of you. Can you?" She met his eyes, and he could swear there was a hint of panic in her gaze.

"Do you need me to?" he asked. He and Cade had a few more questions to ask Jet, but once they finished, Simon would be off the clock.

Hubert sighed. "Wouldn't matter one bit if she did." Simon would place him at about sixty, his white hair pulled back into a low ponytail, his beard thick and long. Guy could have been Santa Claus if he hadn't been skinny as a rail. "Those sisters cause more trouble than a couple of possums in an attic. I just spent five days with them, and I can tell you right now, those were the worst five days of my life. Turned my hair completely white!"

"Your hair has been white for as long as I can remember," Apricot said with a sigh.

"Doesn't mean their shenanigans didn't make it whiter. I swear I've aged a thousand years these past few days."

"You don't look a day over twenty, Hubert."

Apricot's dry response made her father smile. "You still got it, kid. But all the flattery in the world isn't going to make me feel better."

"How about I get you some coffee. Will that help?"

"Whiskey would be better."

"I don't have any whiskey in the house. Even if I did, it's too early in the morning."

"It's never too early for a shot of moonshine, little lady! I'll take the coffee, though. Better bring some for your mother and aunt. We drove straight through, and we're all feeling it." He shuffled into the living room, and Apricot ran a hand down her face. Shook her head as if she couldn't quite believe what was happening.

"I take it you're not real happy about them showing up?" he asked.

"What clued you in?"

"The horror in your eyes was a dead giveaway."

She cracked a smile at that. "Them showing up on my doorstep is just about the last thing I wanted."

"Just about? There's something you'd want less?"

"Yeah," she admitted as she walked down the hall. "My ex showing up with his new wife. *That* would be even worse."

She walked into the kitchen, and he followed.

Cade didn't look happy.

Jet didn't look happy either.

As far as Simon could tell, Jet had been honest about where he'd been and what he'd done the previous day. His gut said the kid was innocent. Add to that the fact that everyone who met Jet liked him, and it was Daisy's story Simon was questioning.

He didn't feel all that great about that.

Daisy might drive him crazy, but she was family. He didn't want to doubt her. Facts were facts, though, and the fact was, Daisy's story wasn't adding up. At first, she'd said she'd barely caught a glimpse of the guy who'd grabbed her purse. It wasn't until hours later that she'd remembered exactly who she'd seen— not just some nameless stranger, a young guy she'd often said she was suspicious of.

She'd called Cade immediately, not even bothering to get Simon out of bed to tell him about her epiphany.

If Simon had to guess, he'd say that Daisy had confused a dream with reality. That maybe she'd been trying hard to remember something she didn't, and she'd managed to convince herself that she had.

"Who was ringing the doorbell? More company?" Cade asked, an edge of impatience in his voice. "Because we don't need anyone else in here trying to help with the interview."

"Trying to collect information to share with everyone in town, you mean?" Jet snarled, his eyes blazing with anger.

"Dusty agreed not to tell people that we were out here questioning you," Simon reminded him.

"Do you think he'll keep the promise?" Apricot asked as she levered up on her toes and grabbed mugs from the cupboard. Her tank top rode up, revealing creamy skin and sinewy muscle. Simon wanted to press his lips to that little spot, nibble his way around to her stomach.

He looked away, saw that Cade was watching him.

He shrugged. There wasn't any need for more than that. He was doing his job and doing it well. His private life was his, and he didn't let anyone dictate how he lived it.

"I'm pretty confident Dusty will keep his word," Simon responded, turning his attention back to Apricot. Her shorter hair gave him a perfect view of her profile—the sweet curve of her jaw, the sharp angle of her cheekbones. She was a younger, more exotic version of her mother.

"I hope you're right." She grabbed cream from the fridge and poured it into two of the cups, added a heaping teaspoon of sugar into another. "Jet doesn't need or want any kind of trouble."

"I can speak for myself, Apricot," Jet interrupted.

"Of course you can, but sometimes we all need someone else to speak for us."

"He's got more than one person to speak for him." Cade glanced at his watch. "People in town like you, Jet. So don't get too defensive about this thing, okay?"

"Don't get defensive? Some old spinster accuses me of robbing her, and I'm going to be defensive!" Jet's eyes flashed and Simon could almost hear his teeth grinding. No doubt, the kid had plenty of other things to say about Daisy, and was holding back because Simon was there.

Smart kid.

Which was why Simon was convinced that he was innocent. No one in his right mind would rob an acquaintance in broad daylight in the middle of a town where everyone knew everyone. Seeing as how Jet appeared to be in his right mind, it seemed implausible that he'd actually been the one to rob Daisy.

That put Simon in a tough position.

Daisy was family, but she was high-strung and dramatic—even more so since Dennis had flown the coop. Just like her sister, she had a tendency to see what she wanted to see. Usually what Daisy wanted to see amounted to monsters in the closets and boogeymen under the bed.

"Give us a little time, Jet. We'll sort it out." Cade stretched, barely hid a yawn.

"A little time is just enough time to get me hung in this town," Jet muttered, pushing away from the table and standing. "If you don't have any more questions for me, I promised my grandmother I'd drive her to church service. My granddad isn't feeling too hot. Thanks to dingbat Daisy, he's going to be feeling even worse when Grandma gets home from church."

"I'm sure people won't be gossiping about this at church," Apricot said as she set the coffee mugs on a wooden tray.

Simon couldn't help himself. He laughed.

She frowned. "What's so funny?"

"When was the last time you were in church, Apricot?"

"Easter."

"Ah," he responded. "That explains it."

"Explains what?"

"Why you don't understand that church is the best place for the blue-haired ladies of any community to gossip."

"Wrong," Cade said. "That would be the diner. Church is second, only because gossiping there requires a good bit of whispering and none of those ladies hear that well."

Apricot laughed, and even Jet cracked a smile.

"Come on." Cade slapped the kid on the shoulder. "I'll give you a ride home so you can get your grandma to church."

"I'm not sure my grandparents are going to be happy to see me coming home in your squad car," he muttered, but walked out of the kitchen with Cade.

"I should probably head out too. Want to walk me out after we bring these to your folks?" Simon took the tray from Apricot's hands and was more than pleased to see a hint of pink spreading across her cheeks. "You're cute when you blush," he said, and the pink deepened to red.

"Cut it out, Simon."

"Why?"

"Because my family is here, and I don't have time to think about anything else."

"Like us, you mean?"

She stomped from the room, and he followed, feeling better than he had since he'd gotten the midnight phone call from Cade. Honest to God, Simon didn't know what went through Daisy's head sometimes. She'd been at his house, sleeping in his guest room. She could have easily gotten him out of bed and shared her sudden epiphany about who her attacker was. Instead, she'd called Cade *at home*, talked his ear off for about fifteen minutes before Cade had finally ended the conversation and called Simon. He'd dealt with Daisy, convincing her to go back to bed, assuring her that they'd pursue the new lead, cautioning her to keep her suspicions to herself, all the while knowing she wouldn't.

More than likely, she was already at church with the girls, the tiny little Band-Aid she'd covered her scratches with on prominent display.

He stepped into the living room, the tension so thick he could have cut it with a knife. Hubert stood at the front windows, looking like he was plotting a way to escape. Rose was smiling into poor Dusty's eyes, and the guy looked like he was about to float off the sofa and straight through the ceiling. Lilac was studying a painting that hung above the fireplace. A landscape scene, it depicted the Shaffer place several decades ago. It looked like it had been painted by an amateur, the proportion of the house, trees, and grass all slightly off.

"This is lovely," Lilac crooned. "Just lovely. Don't you think so?" She looked at Simon instead of Apricot. Probably because Apricot was making a show of handing out the coffee mugs.

"I think it looks like someone who loved it painted it," he responded.

Lilac raised a brow and nodded. "You're honest. I like that."

"I'm not sure he cares, Lilac." Apricot sighed, handing her mother some coffee.

"I care," he responded and was rewarded with a warm smile from Lilac and a scowl from Apricot.

"Don't encourage her, Simon." Apricot left the tray. "I think I'll bring this back to the kitchen and . . . wipe it down."

"Or you could stay here and talk to the people who traveled thousands of miles to see you." Hubert sipped coffee and stared at his daughter over the rim of the mug.

"Twenty-five hundred, but who's counting." Rose stood and yawned. "Speaking of the trip, I know it's early hours, but I'm exhausted. I think I'll tuck myself in for a nap. Thanks for taking care of things for me, Dusty."

Dusty nodded mutely, following her with his eyes as she made her way upstairs.

"What a woman," he whispered, then walked out the door without a second look at anyone else.

"Maybe you two should rest too," Apricot suggested. "It was a long trip, and I'm sure you're exhausted."

"I slept during the last shift, so I'm feeling pretty good. Your mother, on the other hand, is looking a little worse for wear. She should probably nap."

"Give me a break, Hubert!" Lilac put her hands on her hips and glared. "I look fantastic. Just like I always do, and I'm not taking a nap when my brokenhearted daughter needs me." She tossed an arm around Apricot's waist and tugged her into her side.

"I'm not brokenhearted," Apricot protested.

"Of course you are! You were cheated on, dumped, left for another woman. It's like the story of—"

Apricot moaned. "Lilac, please. I have a splitting headache. I don't want to hear one of your stories."

"It's not just a story. It's a myth, a piece of native lore. It has value far outside of simple literature. Let's go in the kitchen and get some ginger for your pain. Then we'll talk, and you can tell me everything that you're thinking and feeling."

Apricot paled. "I—"

"She's going to church with me," Simon broke in. "So maybe you could take that nap she suggested, and you can all talk when she comes back."

"Going to church dressed like that?" Hubert scratched his head. "It's been a while since I've been in a house of worship, but I'm thinking that's not the right outfit to wear, sweet cheeks."

Apricot blushed three shades of red. Simon figured that was because of her pet name rather than her father's comment about her outfit.

"I'm not going to church," she said.

"Of course you're not!" Lilac nodded sagely, her dark curls bouncing. There were a few silver streaks woven into her hair and just a hint of crow's-feet at the corners of her eyes. She looked artsy, hippy-ish. She didn't look all that maternal. "You're going to stay right here. I'm going to make some of my chicken-foot gumbo—"

"On second thought, I think I'll put on something a little more church friendly. Be back in two shakes of a stick, Simon. Don't leave without me." She ran upstairs.

Lilac dropped onto the sofa, swung her legs onto the cushions and reclined there, a contented smile on her face. "The girl is so predictable."

"The girl hates your chicken-foot gumbo. Everyone does. It tastes like dog puke," Hubert replied.

"Only you would know the way dog puke tastes," Lilac shot back, her hands folded in her lap, her legs crossed at the ankle.

"I don't *know.* I'm *assuming* based on the taste of your gumbo. I can tell you right now, if you were going to make that crap for me, I'd be running off to church too."

"You *need* to go to church. You're a reprobate, leaving your wife and coming all the way across the country like you have. It's just plain sinful."

"The wife ran off with Stan, and you darn well know it!"

The two were getting ready for a rip-roaring fight, and Simon was just curious enough to stay and listen to it. They seemed . . . charged by the exchange. As if their batteries had run down and a good fight with each other was the only way to bring them up to full power again.

He leaned his shoulder against the wall, listening as the two lobbed good-natured insults at one another. Upstairs, someone was singing, the high-pitched soprano just slightly off-key. Rose? Probably. He didn't imagine Apricot's voice would be quite so high.

Handsome bumped his calf.

"What?" he asked, lifting the kitten and stroking its coarse fur. "You hungry?"

"Look, Hubert." Lilac sighed, smiling softly in Simon's direction. "He likes animals!"

"And?" Hubert griped.

"He is polite." She held up one finger. "He is honest." Up went another finger. "And he likes animals." A third finger extended, and she jabbed her entire hand in Hubert's direction.

"And?" Hubert said again.

"*And*, he'll be perfect for our Apricot."

Simon probably should have corrected whatever assumption she was making, but Apricot picked that moment to rush down the stairs, a pretty sundress floating around her legs. Her lips were slick with gloss, her hair brushed to a high shine. When she smiled, he forgot all about her parents, Daisy, church. He forgot that there'd been a robbery, an accusation, an investigation that had kept him up most of the night.

He forgot everything except Apricot.

She grabbed his hand and dragged him out of the house, and all he could think was—he might not be perfect for her, but she was absolutely perfect for him.

Chapter Twelve

Simon dragged Apricot straight to the front of the church. Right in the middle of a hymn. Which was just . . . *awesome.* That was *exactly* what she'd wanted on a morning when she was supposed to be tucked into bed, sleeping the day away—to be marched up an aisle in front of a hundred or more total strangers. Good times!

Now she was sitting smack-dab between the twins, Daisy shooting daggers at her over Rori's head. Surprising, since Jet was just across the aisle, a tiny gray-haired woman at his side. If Daisy really thought he was the one who'd robbed her, shouldn't *he* be the one getting the death glare?

Apparently not, because as the congregation stood for a final hymn, Daisy tugged Rori to her side, her scowl deepening.

I'm not contagious, Apricot wanted to whisper, but everyone was singing a cheery song about being part of God's family, and she didn't think a catfight would fit well in the venue.

The song ended, and she thought they were done.

She *hoped* they were done, because the way Daisy was looking, she might just march to the front of the church and accuse Apricot of robbing her.

Someone shuffled past the pew, and Daisy's gaze shifted.

Thank God!

Apricot had probably been three seconds from seeing lasers shooting from the woman's eyes!

A young boy walked to the piano as the last strains of the song drifted away. Small and blond, his shoulders slightly stooped, he moved like an old man—as if every step was a chore and a challenge. Apricot thought he might be nine or ten, but he raised his head as he approached the piano, and his face looked more mature than that, his cheekbones sharp, his jawline well-defined. He had ice-blue eyes that were just a little vague, and a sweet, befuddled expression that made Apricot's heart ache.

Evie tugged at Apricot's hand.

"That's Alex," she whispered loudly.

"Shhhh!" Daisy hissed, holding a finger to her lips, her eyes flashing dark fire. No doubt, she thought her niece was being tainted by Apricot.

"He plays piano," Evie continued as if her aunt hadn't just shushed her so loudly she'd created her own breeze with the force of her breath.

Simon bent and whispered something into Evie's ear.

Whatever he said worked.

Evie crossed her arms over her chest and scowled, but she kept her mouth shut. Somehow everyone in the congregation seemed to understand that the boy's appearance at the front of the church meant they should sit.

They sat as one accord, the swish of clothes and shoes and butts hitting wood surprisingly loud and just a little jarring. Had Apricot known the correct signal, she'd have probably sat with everyone else. Instead, she was a heartbeat behind the throng, dropping down hastily and nearly squishing Evie in the process.

Only it wasn't Evie.

Somehow, Simon had pulled a sleight of hand. Sleight of lap?

Whatever the case, he was sitting beside her, and the truculent eight-year-old he'd shushed was sitting on his other side.

"Sorry," she murmured as she tried to scoot away. There wasn't really anywhere to go. Rori was pressed up tight against her other side, and Daisy was back to shooting daggers.

"Shhhh," he murmured in her ear. "Just listen. You're going to love this."

She didn't know what she was going to love, but she decided it might just be his hand that had suddenly found its way to hers, or maybe it was the way their fingers were woven together.

She was so distracted by his hand, his warm thigh pressed against her, his soft smile, that she didn't realize Alex had taken a seat on the piano bench until he started playing.

Music filled the church. Not the quick, lively sound of the last song. Not the quiet strains of a recessional. This was a light and easy tune. Like spring rain falling on dry ground or snowflakes dancing around a streetlight. It seemed to seep right into Apricot's soul and she couldn't help smiling in response to it.

"Pretty, isn't it?" Simon whispered in her ear.

She shivered, because it *was* pretty and *he* was nearly perfect. She could have sat there with him, listening to the music, sunlight streaming through beautiful stained glass windows, all day and been perfectly content to do it.

She let the music and the warmth of Simon's hand carry her away from the anger and anxiety that had been niggling at her gut since she'd left LA.

Eventually, the last strains of the music faded away and the sanctuary fell silent. Not a sound. Not a shift of impatient congregants wondering when they were going to be dismissed. No gathering of papers or Bibles or purses. Just . . . silence.

Alex stood slowly. He shuffled back down the aisle, took a seat somewhere behind Apricot. She would have glanced back to see where, but as she turned her head, she met Daisy's gaze.

She smiled.

Daisy scowled.

Whatever spell the congregation had been under lifted, and the kind-looking pastor dismissed everyone.

Daisy jumped up and marched out, her nose so high in the air, Apricot thought she might trip on her way through the vestibule and fall on her face.

"Obviously," Apricot said to no one in particular, "I am not her favorite person."

"Who?" Simon tugged her to her feet and took the girls' hands. "Daisy? No one is her favorite person. Except for the girls. She loves them to pieces."

"And you," Apricot pointed out, because it was dang obvious that Daisy had a massive crush on her brother-in-law.

"Me?" He laughed, leading the way through the throng of people who were gathered in the aisle.

"Yes, *you.*"

Jet was just up ahead, moving as quickly as he could. His grandmother wasn't in as much of a hurry. She stopped to talk to a friend, and he stood with his head down, his hands shoved deep into his pockets, not making eye contact with anyone. Not even Apricot. She moved toward him, but Simon grabbed her hand and pulled her back.

"Leave him alone, Apricot."

"He looks miserable."

"He looks like a young man who can take care of himself. You go running to the rescue, and you're going to embarrass him."

"But—"

"Trust me on this," he said as they stepped outside. "He doesn't need you to bail him out."

They stepped outside, the girls charging ahead and joining a group of kids who were chasing each other around the churchyard.

"I wasn't going to bail him out. I was just going to chat with him."

"So that people know he's got allies?"

"Something like that," she admitted.

"Not necessary. People around here like Jet. They're not going to convict him without a fair trial. They'll give things a few days. See what comes of the investigation."

"Most of them."

"The ones who won't, don't matter." Simon stopped at the edge of the yard, his gaze focused on the girls. "You've got me worried, Apricot. I'm not going to lie."

"About?" She moved closer, because the sun was

bright and the kids were laughing and it just felt . . . good to be next to him.

"Daisy."

"What's to worry about?"

"It never occurred to me that she might . . ." He shook his head.

"Be madly in love with you?" she suggested.

He frowned. "She's not in love with me. She's just—"

"Infatuated? Enamored? Smitten? Besotted?"

He laughed. "Enough. I get it. You have a great vocabulary."

"And keen insight into people." Most people anyway. She'd kind of missed the boat with Lionel. Or maybe she hadn't. Maybe she just hadn't wanted to admit the truth to herself.

"Well, your insight is off on this one. Daisy is Daisy. She's a little nuts, but she means well. She's just trying to help out since Megan isn't around to mother the girls. That doesn't mean she's smitten with me."

"I'm sure it doesn't." Apricot agreed because . . . what else could she do? Daisy, Simon, and the girls were family. They had something that worked for them, and it wasn't her business to start mixing things up. On the other hand, Simon was wrong.

Daisy *was* smitten.

Worse, she was desperate to get a ring on her finger.

She probably didn't care all that much who put it there.

Simon was convenient. Add to that his natural kindness, his charm, his good looks, and you had a recipe for an infatuation so deep Daisy was probably convinced it was the love of a lifetime. She'd probably written him into her diary as her soul mate on the same page where she'd written her first name followed by his last name dozens of times. With little hearts and flowers and swirls all around them.

"Seriously, Apricot. She's not," Simon murmured, and she didn't think he believed a word he was saying.

"Okay," she responded.

That one word said a million things that Simon didn't want to hear.

She wasn't convinced.

She really believed that Daisy had her eyes on Simon.

She was amused by the whole thing.

Simon was not.

Daisy was nice in a high-strung, overpowering sort of way. He loved her like a sister, and he didn't want to hurt her. But there was no way in hell he was interested in her, and he was absolutely sure he'd never given her the idea that he was.

If she hadn't been loping across the churchyard, heading straight for him, he'd have told Apricot that.

"Speak of the devil," Apricot murmured, an impish grin making her look young and fresh and unbelievably kissable. If they hadn't been standing in the churchyard, dozens of people all around, he might have tugged her into his arms, nibbled his way up her throat, found his way to those beautiful lips.

"Simon!" Daisy shrieked, her voice sharp.

Everyone who'd been happily talking in the churchyard went silent.

Apricot's grin broadened, her eyes twinkling with amusement.

He was not amused.

"What is it, Daisy?" He kept his tone neutral. Barely. Lately Daisy had been getting under his skin, taking up a little too much of his energy.

"Did you see who was here?" She grabbed his arm, pulling him around so that he was looking directly at the church door. The pastor and his wife were there, chatting with Jet and his grandmother. Jet shifted uncomfortably, his dress shirt a little short in the sleeves, his dark slacks about two sizes too big.

"There were a lot of people at service today." He was purposely obtuse. Sometimes, with Daisy, it was best to feign ignorance.

"You know who I'm talking about," she whispered. "Jet. Aren't you going to say something to him?"

"He's already been questioned."

"Why hasn't he been arrested?" she demanded, her voice getting a little louder and a little higher with each word.

"Because Cade and I didn't find any evidence to support doing it."

"Evidence? I told you he's the one who did it. Isn't that enough?" She blinked rapidly. A sure sign she was about to cry.

"I'm afraid it's not, Daisy. Evidence is what convicts someone. Until we have it—"

"You think I'm lying, don't you?" she said loudly.

"Why would I?" he volleyed back.

The churchyard had gone quiet, people grouped around trying really hard to pretend they weren't listening to the conversation. Jet had his grandmother's arm and was trying to hurry her down the stairs.

Problem was, there wasn't a whole lot of hurrying a woman Dorothy's age could do.

Simon hoped to God Daisy wouldn't decide to go over and confront the two.

"If you didn't, you'd have already arrested him." She swallowed hard, her eyes skittering away. "He'd be in jail, and I'd be safe."

"You are safe."

"I don't feel safe." Her lower lip trembled, and he felt just sorry enough for her to pat her shoulder.

"You are. Cade and I aren't going to let anything happen to you. Besides, you weren't injured—"

"Not injured!" she cried. "What do you call this?!" She lifted the hem of her long jean skirt to reveal three small brightly colored Band-Aids. One on her knee. Two on her shin. If he remembered correctly, she had a couple of tiny little scratches there.

Apricot coughed, and he met her eyes.

She was fighting the urge to laugh.

Fighting it desperately, her lips twitching, her chest heaving.

"Don't," he cautioned, because if she laughed, Daisy would cry, and he needed that like he needed a hole drilled through his head.

"Don't what?" Daisy demanded. "Show my legs on church property? This isn't the Dark Ages, Simon. Women wear all kinds of revealing clothes. Even to church. I try to be modest, but not everyone feels it's necessary." Her gaze settled on Apricot, dropping to the neckline of her sundress.

It wasn't at all revealing.

But now that Daisy had called his attention to it, the creamy swell of skin peeking out from light blue fabric was one of the sexiest things Simon had ever seen.

"You don't think my dress is appropriate?" Apricot asked, smoothing her skirt.

"I never said that."

"You seemed to be implying it, but I might just be misreading you. You've been through a lot, and your aura may be a little off because of it."

"Things have been tough," Daisy conceded. "I guess you've been too busy doing other things to see how much this has affected me, Simon." She turned her gaze back on him. "I'm just exhausted. I didn't even sleep last night, I was so scared."

Not true. She'd been snoring loud enough to wake the dead. Simon had closed her door to try to mute the sound.

He kept his gentlemanly manners his parents had instilled in him and didn't mention it.

"You need a nap," he suggested. "Why don't you go on home and rest?"

"I'm making meat loaf for the girls this afternoon. I promised I would while we were on the way to church this morning." She was still eyeing Apricot, who was eyeing her right back. The difference was, Apricot looked pleasant, a smile curving her lips. Daisy's lips were pressed tight, her eyes hot with irritation.

"There's no need to make me and the girls a meal, Daisy. We can manage just fine on sandwiches."

"I always cook on Sunday."

True. And he always tried to get her to *not* cook. "You haven't always been recovering from a trauma."

"I need to keep my mind off things. Cooking will help."

"There are probably better ways to get your mind off things. You could go out with a couple of your friends. Maybe see a movie or go to the diner," he suggested.

"You don't want me around!" she accused.

His blood pressure was rising, and he was about out of patience, but he did everything in his power to keep it from showing when he answered. "Me saying you need to relax and get your mind off things, doesn't mean—"

"Can it!" she snapped. "You just want to spend more time with her!" She jabbed a finger toward Apricot. "And that's just fine. You just go ahead and do what you need to do. I'll be here when she's moved on to the next man on the list!"

She stomped away.

Apricot let out a soft, low whistle. "Sorry about that, Simon. I didn't mean to cause trouble in your family."

"You didn't. Her ex-boyfriend did. Ever since he ran off with someone else, she's been a little nuts." Although, truth be told, Daisy had been a little nuts before Dennis left. She'd just had someone else to focus the crazy on.

"She's heading for thirty, isn't she? She's probably hearing her biological clock ticking away."

"You don't need to make excuses for her. I'm not going to boot her out of the family because she's a little more high-strung than usual."

"A little, huh?"

"A lot, but I'm hoping she'll get over it and things will calm down a little."

"How long have you been hoping that?"

"Six months."

She laughed, her cheeks pink, her hair shining in the sunlight.

"You're beautiful, you know that?" The words slipped out, and Apricot's laughter died away.

"I'm not," she said, and he knew it wasn't false modesty. Knew she wasn't fishing for compliments or looking to be reassured.

And, God! That made her even more gorgeous.

"There is nothing more beautiful than a woman's laughter," he responded lightly. "And nothing more attractive than someone who is comfortable in her own skin."

Her eyes widened. "Wow!"

"What?"

"Just . . . wow. Your breed of men supposedly died out decades ago. But there you are. In the flesh. Alive and well."

That made *him* smile. "I didn't realize there were breeds of men."

"Of course there are. Playboy, workaholic, little boy, momma's boy—"

"Good old boy?" he offered.

"That too, but I've never dated one."

"You've dated all the others?"

"Lionel was all the others. But I've also dated the pessimist, the narcissist, the randy dog."

He laughed. "You're kidding."

"Only a little."

"So, what kind of breed am I?"

"You?" She studied him for a moment. "That's easy. You're—"

A scream rent the air, the shrill sound making the hair on Simon's arms stand on end. Another scream and another, and Daisy came tearing across the parking lot, her jean skirt tangling with her legs as she sprinted back toward the church. She fell, righted herself, and just kept coming.

He ran toward her, a throng of people rushing with him.

Everyone was talking at once, the murmur of the crowd making it impossible for Simon to hear what Daisy was saying. And she *was* saying something. Her mouth was moving, her eyes wild.

"What is it?" He took her arm, scanned the parking lot, expecting to see someone fleeing the area.

"My car. Someone vandalized my car!" she cried, tears pouring down her face.

"Did you see who it was?"

"Of course, I didn't! I was in church!" she wailed.

"There, there, dear." Ida Cunningham appeared at her side and offered her the kind of motherly embrace that Simon couldn't have managed.

Daisy buried her face in poor Ida's shoulder and cried hysterically.

"Could someone get her some water?" Ida asked, and a group of women rushed back into the church. "Come on, let's sit you down on the steps while Simon checks on your car."

Ida led her to the church stairs, and Daisy plopped down like her legs couldn't hold her. The congregation moved in, and Simon could barely see her sitting there.

The twins had somehow made their way into Apricot's arms.

"I've got them," she mouthed.

And he knew she did.

As long as it took him to check out Daisy's car, she'd be there with the girls, distracting them from the hysterical sobs that were being wrenched from their aunt's throat.

There was something really nice about that.

He didn't mind acknowledging it.

It took him a couple of minutes to find Daisy's car. She'd parked at the far end of the lot, to the side of the church. A few other cars were there.

He walked around the vehicle, realized the front tires had been slashed, snapped a couple of photos with his camera phone, and texted Cade for backup. Simon wasn't on duty, but he could at least secure the scene while he waited.

There was no sign of any other vandalism. No eggs. No scrawled words. Just the tires.

"Simon!" Jethro Fisher hurried toward him. Pastor of Apple Valley Community Church, he had a reputation for being kind and generous. As far as Simon knew, no one in town had a bad word to say about him or his wife, Natalie.

"Sorry, Pastor. This is a crime scene. You're going to have to stay back."

Jethro stopped a dozen feet away. "Looks like those tires are good and flat. Anything I can do to help?"

"Just keep everyone out of the parking lot until Cade gets here. He might want to interview people, so if you wouldn't mind getting the names of people who are here, that would help."

"No problem." Jethro didn't leave. Just stood watching as Simon peered under the car.

"If you want to do that now, that would be great," Simon suggested, and Jethro smiled.

"Actually, it's already being done. My wife loves a good whodunit story. She thought it would be a good idea."

"Natalie is a smart lady," Simon responded absently.

Nothing under the car. Nothing under the cars to either side. Too bad.

"Yes. She is," Jethro responded, and there was something in his voice that made Simon look away from the tamped-down grass near the curb.

"Everything okay, Pastor?" Not that it was his business, but Natalie and Jethro had always been good to the girls. They'd even babysat on a few nights when Daisy hadn't been available. If they were in trouble, he'd do what he could to help.

"Sure. Of course," Jethro responded a little too quickly. "I'd better go help my better half. If you need anything, just holler."

He hurried away, his lanky frame nearly skeletal beneath his worn suit. Had he lost weight? Was he having health issues? Marital problems?

The last seemed improbable. Everyone in town knew how deeply he loved his wife.

Simon's cell phone buzzed, and he glanced at an incoming text, expecting it to be from Cade. Instead it was an unknown number, the words making him smile. Daddy, can Apracot take us to the park. Daisy is screeming so loud our ears hurt and Rori is crying. This is Apracots phon.

He typed a yes and sent the text, tucked his phone

back in his pocket and headed into the cemetery. He was looking for footprints pressed into the grass or some other sign that someone had run through the area. He wove his way through old headstones and around new ones, the sun warm and bright, the day alive with the subtle noises of small-town life.

Far below, Riley Pond shimmered in the afternoon light.

It was a beautiful town with beautiful people in it, but someone had stolen Daisy's wallet and someone had slashed her tires. Since Jet had been sitting in plain sight of the entire congregation of Apple Valley Community Church, Simon thought it was safe to say he wasn't the perpetrator.

He turned back toward the church, saw Cade's patrol car pulling into the parking lot.

He was a few steps from the lot when he spotted something glinting in the sunlight.

A knife?

He took a couple steps closer.

Yep. A knife.

It looked like something that could have been used to slash a couple of tires.

He left it where it was and motioned for Cade to come over.

Chapter Thirteen

Cold lemonade on a warm day. In Apricot's estimation, there wasn't a whole lot that could top that.

She took another sip of the icy drink, swiped moisture from her lips and waved at Evie, who stood at the top of the slide.

"Watch me!" she screamed loudly, then whooshed down the slide with wild abandon.

Rori followed a little more cautiously, her skirt wrapped snuggly around her knees, every hair on her head still neatly in place.

Evie looked like a ragamuffin, her hair flying in a thousand different directions.

Daisy would not be pleased.

Hopefully, she'd gone home to recuperate and wouldn't ever see the giant rip in Evie's tights or the chocolate stain on the front of her dress.

Getting the girls chocolate bars from the ice-cream truck might not have been the best idea. Especially since they hadn't had lunch yet.

Her cell phone rang, and she answered, still

tracking the girls as they moved from the slide to the swings.

"Hello?"

"Hey, you guys still at the park?" Simon's warm, gruff voice washed over her, and her insides turned as melty and soft as warm butter.

"Yes. How are things going?"

"We're done. I'll swing to the front gate of the park and pick you up. How about lunch at the diner?"

"After my last visit, I think I've been banned."

"Right. I'd forgotten about that." He paused. "I can cook something for you."

"Really?"

"I'm a fair hand in the kitchen, but today we're going to do something simple."

"In other words, bread and peanut butter?" She laughed.

"More like my ham and cheese on rye."

"Sounds better than chicken-foot gumbo."

"Does that mean yes?"

No! Of course it didn't, because she was absolutely not in the market for any kind of relationship. And going off to some guy's house for lunch? That could be misconstrued as interest.

"Apricot? You still there? You want to come to lunch? If not, I'll just take you home." Simon broke into her thoughts, and she opened her mouth to say exactly what she should.

"Sure," she said instead. "Why not?"

He chuckled. "I'm glad you're so enthusiastic. I'll be there in five." He disconnected, and Apricot stayed right where she was for sixty seconds, just thinking back over the conversation and wondering how she'd gone from *no way* to *sure.*

She called the girls and followed them as they skipped to the park entrance. The afternoon sun had just crested its zenith and was drifting lazily toward the western horizon. The twins were chatting and giggling and acting exactly the way little girls should. Apricot thought she probably should have been thinking about how sad it was that she wasn't in Aruba with Lionel or that she wasn't going to be trying for the family she'd wanted, anytime soon. She probably should have even been a little bitter that Lionel had moved on so quickly. She'd certainly spent a couple of sleepless nights thinking about it. She'd spent more than a few hours feeling lonely and unhappy, as though life were suddenly passing her by.

Right then, though, with the sun bright and the sky blue and the girls giggling, those things didn't seem all that important.

She grabbed the girls' hands as they walked through the park gates. All around them, Apple Valley drifted along at its own pace. People meandered along Main Street window-shopping as they sipped soda or iced tea. A few teens skateboarded along the sidewalk. A small group of bicyclists passed on their way into the park, and the girls waved, calling hellos to people they knew.

It seemed almost perfect, this little town on the eastern side of Washington. It wasn't, Apricot knew that, but she imagined it was about as perfect as any place could be. The longer she stayed, the more she liked it. The more she liked it, the more she thought about all the things she could do with Rose's property, all the ways she could turn it around and make it into the productive orchard it used to be.

Simon pulled up to the curb, and every thought

about the town and Rose's property flitted out of Apricot's head.

He looked good, the sunlight adding burnished red to his dark hair, his uniform shirt hugging firm biceps and a broad chest. He smiled as he rounded the SUV and opened the back door for the girls, and Apricot didn't think she'd ever known anyone with a smile as warm as his.

She must have been staring.

He raised a brow and cocked his head to the side. "What?"

"Just thinking that you have a nice smile."

His gaze dropped from her face to her lips.

"You have a nice everything," he murmured, opening the passenger-side door.

She slid in, inhaling the clean, fresh scent of soap and shampoo and something indefinably Simon. She wanted to bottle the scent, use it to create candles that every woman on the planet would want to have.

She was kind of drifting in a haze of happy contentment when she realized she and the girls weren't alone.

Daisy was in the backseat, head back, eyes closed. She looked like she'd been through the wringer. Poor thing. She had some issues, but she didn't deserve the trouble she'd found herself in.

"How are you feeling, Daisy?" Apricot asked softly.

Daisy sighed and shook her head. "Terrible. I have one of those migraines I get when I'm really stressed out."

"I'm really sorry to hear that. If there's anything I can do—"

Daisy moaned. "I don't think any of your oils or

teas are going to help with this." She did look pale, her eyes hollow and deeply shadowed.

"Do you have a prescribed medicine?"

"I don't get them often enough to have a prescription." She groaned as Simon got in.

"How you holding up, Daisy?" he asked.

She moaned again. "Not good," she said and closed her eyes.

"I'm going to drop her off before we go back to my place. I hope you don't mind," Simon said quietly.

"Not at all."

"I'd have mentioned it before, but she was fine until right before I left the church."

"I wasn't fine," Daisy interrupted. "I was trying to be. It didn't work."

"You'll feel better once you're home and in bed." Simon turned onto a side street and pulled up in front of a tiny white rancher.

"I hope so. I don't even know if I should be alone. My eyes aren't working properly."

It might have been Apricot's imagination, but she was pretty sure Simon's jaw tightened imperceptibly. "Do you want to stay with me and the girls again tonight?"

"It might be for the best. I know it's a little tight since you only have the one bathroom, but I think it would be safer."

"Safer than what?" Simon muttered, but he pulled back out onto the road.

"You're going to have lunch with us, right, Apricot?" Evie hollered as if she weren't sitting right behind Apricot.

"Evie!" Daisy barked. "I have a headache. Don't be so loud."

"Sorry, Aunt Daisy," Evie whispered. "Are you, Apricot? Because that would be the most fun thing ever."

"Even more fun than eating chocolate bars at the park," Rori added. "I'll make your sandwich. I'll put pickles on it. You like pickles, don't you?"

"Sure."

"Don't talk about pickles. I might puke." Daisy groaned, and she sounded so miserable, Apricot shifted and motioned for both of the girls to be silent.

They quieted down immediately.

"You're really good with them," Simon murmured, patting her thigh absently. Heat shot straight from her leg to her gut, and she shifted away, her cheeks hotter than a Savannah sidewalk in midsummer.

Thanks, she wanted to say, but the word just stuck in her throat, because his hand settled on her thigh, just kind of sat there all warm and nice.

"I don't want to be rude," Daisy grumbled, "but I have got to have quiet. Every single word you say is like a thousand fireworks going off in my head."

This time, there was no doubt about it. Simon's jaw tightened. He rubbed the back of his neck but didn't say another word. The silence felt thick, heavy, and uncomfortable. Apricot wanted to break it, but she didn't want to cause Daisy more pain.

Simon turned onto a narrow street lined with tidy houses and neat yards. Mature trees and landscaping added charm to what might otherwise have been a typical neighborhood. Apricot had been to Simon's house before, and she still found the little yellow cottage charming. The porch swing added a touch of whimsy to the bungalow. A few flower baskets hung from porch hooks and a little garden gnome peeked out from behind a shrub.

Daisy's doing?

Apricot would have laid odds that Simon hadn't set it there.

She didn't ask, though. Even the twins were silent as everyone got out of the SUV and walked to the house.

Daisy, on the other hand, groaned loudly as Simon helped her inside. "This is terrible. The worst I've ever been. Maybe that knock on my head yesterday did more damage than the doctors thought."

"You didn't get a knock on the head, Daisy, remember?" Simon reminded her gently.

"I feel like I did." She touched her forehead and swayed. "I think I'd better lie down."

"I'll help you upstairs." Simon nudged her toward the stairs, but she walked into the living room and dropped onto the couch.

"I think I'll just lie here for a while. Don't let me stop you from having your lunch, Apricot." She covered her eyes with her forearm and lay still.

Sticking around and eating lunch when Daisy was feeling so crappy just seemed . . . wrong. Which didn't mean that Apricot wasn't tempted to do it anyway.

She liked Simon and the girls.

Not to mention the fact that returning home meant facing Rose, Lilac, and Hubert.

She'd been trying hard to forget they were there. In the house. Waiting for her to return.

She hoped to heaven there wasn't any chicken-foot gumbo waiting with them.

"I'd probably better leave," she said, because it was

the right thing to do. "I'll come for lunch another day."

"Really," Daisy said weakly. "Stay. If I smell pickles and need to puke, I'll do it quietly so that I don't ruin your meal."

Simon snorted. "That's really gracious of you, Daisy, but I think Apricot is right. We'll do lunch another day. How about tomorrow?" His gaze settled on her, all foresty green and compelling, and she thought that she'd agree to just about anything he wanted.

"Sure."

"I'll pick you up at your place."

"You're working tomorrow," Daisy reminded him.

"I have an hour for lunch. That'll be plenty of time to eat a sandwich. We can eat in the park, if that sounds good to you."

"It sounds . . ." *Fantastic! Wonderful! Heavenly!* "Great."

"Good. Now, I've got to get you home and get back here to Daisy. Girls! Apricot has to leave!" he called. There was a flurry of footsteps and a frenzy of wild protests as the girls ran down the stairs, fuzzy kittens following along behind them.

"We were going to have sandwiches with pickles," Rori cried. "I was going to even put mustard on your sandwich so it would be fancy."

"That sounds delicious, but your aunt needs to rest, and I don't want to keep her from doing it."

"She wouldn't need to rest if she hadn't gone out last night," Evie griped.

"I didn't go out last night," Daisy muttered from beneath her forearm.

"Yes, you did. I heard you leave."

"That was me," Simon cut in. "I had to go into work."

"It was Daisy. She went out after you came home, so it's her own fault that she's tired, and she should have to get the consequences." Evie scowled. "I think Apricot should just stay here. If Aunt Daisy doesn't like it she can go home."

"Evangeline Rose!" Simon barked. "You're being very rude to your aunt."

"I'm not. I'm being truthful."

"How about you be truthful in your room? Because that's where you're going to spend the next hour."

"But—"

"Go." He pointed to the steps, and she went, shoulders slumped, wild hair hanging listlessly.

"Sorry about that," he said after she disappeared from view.

"I think we're all feeling a little tense. Ready?" He sounded so tired, so worn out, that she did the most natural thing in the world—linked her arm through his and tugged him outside.

"It will get better," she assured him, even though she didn't know if it was true.

"After Daisy leaves," he murmured so quietly that she almost didn't hear.

"You don't want her here?"

"To put it bluntly, no."

"Evie isn't the only one who likes to tell the truth," Apricot said with a laugh.

"As long as Daisy isn't around to hear, I guess the truth won't hurt her." His gaze dropped to her lips and settled there. "I've been thinking, Apricot."

"I'm not sure that's a good thing."

He smiled, but there was no humor in his eyes.

"It's funny how life is. You're just walking along, doing your thing, thinking that what you have is all you need. Then something happens and you realize you're missing something important."

"Simon—"

"Thanks for watching the girls again." Just like that he changed the subject, and she wondered if he'd really been saying what she thought he was—that he hadn't known what was missing until she'd walked into his life.

"It was no problem."

"Maybe not, but I do appreciate it. The girls really enjoy spending time with you, and it gives them a little freedom from . . ." He didn't finish the thought, and she didn't ask. She had a feeling she knew. Freedom from Daisy's rules, from her fancy dresses and need to make the girls into beautiful little dolls. That was fine for Rori. She seemed to enjoy the girly clothes and perfect manners, but Evie was a rebel.

"How long has Daisy been helping with the girls?" she asked as he backed the SUV out of the driveway.

"Close to six years. I moved here after my wife died, and Daisy stepped in to lend a hand."

She wanted to ask him about his wife.

She wanted to know what she was like, if he'd loved her. If he still did.

"Daisy must have been really young," she said instead.

"She was. Just out of college. She'd accepted a job at the library here, and she kept begging Megan to move back to town."

"Is that why you moved here with the girls after Megan died?"

"It was one of the reasons." He shrugged. "We buried Megan in the church cemetery. I was standing there, listening to a pastor who didn't know my wife talk about her life, and I looked at all the people who *had* known her—people she'd grown up with, people who understood her—and I thought that this was the right place for the girls. I guess I was afraid if we stayed in Houston, they'd never know anything about their mother except for what I could tell them."

"That's . . ." Sweet. Beautiful. Lovely. None of the words seemed adequate. "I bet your wife would be happy if she knew they were here."

"Maybe. Maybe not. Megan was a woman full of contradictions. She'd smile for the world and be completely broken inside. She'd say she was content, but inside, she'd be wanting a hundred things she'd never ask for."

"Did you love her?" The question just kind of slipped out, and she couldn't regret it. She wanted to know. She even felt like she might need to know, because Simon wasn't a guy full of contradictions. He was exactly what he seemed to be—a good father, a good cop, a good friend.

"Now, that's a loaded question, isn't it?" He turned onto the dirt road that led to Rose's house, and she thought he might not answer. After several heartbeats of silence, he continued. "I guess the simple answer is that I did love her."

"What's the complicated one?"

He glanced her way, his face craggy and a little worn in the late afternoon light. "You're asking a lot of questions, Apricot Sunshine. Better be careful, or I might think you've got a reason for it."

"I do. I want to know."

"Why?"

Good question.

She didn't have a good answer. "Most people ask questions when they're getting to know someone. It's just what's done."

"Uh-huh," he responded, and she scowled.

"What's that supposed to mean?"

"It means there's more to it than that, and I'm not sure why someone as bold as you are is afraid to say it."

"I'm not afraid to say anything."

"Except that you're curious and interested."

"Of course I'm interested. Megan was your wife and the girls' mother, and I like all three of you. I can't help wondering about her."

"Can't help asking if I loved her? Can't help asking why my answer to that is complicated?" He pulled into Rose's driveway and parked the SUV, then turned to face her. "I'll tell you the truth, Apricot, since that's what you seem to want. I met Megan my first year of college, and fell for her hook, line, and sinker. She was pretty and fun and bright. I'd say that was just about everything a nineteen-year-old kid could want in a woman. I was still in love with her when we got married, when we had the girls, when she died."

"You don't have to talk about this."

"I don't, but I will, because you asked, and because I want you to know." He smiled, and her heart just kind of reached out for his, just kind of flowed toward him like a wave flows toward shore. "I loved Megan, and I know she loved me, but she had problems that she hid really well. I don't think she was ever as honest with me as I was with her. She'd gown up tough. Both her parents died before we met, and she'd been raised by her grandparents. They weren't all that nice, the way I hear it. I don't know if that made a difference in the way she was, but I do know that she had a lot of big ideas about the way love was supposed to be. When we met, she thought I was her knight in shining armor. A few years later, she was in a car accident. I stood by her, helped her heal. We both figured if we could get through that we could get through anything."

"It sounds like you did. Until she . . ."

"Died of an accidental overdose. She was addicted to prescription painkillers."

"I'm sorry, Simon." She touched his arm, and he covered her hand with his.

"Me too, but sorry can't bring her back, and it can't change the fact that I didn't know. After the girls' birth, I'd noticed that she seemed forgetful, tired, that she fell asleep on the couch watching TV. I worked long hours, and she had full responsibility for two babies. I figured that was why. In reality, she was an addict and fed her addiction by going to urgent care, complaining of back spasms and migraines. The coroner thought it probably started after the car accident. When the girls were born, the back pain got worse, and she started relying on the medicine more and more. Eventually, it got the best of her."

"You can't blame yourself for that."

"Wouldn't you?" he asked, meeting her eyes.

"Probably," she admitted, because she knew that she would have.

"Then you understand why I can't forgive myself."

"Simon—"

"Here's the thing, Apricot. You asked if I loved

Megan. I did, but I don't think I really knew her. Not the way I should have. She kept her prescription pill bottle on the windowsill in the kitchen. I had no idea she was having it refilled over and over again. Sometimes I lie in bed at night, and I think about that bottle, and I wonder what would have happened if I hadn't trusted Megan so much, believed in her so deeply. It never, ever occurred to me that she was struggling, because she kept smiling at me and telling me everything was great."

"You are the most honest person I have ever met," she said, touching his cheek, feeling the warmth of his skin and the tension in his jaw. "You thought she was being honest too."

"And she died because of it." He lifted her hand, pressed a kiss to her palm. "I like you, Apricot. A lot. I'm not going to lie about it. I'm not going to pretend it's something that it's not. But I'm not going through what I did with Megan ever again. If I'm with someone, she has to be as honest with me as I am with her."

"I understand," she said, her heart thundering in her chest, her fingers curving around that warm spot on her palm. The spot where his lips had been.

"Good. Now . . ." He glanced at the house. "You'd better head in. I just saw your mother peeking out of the door."

"I don't care about my mother," she replied, her body finding its way closer to his, her lips finding their way to his mouth. She meant to offer a hug, a light kiss of sympathy, compassion, empathy. But he tasted like rich dark chocolate and whiskey. Like strawberries straight from the field. He tasted like everything wonderful she'd ever had, and she didn't want to move away.

"Apricot!" Lilac called.

"Dear God in heaven, that woman!" she muttered, moving away, her heart still pounding frantically.

Simon laughed. "She's got great timing. I'll give her that."

"Planned timing," she responded, climbing out of the SUV and bracing herself for a bowlful of chicken-foot gumbo and whatever advice Lilac was preparing to give her.

She would have marched to the front door herself, but Simon fell into step beside her, his arm brushing hers as they made their way up the porch steps.

She felt like a high school kid coming home from her first date, giddy and a little disconcerted. Not quite sure if she'd see the guy again, but hoping that maybe she would.

He pulled her to a stop in front of the door, his hands cupping her elbows as he looked into her eyes. "I've been thinking again."

"Should I ask what about?" Her heart pounded heavily and her mouth was dry, but she managed to smile, because she always felt like smiling when she looked into Simon's eyes.

"Your name," he responded, his hands sliding to her shoulders and then to her cheeks. "It's perfect for you."

"It is?" she squeaked, and he chuckled.

"More perfect than Anna or Annie."

"Anna is a pretty name," she murmured, backing away a little so she could think. Because when he was near? Yeah. He was all she could think about.

"Sure it is, but Apricot Sunshine suits you." His

thumb ran along the underside of her jaw. "Kind of like biscuits and sausage gravy. You and your name just go together."

That made her laugh.

He cupped her jaw so gently, so sweetly, she wanted to cry from how beautiful it was. When he kissed her she wasn't surprised. Not with the kiss. Not with how tender it was. Not with the longing that swelled up from the deepest part of her heart.

Someone knocked on the living room window.

"What are you doing out there?" Lilac called as if she couldn't see for herself.

Simon glanced at the window, offered a quick wave. "I guess this is my cue to go."

"You don't have to," Apricot responded, and she felt just a little desperate and a whole lot foolish, because Simon did have to leave. He had Daisy to take care of and the girls to worry about.

"The girls are probably driving Daisy batty." He kissed her forehead, the gesture as easy and friendly as a handshake or a hello. To Apricot, it felt like so much more. "I'll see you tomorrow."

"Tomorrow?"

"Lunch, remember?" He threw the words over his shoulder as he jogged down the porch stairs. "I'll pick you up at noon."

He was in the SUV and driving away before Apricot's brain reminded her to breathe. And move. And, actually, think.

"He's a winner!" Lilac called, her face pressed against the window. "Don't you let him slip through your fingers."

"Shut up, Lilac!" Hubert shouted from somewhere inside the house.

Lilac turned away, her response muffled.

No doubt they were heading for another rip-roaring fight.

Apricot could stay and listen to it or she could go for a walk through the orchard. Maybe do a little pruning. Get herself as far away from her parents' bickering as possible.

It was a no-brainer.

She'd spent her childhood listening to Hubert and Lilac ripping each other to shreds verbally. As amusing as they could be, they grew boring when they were together—just one swipe after another.

She could hear them shouting as she walked around the side of the house. It reminded her of long-ago summer nights spent sitting on the tire swing, the sound of her parents' arguments filling the quiet night. She'd never thought much about it. The arguing was all she'd ever known, but she'd promised herself that she wouldn't have the same. That when she grew up, got married, had her own life, things would be nice and quiet and peaceful.

They had been.

Her life with Lionel had been just exactly what she'd wanted. That had been enough. Or maybe it hadn't, because Lionel had found someone else, and she was alone, thinking about a man who made her laugh more than anyone else ever had.

Chapter Fourteen

Two days. Two! Listening to Daisy moan about her head, her scrapes, her invisible wounds.

And, God help him, Simon was about to lose it.

In a big way.

He gritted his teeth, the phone pressed to his ear as Daisy went on and on and on about the MRI she had scheduled for the following day. He should never have brought her to pick out a new cell phone. Shooting himself in the foot would have resulted in a lot less pain.

"Daisy," he finally cut it. "We've been over this. You don't need an MRI."

"Then why did my doctor write me a referral for one?" she demanded in the high-pitched breathy voice she'd been using nonstop since she'd been mugged.

Because you are driving her *as crazy as you're driving me, and she wanted to get you out of her office* didn't seem like the right thing to say.

"An overabundance of caution?" he suggested.

"It isn't an overabundance of anything!" she

protested so loudly Max looked up from his cubicle across from Simon's and frowned.

"Problems?" he mouthed, his smirk only adding to Simon's irritation.

He shrugged, turning so he was facing away from Max. "How about you fill me in on the rest of this when I get home?" he suggested. "Work is hectic today."

Not really, but it was as good an excuse as any to get her off the phone.

"Isn't this your lunch break?" she asked.

"It would be if I weren't on the phone with you," he muttered.

Behind him, Max snickered.

"Shut up, Max!" he barked, and Max laughed full-out.

"If I'm bothering you, I'll just hang up and let you go on with your day!" Daisy said shrilly, the words drilling into his head.

He'd been up half the night working leads with Cade, trying to find the guy who'd mugged Daisy. He'd been up the other half listening to her moan about what she was sure was a concussion.

Sleepless nights, hyper girls, and an overly dramatic sister-in-law? Not a good way to start the week.

"You're not bothering me, but I have an appointment in ten minutes."

"A date, you mean. With Apricot." She sniffed. "You could do a lot better than her, Simon. There are dozens of women in town who would be a better match."

"It's lunch. Not a lifetime commitment." He bit the words out, his jaw so tight from not saying what he wanted to, that he was pretty sure it was going to snap.

"She's nothing like Megan. You know that, right?"

"I'll be home at five. I'll give you a ride back to your place. I think you'll probably sleep better in your own bed, and a little more sleep will probably help with the headache."

"Now you're upset."

"Actually, what I am is tired. I need sleep too. So do the girls. See you at five." He hung up, and he felt a little like a bully who'd just tied a bunch of cans to a kitten's tail and sent her out into a yard full of dogs. Daisy had helped him out more than he could ever repay her for, but he needed space. The girls needed space. And, honest to God, he didn't think Daisy was hurt. Not a concussion. Not a bruise. Not even a scratch.

"So," Max said, "Daisy is one crazy lady."

"Thanks. Without you to keep me informed, I don't know what I'd do," he said drily.

"No need to be pissy. I'm just making a comment."

"Why?"

"Because Cade asked me to run some prints that were on Daisy's purse. No matches to anyone but her. And, she *is* in the system."

"I'm well aware of that." Daisy had been arrested for breaking and entering when she'd tried to steal the recipe for Charlotte Garrison's famous chocolate cupcakes. Fortunately for Daisy, Charlotte had refused to press charges. Otherwise, Daisy would have a criminal record. Not good for someone who worked for the county.

"And you're well aware she's crazy. Has it occurred to you that she made this whole thing up?"

Yes. But he wasn't going to admit it. Not out loud. "Why would she?"

"How should I know? She's your relative."

"By marriage."

"Doesn't matter."

"What exactly do you want to say, Max? Because I've had a heck of a weekend, it's not shaping up to be a very good week, and I don't have the patience to wait while you beat around the bush."

"Someone needs to ask Daisy if she's telling the truth about what happened. I think that should be you."

"I'm thinking that I'd rather listen to you blabber on for another six years," he commented.

Max shrugged. "I don't blabber. I get to the point, and my point is, you need to be the one to ask. She's your relative, she trusts you, you have a relationship that allows you a certain amount of leeway when it comes to your dealings with her."

"In other words, you don't want it getting out that you bullied her?"

"Bullied? She'd end up accusing me of police brutality. I've got a kid, and I don't need any smears on my reputation."

"I think it may be too late for that."

"Bullsh—crap," he growled. "If there's one thing I've never done, it's anything that would tarnish my professional reputation."

"It was a joke, Max. And I wasn't talking about your professional reputation. I was talking more along the lines of personal things." He rubbed his neck, tried to ease a boatload of tension from it.

Max glared at him for about three seconds before his expression eased and he shook his head. "Right. A joke. I'm not feeling all that amused this morning. The kid kept me up all night. Zuzu was puking from midnight to four. Must have gotten sick from one of those little demons she goes to day care with. Guess I'm a little on edge."

That made two of them. "You need to take time off to bring her to the doctor?"

"Charlotte is bringing her in this afternoon. She said it probably wasn't necessary. Zuzu has been bouncing off the walls and begging for cookies since she woke up. I still want her to be checked out. Just to be on the safe side."

"Makes perfect sense." Not really, but that was something a parent learned over time, and Max had only been parenting Zuzu for a few months.

"Right." Max snorted. At least he knew he was being a little nuts. "So, how about we stop talking about my craziness and get back to your crazy sister-in-law? *You* need to ask her. Flat out. If she made this up, she needs to admit it now before things go any further. Otherwise, she is going to be in a lot more trouble than she was when she tried to get her hands on Charlotte's recipe. Speaking of which"—he glanced at the clock—"Charlotte and Zuzu are dropping cupcakes off at the front desk. I want to make sure I'm there when they arrive."

"Want to get first dibs on the cupcakes?"

"I can have cupcakes any day. I want to find out how my kid is doing. If she looks pale and listless, I'm calling an ambulance."

"You know Charlotte would have called you if she had any worries, right?"

"Yeah, but I'm worrying anyway. Plus, I want first dibs on Charlotte. As soon as she walks into a building, every single person around comes to visit with her. When she's with Zuzu, it's even worse. You'd think a guy could spend five minutes with his lady and his kid, but I'm lucky if I get five seconds with them. See you around." He tossed the last few words over his shoulder as he hurried away.

Which left Simon alone in the office area, Max's words ringing through his head.

He'd been trying, *really trying*, to convince himself that Daisy wouldn't have made up the story about being mugged. He hadn't been successful.

He needed to talk to her. That much was for sure, but approaching Daisy about the matter wasn't going to be easy.

Basically, he'd be accusing her of fabricating a lie to get attention. She wasn't going to like it. Whether she'd actually lied or not, their relationship was going to be changed.

Why that bothered him, he didn't know.

He cared about Daisy, the girls cared about her, but she had some really weird ideas, lots of superstitious beliefs. The older the girls got, the more worried he became about her influence over them. A little less time together might not be a bad thing.

He grabbed his jacket and headed toward the back exit. He didn't have the energy to field a hundred questions about the mugging or to explain to anyone who happened to be around why Jet hadn't been arrested. No evidence. No arrest. Simple as that, but the good citizens of Apple Valley didn't see it that way. The town seemed divided, half of them siding with Daisy and the other half siding with Jet. Not good, and if Daisy was responsible for the squabbling . . .

Yeah. Not good.

He stepped outside, watery sunlight painting the blacktop gold. The air held a hint of rain and just a touch of cold. Soon the foliage would start changing color and the days would shorten. Fall would usher in winter and then spring again. Summer would come. Just like it always did, the girls closing in on another full year of life, and Simon just kind of drifting along with them. He'd been content to do that. He liked the way one day flowed into the next, time just kind of unfolding, dawn to dusk and back again. Sure, there were times when he missed the hustle and bustle of Houston life. There were days when he longed for the kind of case that made his pulse pound and his heart race, the kind that made adrenaline pump through him, made his brain function at such a high level, he couldn't sleep, couldn't rest until he solved it.

Those days were few and far between, though.

He didn't miss the crazy schedule, didn't miss not seeing the girls in the evenings and mornings. He didn't miss his marriage, either. Though there were moments when he missed what he'd thought he and Megan were building together.

A house of cards, that's what his dad had called it. His parents had come and stood beside him during the funeral, waiting with him while the casket was lowered into the ground. Simon had been sobbing. He wasn't too macho to admit it. He'd missed the boat, not seen the signs that Megan desperately needed help. He'd lost his wife because of it and the girls had lost their mother. They'd been tiny little things, and he'd been thinking of that. Of how they'd have the birthday presents Megan had been buying for them, but they wouldn't have her.

"*My fault,*" he'd said as the first scoop of dirt fell onto the casket. "*I did this.*"

"You loved her like the morning loves the sun, and you thought you were giving her what she needed, because she let you think that you were. It was a house of cards, son," his father had said. *"One built by Megan and maintained by Megan until she just couldn't maintain it anymore."*

Maybe so, but that didn't make Simon feel better about his failure. Megan had died and he'd gone on, but the weight of responsibility? It never left.

He'd parked in the back lot, and he walked to his SUV, trying to brush off the mood he'd fallen into. September was always hard, but this year, Daisy was making it even more difficult.

He needed to find her a man.

One who didn't mind a little craziness.

One who could overlook Daisy's high-strung nature.

One who was . . .

A saint?

Or desperate. That might work too.

Even if it was only for a few weeks or months, a little distraction would do Daisy good. Problem was, he couldn't think of anyone. Not off the top of his head. Not anyone who was good enough, anyway, because he sure as heck didn't want her with another loser.

He thought about it all the way to Apricot's house, was still thinking about it as he pulled into her driveway.

Apricot came running out, a look of abject desperation on her face. He planned to open the door for her, but she jumped in, her skin dewy from heat, her cheeks pink from sun. She wore a white sundress that revealed smooth muscular shoulders and long slender legs.

"Go! Go, go, go!" she nearly shouted, her short hair flying around her face as she slammed the door and reached for her seat belt.

"That hungry, huh?" he asked mildly, and she blinked, her hands stilling on the belt as she met his eyes.

Slowly, her lips curved, her frantic expression faded.

"You asked for it." She sighed, the smile on her lips and in her eyes.

"For wh—?"

He didn't finish the question, because Lilac swooshed out onto the porch, her long dress touching the ground as she made her way down the steps. Rose followed, dressed in white slacks and a bright pink shirt that fell almost to her knees. Both held baskets. Both looked like trouble waiting to happen.

Lilac knocked on Simon's window, and he unrolled it.

"Afternoon, Doctor," he said, and she smiled the same beguiling smile as her daughter's.

"It is a beautiful one. Not meant for ill-prepared food filled with GMOs and preservatives. I'm sure you'll agree."

"I don't suppose you're wrong," he responded.

"Lilac," Apricot broke in, "I told you. We are not—and I'm going to repeat this to make sure you're hearing me—*not* eating your cow tongue sandwiches."

"The native people of every land know the importance of using each and every part of their natural resources. To turn up your nose at a particular food because you are too highbrow—"

"Ma'am," Simon cut in. He was hungry and tired, and he didn't want to spend fifteen minutes of his hour lunch break listening to Apricot being lectured. "With all due respect, a woman who makes her living out of using what nature has provided in abundance probably isn't too highbrow to eat cow tongue."

"And yet she's turning up her nose at my offering."

"Maybe she just doesn't like the way it tastes. Unless you're raised on the stuff, it can be a tough thing to choke down." Simon had eaten his fair share of cow tongue, liver, and heart when he was growing up. He didn't hate it. That was about as much of a compliment as he could give.

"I *was* raised on the stuff," Apricot said drily. "And that is exactly why I'm not eating it today. You can't cook, Lilac. Not tongue. Not pasta. Not rice. If you'd just accept that fact, the world would be a better place."

"The people of Papua New Guinea loved my food!" Lilac argued, but her eyes were sparkling.

Perfect! Apricot thought as she looked into her mother's gleaming eyes. Lilac was pushing her buttons.

Again.

The woman was an expert at it.

And, generally speaking, once the button pushing began it didn't end.

Which meant that Apricot was going to have to end it herself, because time was ticking away, her stomach was growling, and she needed to get away from her family and eat something in exactly that order or she just might be tempted to kill someone. Namely, Lilac. Or Rose. Or even poor Hubert, who was peering out the living room window probably wondering if he should come running to the rescue.

"Good. Great." Apricot sighed. "Ship the sandwiches there, because they are definitely not what I feel like eating today."

"This isn't about what you feel like eating. This is about what's healthy. Look at your skin!" Lilac jabbed a finger in her direction. "Pasty. You've been eating refined wheat again, haven't you? Is that a zit I see on your nose? You know how you break out when you eat processed food."

Good gravy! How in God's name had this situation gotten so completely out of control?

"I think she's got a bit of sun on her nose," Simon drawled, his beautiful eyes skimming over whatever offending mark Lilac had noticed. "And I think it looks beautiful on her."

"Cow tongue! That is the key to clear skin and energy. You're going to need the former if you're going to find yourself a new man, Apricot. You're going to need the latter if you really plan to bring the orchard back up to snuff," Lilac proclaimed as if she hadn't heard a word he'd said.

Apricot had heard, and her heart was doing a funny little dance of happiness. Not so much because of his words, but because of the way he looked at her, as if she were the most beautiful woman he'd ever seen. Even with her sunburned nose and wild hair.

"What *do* you feel like eating, Apricot Sunshine?" Simon asked, ignoring Lilac's lecture. For a moment, she was so caught in the deep green depth of his eyes, she wasn't sure what he was asking or why an answer mattered.

Then Rose started gesturing wildly from behind Lilac. Apricot wasn't exactly sure what the wild gestures were meant to convey, but they served to pull her out of the happy little spell she'd fallen into.

"A ham and cheese sandwich on rye would be really nice," she said quickly, hoping her long pause wasn't too noticeable.

Based on the amusement in Simon's eyes, she'd say it had been. He was too much of a gentleman to point it out.

"I think that can be arranged," he responded easily, smiling into her eyes with just the right amount of focus and interest and humor.

Dear God above, she liked him!

He made her feel . . . happy, excited, beautiful.

It had been a heck of a long time since she'd felt any of those things.

"Ham and cheese?!" Lilac leaned into the car, thrusting her upper body through the window. Simon had to lean back to avoid getting a face full of cleavage.

Apricot wanted to pull Lilac's V-neck closed, but that would just start a tirade about another one of Lilac's pet subjects—the beauty of the human body. It could even end with a full-out stripping off of the muumuu her mother was wearing.

Nope. Better to keep her mouth closed.

"They process the crap out of that stuff," Lilac spat. "It's not even real food."

"Give the kids a break." Rose dragged Lilac out of the window. "They don't want your disgusting cow tongue sandwiches. Take this instead." She passed a basket in through the window. "Huckleberry jam and homemade bread. Goat cheese and quinoa salad. Flaxseed crackers. A little wine. A nice cold ginger tea. Perfect picnic food."

"Thanks, Rose." Apricot set the basket on her lap. "We'd better go. Simon has a limited amount of time for lunch, and I have more work to do in the orchard."

"If you're picnicking, why not just stay here? That will save Simon a drive into town and back and give you two a little extra time to enjoy . . ." Rose glanced at Simon and offered a sly wink. "The food."

"What do you think, Apricot? The park or the orchard? I'll be happy either way," Simon responded, ignoring Rose's obvious hint.

"Well?" Lilac pressed. "You going to drive around in the gas guzzler and contribute to global warming and the death of our beautiful planet? Or are you going to do the decent, the humane, the *right* thing and just stay right where you are?"

"You're not on the political circuit, Lilac. No need to get overly dramatic in your pitch," Apricot said, sidestepping the question, looking out the window at the beautiful sunny day, the bright blue sky, and the clouds just kind of meandering across the horizon.

It *was* a good day for the park *or* the orchard.

The thing was, one idea seemed a heck of a lot more romantic than the other. The park was public, the chance of finding herself in Simon's arms slim to none. The orchard, though? She could picture herself sitting on the little bench with Simon, the soft rustle of leaves all around them, the quiet solitude, the sun just warming them through the trees. She could imagine eating cheese and sipping wine and listening to him talk about his girls and his crazy sister-in-law. Anything could happen in the orchard, and she had to admit, she kind of liked that.

"You're wasting precious time," Rose pronounced, yanking open Simon's door and pulling him out of the SUV. "There's an absolutely perfect picnic spot in the orchard. A lovely little bench right in the middle of a clearing. You know it, right, Apricot?"

"Yes, but—"

"But what?" Lilac demanded, hands on her hips, the neckline of her muumuu still drooping a few inches too low.

"The park may be—"

"Boring." Lilac cut her off again. "I did not raise a boring child. You might live a boring life, but there's got to be a little bit of wildness in you. Embrace it for a change, Apricot Sunshine."

"There is nothing boring about lunch in the park," Apricot protested, but her mother and aunt had Simon by the arms and were jabbering away at him as they walked toward the house.

Simon didn't seem to mind being shanghaied. As a matter of fact, he smiled and waved at Hubert as they passed the living room window.

Hubert mouthed something that looked an awful lot like *you poor son of a monkey's uncle* and Simon laughed.

He didn't seem at all bothered by her family's intrusiveness. Which made Apricot's heart melt just a little. In all the time she'd been with Lionel, he'd never been comfortable with her family. When they'd come for their once-in-a-blue-moon visits, he'd moved in with his mother to "give them room in the condo."

Her family hadn't appreciated the effort. As a

matter of fact, Lilac had complained bitterly about it on more than one occasion.

"Too good for us. That's the problem. He's got his fancy clothes and fancy way of talking, and he thinks we're a bunch of clueless hippies. What you see in that guy, I'll never know."

Apricot had known *exactly* what she'd seen in him—the opposite of what she'd had with her family—predictability, order, manners, and a bit of polish. She'd wanted that for herself, because she'd never, *ever* wanted to be like Lilac and Rose or any of the rest of the clan. She'd wanted to be . . . normal, because normal had seemed like the easiest way to live her life. She hated the overwrought emotionalism, the extremes of passion. She wanted to raise her kids in an environment that embraced individuality but didn't thumb its nose at conformity.

She and Lionel had talked it all out, and they'd agreed on Montessori school for the first few years, then a private middle school and high school to polish things off. No one-room schoolhouse in the middle of a tiny little village where everyone knew everyone. *Their* children would be exposed to art and culture and sports.

Their children who would never exist, because she and Lionel no longer existed as a couple.

She should have known that was the way it would be. The women in her family weren't meant for long-term relationships. If she hadn't been so caught up in her dream of wanting one, she would have realized that and saved herself a little heartache.

Simon glanced over his shoulder as Lilac and Rose led him away.

"Help me," he mouthed, and she couldn't help

smiling. He had a sense of humor, and she liked that. She liked him. She liked his girls. She liked the way she felt when she was with them. As if all those years she'd spent with Lionel weren't a waste because they'd led her to Apple Valley and all the wonderful people she'd met here.

That had to mean something.

Didn't it?

Right then, she wasn't so sure, but she knew she couldn't just let Rose and Lilac drag Simon off. Lord alone knew what those two women would do with him.

She caught up with them quickly, Rose's basket slapping against her thighs, the little white sundress that Apricot had planned to wear in Aruba sliding up her legs. The weather in Apple Valley was almost too cool for the dress, but the eyelet fabric made her feel pretty and feminine, and for some reason that had seemed important while she was getting ready.

"It's going to be a little difficult for Simon and me to have lunch together if you two are around," she said pointedly, hoping Lilac and Rose would take the hint and leave.

"We could all eat together," Lilac suggested.

"I'd rather starve," Apricot responded.

Simon chuckled.

Lilac scowled.

"I'm shocked at how inhospitable you sound, Apricot. You were raised on the idea of the communal meal, of breaking bread together as a sign of solidarity in mind and heart."

"Right now, I'd just like to have a little solidarity in my stomach. I didn't eat much this morning, and I'm starving." As if to prove the point, her stomach growled so loudly a couple of magpies flew from an apple tree.

Simon glanced her way and winked, and her heart thumped so hard in response she thought it was trying to leap from her chest.

"And what have I told you about that?" Lilac sighed. "How can you possibly keep your metabolism working properly if you refuse to nourish your body?"

"Lilac, how about you hold off on your advice for a while? I'm seriously going to tear someone's head off if I don't get some food in my stomach soon."

"No need to get snippy. I'm simply informing you because I care." Lilac thrust the second basket into Apricot's free hand. "Eat the tongue," she whispered loudly. "It will help with the wrinkles you're getting on your forehead."

With that, she grabbed Rose's hand and dragged her away.

There was a moment of silence, the day just kind of pausing as Lilac and Rose walked inside the house.

"Wow!" Simon breathed. "Just . . . wow."

"Yeah. I know. Imagine being raised by those two."

"And Hubert?" He took both baskets and used his hip to shove open the gate that led into the orchard.

"And with an entire gargantuan family of crazy people," she responded.

He laughed, and the muted sunlight seemed a little brighter, the leaves a little greener.

That was not good, because she was not heading down the relationship path again. It wouldn't lead anywhere but heartache, and she'd had enough of that to last a lifetime.

"What's wrong?" Simon asked as she led the way to the clearing and the pretty little bench that had been placed there by a man who had loved his wife so much that he'd spent every minute without her mourning what he'd lost.

At least, that's what Apricot had been imagining late at night when she couldn't sleep, when all her dead dreams just kind of piled up in her mind and made her wish she'd made different choices.

"Just thinking that this probably isn't a good idea," she responded honestly.

"What? Lunch?" He sat and pulled her down beside him, his arms somehow winding around her shoulders, his fingers playing in the ends of her hair.

"Lunch is fine. It's *us* I'm worried about. That's what this feels like to me. Not just lunch with a friend, lunch with someone I really like, someone I want to get to know better, someone I think I could spend a lot of time with and never get tired of."

"Whatever kind of lunch we're having, it doesn't mean a lifetime commitment. It just means today, right now, this moment. Let's just relax and enjoy it." He smiled, stretching his legs out in front of him, the sunlight dancing in his hair. She wanted to run her fingers through the soft strands, run her palm along the rough stubble on his jaw. She wanted to hold his hand and bask in the warmth of the day and just let herself enjoy the deliciousness of new . . .

Love?

Good God almighty! That was not where they were heading!

"Right. Enjoy it," she muttered, thinking that she wouldn't be enjoying it in two or three years when the newness wore off and he went and found someone else.

"Get a little cranky when you're hungry, huh?"

"Sometimes," she admitted, but she took a cracker that he held out and ate it. "And you know this is more than lunch. If you say anything else it will be a lie."

He didn't say anything, just sat beside her silently for so long, she finally had to speak.

"No comment?" she asked.

"What do you want me to say?" he responded, lifting her hand, his thumb sliding across her knuckles. "That we're making a mistake spending time together? That it would be wrong to walk down this path and see where it leads?"

"I . . ." *Was* that what she wanted him to say? "Just got out of a relationship."

"I'm well aware of that," he said, looking straight into her eyes. "I did see you the day you drove into town in that fluffy pink monstrosity of a wedding gown, remember?"

"How could I forget? Dusty had his rifle pointed at my heart."

"Not quite," he said with a smile.

"It seemed like it to me."

"You were having a bad day, but I still thought you were beautiful and spunky."

"Spunky, huh?"

"I'm not into women who aren't," he replied, suddenly serious again. "Here's the thing, Apricot. You just got out of a relationship. I've been out of one for six years. Up until recently, I didn't think I wanted to ever be in one again, but here I am, having lunch with you." He kissed her palm and folded her fingers over the spot the way he'd done the day before. "If that bothers you, I can go have lunch with my crazy sister-in-law and you can have lunch with your crazy family, and we can call it good. The choice is yours, but make it quick, because my stomach is growling and, like you, I'm not all that pleasant when I get hungry."

"You're always pleasant," she responded, lifting Rose's basket, her cheeks hot, her heart running like a mad thing in her chest. "But, just to be safe, let's go ahead and eat."

He smiled, smoothing a strand of hair from her cheek, tilting her chin just enough for a kiss that should have been nothing at all, but seemed like everything Apricot had ever wanted.

Chapter Fifteen

Simon could have gone on kissing her forever if his cell phone hadn't buzzed.

"You'd better get that," Apricot said, her cheeks pink, her lips rosy from his kiss.

"I can think of a few other things I'd rather do." He pressed his lips to her nape, felt her pulse racing beneath the skin. His hand found its way to her thigh, and he ran his palm along the silky flesh, loving the feel of firm muscles and smooth skin.

His cell phone buzzed again, and he finally dragged it from his pocket, glanced at the number.

"Daisy," he muttered.

"Of course," Apricot responded, reaching down to grab the plate that had dropped onto the ground. She put it back in the basket, tossing the spilled crackers and cheese farther into the orchard. "Aren't you going to answer it?"

"It can wait."

"What if it's something to do with the girls?"

"They're at school. If something happened to them, the school would be calling."

"But—"

"Tell you what," he said, a little more sharply than he intended. "How about we forget Daisy? I want to have lunch with you, and I don't want to think about her while I'm doing it."

The orchard went dead silent, both of them sitting on the bench, tense and more than a little frustrated. His fault. Not Apricot's, and it was his job to fix it.

"Sorry," he finally said. "That came out more harshly than I intended. Daisy is becoming a problem, but that has nothing to do with you."

"I think it probably does." She handed him a slice of crusty bread smeared with jam. "She's jealous. She wants you to herself, and she probably thought she was going to have you. Then I came along, and everything just kind of fell apart."

"You said something similar to that yesterday. I don't want to believe it anymore today than I did then," he said, biting into the bread, the sweet, tart taste of the jam nearly making him moan. It was that good. "What kind of jam is this?"

"Huckleberry. I made it yesterday."

"It's good."

"You can't distract me with your compliments, Simon."

"Can I distract you some other way?" he asked, purposely letting his gaze drop to her lips, to the tiny bit of jam in the corner of her mouth. He wiped it away with his thumb.

"Thanks," she murmured.

"You didn't answer my question," he responded, his blood pulsing like lava through his veins, his fingers trailing over smooth skin. He could feel her pulse thrumming just beneath the surface, let his palm sweep along the slender curve of her neck and settle at her nape. Her skin felt like warm silk, and he trailed his lips along the line of her jaw. "*Can* I distract you some other way?"

His cell phone buzzed again, and he wanted to take the thing and smash it against the nearest tree.

"You know what?" Apricot stood, her white sundress swishing around those beautiful thighs. "This really isn't a good idea. You have a really busy life, and I have . . ." She gestured at the trees. "All this to get under control. This isn't the right time to explore a relationship or walk down some path that's supposed to lead to something wonderful."

"That's a cop-out, Apricot, and you know it."

"So?" She grabbed both the baskets. "What if it is? I already made one colossal mistake in my life. I don't want to make another one."

"Another cop-out." He was angry now, pissed because Apricot didn't seem to have the guts to take a risk and because Daisy had interrupted a beautiful day and a pretty damn wonderful moment. Not once, but twice.

"No. It's not. You've got a perfect life, Simon. Two beautiful girls, a sweet house and a nice job. You have a community that loves you and that you love. You don't need me, and I'm not going to get into a position where I find myself needing you."

"It isn't about need. And having something good doesn't mean that adding something else to it won't make it better."

She hesitated, then shook her head. "I think our hour lunch break is up. I'm sorry you drove out here and didn't even get to eat."

Okay. Now he was *really* pissed. "*I'm* sorry that you're too much of a coward to go after what you want."

"I'm not a coward." She huffed, her eyes blazing, her cheeks pink with annoyance and, maybe, embarrassment. "I'm cautious. There's not a dang thing wrong with that."

"There is if it keeps you from having what you want," he responded.

She opened her mouth, snapped it shut again.

"At least you're not going to lie and say you don't want me," he muttered, shoving his phone into his pocket and stalking away. He had plenty to do. He didn't need to waste his time arguing about something that shouldn't need to be reasoned out or talked through. Not at this stage. Not when it was still so fragile and new.

"Sometimes the things we want aren't the best things for us, Simon," she said so quietly, he almost didn't hear.

"And sometimes," he responded, turning so that he was facing her again. "The things we want are."

"Too bad we can't see into the future. We'd be able to take the risk without worrying that we're going to end up worse off than we were before we tried." She lifted both baskets, her movements stiff and tight, her pretty little sundress fluttering. A breeze ruffled her hair, pushing a few short strands across her forehead.

"No one ends up worse off if he goes in with the right attitude. Today wasn't about a lifetime commitment, Apricot. It was just about lunch with someone I'm interested in getting to know better. I'm not sure what it is about that that scares you."

"I'm not scared."

"Remember when I told you I only wanted to be in relationships that are built on honesty?" he snapped. "I meant it."

"I'm not!" she protested, but she *was* lying and they both knew it.

"Tell you what, Apricot Sunshine. If you change your mind and decide we can both handle the truth, give me a call. Otherwise, I'll let you go on just the way you are, fixing up the orchard and dealing with your family and watching one day pass into another without more than a tiny little hiccup to make things difficult."

"Simon—" She started to protest, but he wasn't in the mood for listening, so he turned on his heels and walked away, walking through the gnarled apple trees, past the house where Lilac and Rose were snapping peapods on the back deck, and straight into his car.

He didn't look back as he drove away, because he didn't want to see what he'd almost had. Just like Apricot, he didn't want drama in his life, but he'd have been willing to take a chance on it for her.

It was a helluva shame that she hadn't felt the same.

His cell phone rang again as he sped toward Main Street.

Daisy again. He didn't even have to look to know it.

This time he answered. "What the hell is it this time, Daisy?" he barked.

"Simon! Language!"

"What. Do. You. Need." He bit every word out.

There was a moment of silence. "I . . . well, I'm at the library. Jet is here."

"And?"

"He's watching me with an evil look in his eyes."

"What exactly does that mean?" he growled, because, right at that moment, he didn't have the patience for her high-strung nature.

"He had murder in his eyes, Simon," she hissed. "I saw it as clearly as I see the sun shining outside my office window."

"Did he approach you?"

"No."

"Say anything to you? Imply in any way that he intended to do you harm?"

"No, but—"

"Then he has every right to be at the library," he cut in, because he knew that *but* always led to twenty minutes of illogical reasoning.

"You don't seem to understand."

"I understand perfectly well. I think you're the one who isn't getting it."

"What's that supposed to mean?"

"People are talking, Daisy," he responded, ready to go all out and say what needed saying. In for a penny, in for a pound, that's what his grandmother always said. "They're questioning your story."

"What story?"

"They're wondering if you really were mugged or if maybe you made the whole thing up."

Silence. Not even a breath of air passing across the line.

"You still there, Daisy?"

"I'm . . . I can't believe you would say something like that to me."

"I'm not the one saying it. I'm just bringing it to your attention."

"What you should be doing is defending me. I'm your wife's sister. Your daughters' aunt."

"I'm well aware of who you are," he muttered, pulling into the drive-through line at the local coffee shop.

"Well, then, why aren't you jumping to my defense?"

Because I'm wondering too, he almost said. "What I'm doing is due diligence. I'm checking all the facts and trying to get them to line up. So far, they're not."

"What's that supposed to mean?"

"You were mugged in broad daylight in a well-traveled area, but not one person saw the attack."

"It happened in an alley!" she cried, her voice shaky.

"An alley just about anyone can see into if they take the time to look."

"It happened so fast. There wasn't time for anyone to see it." She was crying. He knew it, and he should have felt bad, but he was still mad as all get-out, and she was part of the reason for that.

"Maybe not, but people are wondering, and I think maybe you should take a really hard look at what you've been saying. I think you might want to consider that there are a lot of people in town who have hired Jet, who have liked the work he's done for them, who find him to be honest and forthright. You, on the other hand—"

"Don't you dare bring up the cupcake thing!" she snapped. "Don't you dare."

Then she disconnected. Just like that. Ended the conversation without ever denying that she'd made the story up.

Which, when he thought of it, was not like Daisy at all. She loved to prove a point, to be right, to commit to something and stick with it.

So why hadn't she shouted her innocence to the world?

Why hadn't she demanded a meeting at town hall, where she could share her grievances and demand an apology?

It worried him, he'd admit it.

Because if Max was right and Daisy had made the entire thing up, if she was accusing someone of something that hadn't even happened . . . that was a crime, and she could be punished with jail time.

He needed to talk it out with someone. Preferably not someone who worked for the Apple Valley Sheriff's Department.

Apricot popped into his head. She'd listen without judging. She'd give whatever advice she could. She'd probably prescribe teas and tinctures to help with Daisy's high-strung nature.

Thinking about that made Simon smile, until he remembered that Apricot didn't want drama, she didn't want risk, she didn't want any of the things he had in his life. She didn't want to be honest either, and that, more than anything else, was the kiss of death to whatever they'd had.

"Can I help you?" the young woman at the drive-through window asked.

"Only if you can shoot me back in time so I can start my day again," he replied.

"Excuse me?" Her smooth brow furrowed, her hand paused over the computer keys.

"I'll take a large coffee and a cheese Danish," he said. Neither would taste as good as what he could get at Charlotte's, but he wasn't ready to face a bunch of questions from a bunch of well-meaning people. He didn't want to talk about Daisy or Jet or the mugging. He just wanted to eat something for lunch, go back to work, and pretend the day had never happened.

The problem with pretending was it didn't change things.

It didn't make fiction truth or truth fiction.

All it did was allow a person to hide his head in the sand and ignore things that were right in front of his nose.

For example, a sister-in-law who was just kooky enough to make up a story that would get her every bit of the attention she seemed to need.

Three days after her disastrous lunch, and Apricot hadn't seen hide nor hair of anyone from the Baylor family. That should have pleased her. It didn't, because she missed them.

Simon.

The girls.

Even crazy Daisy.

She missed them, but she was *not* going to call Simon. What would be the point? No amount of apologizing could change what she'd done. She'd blown something really pleasant because she'd been worried about having her heart broken. Funny thing was, she'd spent the past three days feeling like it had been.

She scowled, dropping an armful of tree trimmings into a wheelbarrow she'd dragged from the dilapidated shed she'd found at the edge of the orchard. It had been filled with old farming equipment. Hand tools. Trimmers. Nothing any of the guys she'd hired would use, but she liked the feeling of history, of constancy that came with holding something that someone else had used decades ago. Of course, she hadn't asked Dusty if the building was on her land, but she figured he'd show up eventually if it wasn't and tell her to put the wheelbarrow back.

Or maybe not.

He'd spent most of the last few days mooning over Rose.

Apricot had spent most of the past few days avoiding her family. Even now, at seven in the morning with rain just starting to fall in a light, sweet mist, she wasn't inside. She was out in the orchard, working her butt off, because that was a heck of a lot easier than listening to Rose or Lilac's advice about her love life.

The one she did not have, because she was a coward.

A boring one.

"It sucks to be me!" She dropped another armload of branches and leaves onto the others.

"What's that, Apricot?" Jet asked from the rung of a ladder that leaned against one of the larger apple trees. His upper body and head were shrouded by leaves and branches, but his thin legs were clearly visible.

"Just talking to myself."

"You know you do that a lot, right?" He peered out from between leaves and frowned. "You might want to go see someone about it."

"How about you just stick to trimming trees and save the helpful advice for someone else?" she responded, bending down to gather a few more fallen branches.

"Bad morning with the family, huh?" he responded.

"Bad lifetime with the family," she muttered.

"At least you have them to complain about. One day you might not, so maybe you should just enjoy what you've got while you got it."

"Do you have to be so smart, Jet? Because I'm trying to bemoan my fate, and you're not making it easy." She dropped the third armful in the barrow, stretched a kink out of her back, and tried really, really hard to be thankful for what she had.

"Hey, I just call it like I see it." He ducked his head back inside the canopy of trees and went back to work trimming the top branches. "Besides, if you ask my granddad, he'll tell you I'm more smart aleck than smart."

"I doubt it. The way I hear things, your grandparents think the sun rises and sets with your smile."

He laughed, tossing a couple of small branches down. "They're pretty great people. I just wish they didn't have to go through all this stuff with the crazy librarian. She actually showed up at our house last night and demanded to be allowed to search my room. She still thinks I took her wallet and phone."

"I hope your grandparents sent her packing." And she wondered what Simon had thought about his sister-in-law's escapades.

Which made her wonder about Simon.

Which made her wonder if she was the biggest fool

in the world for not just picking up the phone and calling the guy.

"Nah. We let her take a look. I've got nothing to hide. Poor lady got to my underwear drawer and nearly had a heart attack. It was right around that time that she decided that maybe she didn't need to search my room after all."

Apricot laughed. Probably her first real laugh in three days, and it was at poor Daisy's expense. The woman really did need to get on a strict regimen of herbs and tinctures. A vegan diet might help too. "Did you report her to the police?"

"Granddad said that would just be cruel. She's already made such a fool of herself in town, people look at her sideways when she walks down the street." He tossed several branches onto the ground, looked down at her again. "It's starting to rain, you know."

"You can stop for the day."

"We've barely started, and I like to get a job done once I sign up for it."

"You didn't sign up for this. I volunteered you." That was nearly the truth. She'd actually asked him to join the orchard crew while he was waiting on custom-ordered windows to be delivered. With everything else on the exterior of the house complete, Jet had packed up and told her he'd be back when the windows arrived. She could have let him go, but he'd had a look that bordered on desperation, and she'd thought that maybe his college expenses were piling up or that he was helping his retired grandparents with their mortgage.

Whatever the case, she'd known he needed the money, and she could certainly use the help.

He tossed a couple more branches down, then climbed halfway down the ladder. "You know I appreciate the work."

"And you know that I appreciate you being the one person on the orchard crew who begins work at the crack of dawn like I do."

He shrugged. "You're the only person I know who is willing to let me make my own work schedule. That really helps when it comes to school. I'm taking full advantage of it." He climbed the rest of the way down the ladder, his hair already wet from rain, his body still holding on to the lean, lanky build of youth. "Of course, today I've only gotten an hour in." He glanced up at the cloud-laden sky. "And it looks like that's going to be all. Might be all for a few days. I heard we've got a storm blowing in."

"That's great. All that rain will be good for next year's growing season."

"That's what I like about you, Apricot." He brushed her hands away from the wheelbarrow. "You're always an optimist. Me? I'm just thinking about the money I'm not going to make and about the fact that I'm standing here in wet clothes." He pushed the load to the edge of the orchard, rolled it onto the cart she'd rented, and dumped it there. "You want me to put the wheelbarrow back in the shed?"

She was going to tell him not to bother. She didn't mind a little rain. She'd grown up walking through the woods while rain poured down, and she loved the sound of it on the tree canopy, the soft slap of it on the ground.

Of course, if she told him she was going to keep working, he'd feel obligated to do the same. "Sure. I'll grab the ladder."

"I'll get it. I took it out. Plus, this place is packed with stuff. It's not easy to get the ladder in and out." He rolled the wheelbarrow into the shed, calling out as he went. "You going to the apple festival next weekend?"

"Of course. Rose has been working nonstop to get ready for it. She's got a hundred cases of tinctures to sell."

"She got anything for arthritis? My grandma's hands are . . ." Something knocked against the wall of the shed, and she figured he must have been shoving the wheelbarrow into place.

"Shit!" He came running out, his face white as a ghost, his eyes dark and glassy.

"What's wrong?" She grabbed his arm, afraid he'd been bitten by something. It was late in the season for snakes, but there were plenty of other varmints that were gathering their stores for the winter. Opossums, raccoons, rats. They could all be mean when they were cornered.

"Holy crap! This is bad, Apricot. Really bad," Jet gasped.

"What? Were you stung? Bitten? Are you having a heart attack?" She probed his jugular, and he brushed her hand away.

"I shoved the wheelbarrow so hard that I knocked over the planter. There was a bunch of dirt inside it."

"No problem. I'll sweep up the dirt. It's been in there so long, it's dry as a bone. I could probably just leave the door open and let the breeze blow it—"

He grabbed her hand, yanked her to the door. Pointed, his finger trembling. The planter was on its side, the dirt that someone had left in it spilled out.

And there, right on top of the mess, was a wallet and a shattered cell phone.

"That's not what I think it is, is it?" she whispered as if being quiet could change what she was seeing.

"I don't know. Shit! What if it is?" Jet wasn't at all worried about quiet. He looked ready to run, his eyes frantic, his face pale.

"Did you look in the wallet?"

"No. I didn't want my fingerprints on it."

"Maybe it isn't Daisy's."

"And maybe it is, and if it is, it's going to lead the police right to me. We need to put them back under the dirt and pretend we never saw them."

She grabbed his arm before he could start hiding the evidence. "You know we can't do that."

"I suppose you're going to say we should call the police," he grumbled.

"First, I'm going to see if they're Daisy's. If they are, we'll call the police. If they're not, we're still going to call the police." She lifted the wallet, brushed dirt off its faux leather cover, opened it.

There was Daisy, staring back at her from a really, really, *really* bad driver's license photo.

"Sweet corn fritters, it *is* hers." She sighed.

Chapter Sixteen

"Daddy!" Rori nudged Simon's shoulder, forcing him from a comfortable doze on the sofa. He was tired as all get-out, so he kept his eyes closed and prayed she'd go find her aunt.

"Daddy!" She nudged him again. "The kittens are missing."

He groaned and opened his eyes.

Her face was about three centimeters from his. She had a couple of little freckles on her nose and a whole lot of worry in her eyes. "What's that?"

"The kittens. They're gone."

"Are you sure?" He'd seen them when he got home at eight. Hadn't he? He couldn't really remember.

"Yes. They were here last night, and now they're gone." Her lower lip trembled, and the first tear slid down her cheek.

So, of course, he did what any good father would.

Made promises that he might not be able to keep. "Don't worry, honey. I'm sure they're in the house somewhere. We'll find them. I promise."

"But me and Evie already looked everywhere, and

they're not here." She pressed her palms to his cheeks and looked deep into his eyes. "Evie said they maybe got eaten by Mr. Plumber's mean old dog."

"Where *is* Evie?"

"She's trying to get into the attic."

"What?" He was up like a shot. "You know I've told you girls to stay out of there." He planned to put down flooring, but currently there was nothing but support beams and insulation.

"But she has to look for the kittens. If they didn't get eaten, they're hungry and scared. I'm just so worried about them, Daddy." She ran along behind him, but he was too busy yelling for her sister to pay much attention.

"Evangeline Rose! You had better not be in that attic!" he hollered as he sprinted up the stairs.

"I'm not. Yet," she responded, her voice muffled.

He ran into his bedroom, scowling as he caught sight of Evie, her legs and lower body dangling out of the hatch door in the closet ceiling. He snagged her by the waist and pulled her down. "What have I told you about going in the attic?"

"What's going on?" Daisy appeared in the doorway, a frilly apron tied around her waist. Seeing as how she hadn't spoken more than five words to Simon since their phone conversation three days ago, he was surprised she hadn't just stayed in the kitchen, cleaning the breakfast dishes.

"Our kittens are gone, Aunt Daisy," Evie said, her face smudged with dust. "Have you seen them?"

"They were here when I woke up." She shrugged. "Maybe your father accidentally let them out when he got home."

The girls both shot horrified looks in his direction.

"Did you, Daddy?" Rori asked, looking like he'd just shot an arrow straight through her heart.

"Of course I didn't. I walked in the front door just like I always do. I didn't see the kittens when I came in. Did you water the flower boxes on the back porch, Daisy? Maybe they got out then?"

"Oh, so now you're blaming me." Daisy's hands settled on her hips, her eyes narrowing.

"I'm not blaming you. I'm asking you a question," he explained, taking both girls by the hands and leading them out of the room. "When was the last time you saw them?"

"Last night at bedtime," they said in unison.

"And you didn't go outside this morning?"

"We brought the garbage out, but they were gone before then, Daddy," Rori said. "I noticed they were missing as soon as we got up."

"They had to have gotten out last night then. It's possible they've found a nice place to sleep and they'll come home in a little while."

"Or it's possible they've been eaten," Evie added.

"They weren't eaten," he assured the girls, even though he wasn't actually sure. The kittens were tiny, and there were plenty of coyotes roaming around the outskirts of Apple Valley. They'd been known to sneak in and take chickens, geese, and even a small domestic animal or two.

"Well, then where are they?" Evie demanded, her hands fisted on her hips, her lower lip out. She was going to cry. He could see it coming.

"I don't know, but I'm going to figure it out."

"I bet Apricot can help us," Rori suggested. "She likes to help people."

Daisy snorted.

"She does!" Rori said. "She helped the art teacher. Mrs. Lauren had a terrible back pain and Apricot gave her tea to make it better. Maybe she has tea that will make the kittens come home."

"There is no such thing," Daisy snapped. "The problem is, you weren't careful enough when you took the trash out. They probably slipped out with you and wandered off. More than likely they will find their way home. If they don't, I guess you'll have learned your lesson about responsibility. It's something both of you could use a little more of."

"No need to be harsh, Daisy. The girls feel bad enough."

"I'm not being harsh. I'm teaching them valuable life lessons." Daisy smoothed a few wrinkles out of her apron and fluffed her hair. "It's called good parenting."

"It isn't good parenting if what you're saying isn't true," Evie pointed out.

"Are you calling me a liar, young lady?!" Daisy demanded, her face beet red.

"She'd better not be," Simon broke in.

"I would never call you a liar, Aunt Daisy," Evie responded, her sweet little face and sweet little smile warning Simon that trouble was brewing.

"Evie," he warned.

Too late.

Her mouth was already open and the words were already spilling out. "I'm calling you mistaken. Besides, it seems to me that if you're so sure someone let the kittens outside, you were probably the one to do it!" She pointed her finger straight at Daisy.

At which point, World War III erupted.

Daisy yelled something about false accusations and started sobbing so loudly the windows shook in their frames. Her sobs made the girls cry. Next thing he knew, the entire house was echoing with the sound of sobs and of a phone ringing.

A phone?

He pulled out his cell phone, glanced at the caller ID.

Work. Of course.

"Enough!" he snapped, and Daisy and the girls fell almost silent, their hiccupping sniffles a quiet backdrop to the still-ringing phone.

"Baylor, here," he answered. "I pulled graveyard shift last night, so if this isn't an emergency, find someone else."

"No need to snap my head off, Simon," Emma responded with a hint of glee in her voice. "I thought I'd be doing you a favor by calling, but if you're not interested—"

"I'm seriously not in the mood for games, Emma. If there's something I need to know, tell me."

"Jet found Daisy's wallet and cell phone."

He glanced at Daisy. She was trying so desperately to hear, her neck was straining as her head jutted toward him.

"Hold on," he said. "Girls, get your schoolbooks. Your bus will be here any second."

"We can't leave until we find the kittens," Evie protested, but he nudged them both toward the stairs.

"I'll look while you're gone. Now hurry up. If you miss that bus and I have to drive you to school, I'm docking a half dollar from each of your allowances."

They went reluctantly, trudging down the stairs, their shoulders stooped, their feet dragging. Even their hair looked lank and sad.

"You mind waiting with them, Daisy? I know you like to get in your car and leave for work as soon as their bus pulls away, so it'll be convenient if you do. Of course, if you'd rather I wait with them, that's okay too."

She mumbled something under her breath, but followed the girls, tearing off her apron and dropping it on the floor as she walked outside.

He pressed the phone to his ear again. "Sorry about that, Emma. I had to deal with my family. That can be a little difficult this time of day."

"You're preaching to the choir on that one, brother," she responded.

"Where did Jet find the stolen items?"

"At Rose's place. Sad thing is, he found the stuff, freaked out and ran. Cade found him heading out of town in his grandfather's Oldsmobile."

"Is he in custody?"

"Nah. You know how Cade is. He's gathering facts. Right now, he's at the grandparents' place with Jet."

"Who's at Rose's place?"

"Max."

"Then why are you calling me?"

"Two reasons. First, Daisy is your sister-in-law, and I thought you'd want to be kept updated on the case. Second, you've been moping around for the past three days, and I'm getting sick of it."

"Real men don't mope."

She laughed. "Okay. How does this sound? You've

been grumpier than a pack of vultures fighting over fresh roadkill."

"Better, but I'm not grumpy. Grumpy is for old men and toddlers."

"Whatever you are, it's got to stop, and I have the perfect way to make that happen. Daisy's stuff being found on Rose's property gives you an excuse to have a little face time with Apricot. I suggest you use that time to iron out your differences."

"What gives you the idea that we have differences?" he asked, because he sure as heck hadn't told anyone about the lunch that hadn't been.

"It's not an idea. It's a conjecture based on a conversation I had yesterday."

"What conversation, and who did you have it with?"

"Rose. I just happened to run into her while I was helping set up some of the stands at the fairgrounds. She mentioned the lunch she packed for you guys. Said that not much of it had been eaten."

"So?"

"She also said Apricot came back inside and looked like she'd seen the ghost of Abigail Shaffer. Rose was pretty excited about the idea, but Apricot said she hadn't seen anything but the end of a really nice dream. Any idea what she meant by that?"

"None," he lied.

"Sure you don't," she spat out, obviously disgusted. "Go to Rose's or not, but don't come back to the office tonight with a chip on your shoulder and a scowl on your face. I get enough of that when I'm at home."

She disconnected, and he was left standing there with his cell phone in hand, the house silent as a tomb. He glanced outside. The bus had come. Daisy was gone. He could search for the kittens and then take the nap he needed.

Or, he could do exactly what Emma had suggested.

He wasn't sure which was better, so he took the easy way out and started hunting for the kittens. He combed every inch of the house and the yard with no luck. He finally had to admit that they were well and truly gone. The girls would be devastated.

I bet Apricot can help.

Evie's words wound their way through his head.

Apricot wasn't the cure-all for everything, and she probably couldn't help, but he found himself in the SUV anyway, winding his way through town, raindrops splashing on the windshield as he made his way to Rose's place.

Max was gone by the time he pulled into the driveway, and Simon got out of the SUV, the cold rain streaming from the sky in a heavy deluge that soaked through his jacket as he ran to the front door.

The door opened before he reached it, and Lilac stepped onto the porch, her long dress swirling around her ankles. "It's about time. I thought you'd never get here."

"I didn't think you knew I was coming."

"Of course I knew. People are people. No matter the era they live in, the place they live, the community or culture. If you observe long enough, you start to realize that we all act in predictable ways." She dragged him into the house and closed the door. "It was completely predictable that you would come."

"Great. Good." He glanced around, hoping Apricot was somewhere close by. He liked her family, but he wasn't in the mood for long, convoluted discussions. He wasn't in the mood for much of anything.

As a matter of fact, if he were honest with himself, he'd admit that he'd been about as irritable and antsy as Emma claimed.

He'd have liked to blame it on the graveyard shift, but he'd weathered that plenty of times without having it affect his mood. No. His irritation had nothing to do with work and everything to do with Apricot.

Or, rather, her absence from his life.

He hadn't realized just how much he was going to miss her quirky attitude and sunny smile. He'd even missed her ugly kitten.

"It was," Lilac continued. "Of course, inevitable that you'd also arrive moments too late."

"Too late for what?"

"To see Apricot before she left."

His blood went cold at her words. "Did she head back to Los Angeles?" Because if she had, he might be tempted to take the girls on a road trip to find her.

"Why in the world would she do something like that?" Lilac asked, smoothing her hair back from her face, an armload of bracelets clinking together. "She loves this little town. She's been talking nonstop about getting the orchard going and starting a new venture here. I've had so much of her apple sauce, apple butter, and apple blossom tea that I'm starting to smell like an apple tree!"

"You said she'd left. I thought she'd gone back to LA."

"Hardly! She went to find that ugly little cat of hers. It disappeared sometime this morning, and she's worried sick." She sighed, walking across the living room and lifting a green vase off the mantel. "Do you see this?"

"I do," he responded, not quite sure where she was headed with the conversation, but fairly certain he wasn't going to be able to follow.

"It has a crack in it." She poked a finger at a wide crack that ran the length of the vase. "According to my daughter, that's my fault."

"Did you drop it?" He glanced out the front window. The rain seemed to be coming down harder, but he wondered if he might be better off out there.

"Of course not. I'm very graceful and coordinated. I simply did what Apricot asked me to do. I took the white feather back to the bakery—"

"Sweet Treats?"

"Yes," she said with exaggerated patience. "Sweet Treats. Apparently the kitten has a thing for feathers. He stole one from the shop while he was there with Apricot. What in the world she was doing bringing a kitten into a bakery, I don't know. But she was there and Handsome was with her and the klepto kitty took the feather."

"I can see that happening." He could, and it made him smile.

"Then I'm sure you know what happened next," she responded.

"Apricot insisted the feather be returned?"

"Exactly!" She slapped her hand on her thigh, her bracelets jingling. "Only she didn't want to make a jaunt into town to return it herself. We all know why that is, don't we?"

"I'm not sure. Maybe you should explain."

She grinned. "I like you, Simon."

"I like you too, but I'd probably like you a mite bit better if you got to the point of your tale."

"Yes, right." She held the vase up. "The feather was in this, and I took the whole thing to Sweet Treats, tried to return it, but Charlotte absolutely wouldn't hear of it. She said she had plenty of happiness and love, and she was happy for the feather to have a new home. So, of course, I brought the feather and vase back home."

"Of course," he agreed.

"And I set them right here." She plopped the vase on the fireplace mantel. "And that devil of a cat knocked them down and cracked this priceless family heirloom."

"Is it really a priceless family heirloom?" Because what it looked like to him was an arts and crafts project from the seventies.

"I have no idea, but it makes for a good compelling detail, which makes for a good compelling story. Which, by the way, I'm getting to the end of." She took a deep breath. "Hubert heard the crash and thought the ghost of old man Schaffer had returned. He ran outside—"

"Let me guess. Handsome ran out with him."

"That's right. And not only did he run out, he took the feather with him. I figured the kitten would return eventually. He's always slipping in and out of the house. But he's been gone for hours. Even the rain didn't chase him back home."

"He might have found a place to hunker down until it passed," he suggested.

"That's what I told Apricot, but she's worried. She loves that kitten. As soon as that good-looking deputy left, she headed out to look for Handsome. That was"—she glanced at her watch—"fifteen minutes ago. I'm not sure when she'll be back, but if you'd like me to give her a message when she returns, I will."

"That's okay." He headed to the front door, mulling things over in his head while he went. It was odd that all three kittens were missing. Almost as odd as Daisy's things being found on Apricot's property. "Did Max find anything while he was here?"

"Max?" She followed him to the front door, jingling and swishing the whole way.

"The good-looking deputy," he responded, the words nearly choking him. Good thing Max wasn't around to hear him say them. He'd never let him live it down.

"Oh. Yes. Deputy Stanford." She sighed dreamily. "He said there wasn't much evidence. Just the wallet and a phone."

"Where were they found?"

"Out in the old shed. It's way back at the edge of the orchard. Apricot and Jet were working back there this morning."

"They'd been in the shed before?"

"Yes, but today Jet knocked over a planter. It had a couple of inches of dirt in it. When that spilled out, the wallet and phone came out with it." She paused. "At least that's the way Apricot described it. Had I been there, I'd have probably had a few more details to add to the account."

"I'm sure you would have." He wasn't able to keep the hint of amusement from his voice, and she grinned.

"One more little tidbit of information," she said, obviously relishing each and every detail. "Apricot saw someone walking into the orchard the other night. She thought it was Dusty, so she didn't bother mentioning it to the police. I'd say it was either old man Shaffer's ghost or the guy who mugged your sister-in-law."

"Sounds like some reasonable assumptions. How about you call Max and fill him in." He opened the door, let cool wind blow in. It carried the scent of apples and a hint of winter, and he wondered if Apricot had brought a jacket and umbrella when she'd left the house, or if she'd gone out to search wearing one of those flimsy long skirt and tank-top combos that she seemed to favor. "I've got a couple of kittens missing myself, and if I don't find them before my girls get home, there are going to be a lot of tears."

"Is that why you stopped by?" she asked, stepping onto the porch as he retreated down the steps.

"One of the reasons."

"Did any of the other reasons have something to do with Apricot?"

"It's possible."

"Humph," she responded, the wind whipping her dress around her legs and making her hair fly around her head in a wild frenzy. "That is a very safe answer."

"It's as much of an answer as I can give."

"Be careful, Simon," she said in a voice that had a hint of mystery in it. "Sometimes two people are meant to be together. Sometimes everything in their lives conspires to make sure that they are. When that happens, they really have no choice. They either walk the road side by side, or they live their lives wishing they had." She grabbed a handful of her hair and frowned. "Now I've got to get inside. This weather isn't good for my hair."

She walked inside, closing the door with a quiet snap.

He had the distinct impression that he'd disappointed her, and he was half-near tempted to apologize.

He glanced around the yard. No sign of Handsome. No sign of Apricot. No sign of the girls' kittens. King Henry was parked in the driveway, the Airstream right behind it. Wherever Apricot was, she'd gone on foot.

He rounded the side of the house, rain soaking through his jeans and sliding off his jacket. He could have gotten in the SUV and gone home, but he'd come for a reason. Despite what he'd said to Lilac, despite what he might even be trying to tell himself, he wanted to see Apricot. It was as simple as that, and maybe even as complicated.

He splashed through a couple of puddles as he crossed the backyard and made his way into the orchard. The scent of apples hung thick in the air, the rain creating a rhythmic melody that the girls would have danced to if they'd been with him.

He headed toward the clearing in the center of the orchard because he wasn't sure where else to go, and because he figured that if Apricot had any thinking to do, that's where she'd be.

He found her there, sitting on the bench, her head bent, her hair plastered to her head. Her black T-shirt was soaked, her jeans coated with mud. It looked like she'd been tromping through the orchard for hours rather than minutes.

He was sure she heard him coming, but she didn't look up as he approached.

"It's a little wet for a picnic," he said, settling onto the bench beside her.

She met his eyes, a soft smile curving the corners of her lips, rain streaming down her face. There were goose bumps on her arms, and her teeth were nearly chattering, but it didn't look like she had any intention of going back inside.

"I thought you were Lilac," she said.

"Are you disappointed that I'm not?"

"Relieved is a better word for it," she responded. "She is driving me batty."

"Is that why you're sitting out here in the rain?" He took off his jacket, wrapped it around her shoulders. His knuckles brushed her jaw as he tugged it closed, and it was all he could do not to lean in, taste her rain-soaked lips.

"I'm out here because Handsome is missing. I've been looking for him. I'm sure Lilac told you all about it."

"She did."

"Did she also give that bunch of blarney about people who are meant to be together?" She made a good show of being disgusted, but there was a hint of sadness in her eyes.

"She did."

"Silly, isn't it?" She laughed, the sound echoing hollowly through the clearing.

"I didn't think so."

"Oh, come on!" She stood and paced to the edge of the clearing, her work boots slapping against the wet earth. "You're not the kind of guy who buys into that sort of stuff."

"Why wouldn't I be?" he responded, closing the distance between them.

Sheets of rain were falling all around them, but he couldn't see anything but Apricot, think of anything but how he felt when she was in his arms. "I'm standing in the rain with you, looking in your eyes, and I'm thinking that every day I don't spend with you is a day with just a little less sunshine in it. I'm not sure if that means we're meant to be together, but I know for damn sure that it means I don't want us to be apart."

"I think," she said, her cold hand settling on his jaw, "that is the most romantic thing anyone has ever said to me."

She levered up, her lips brushing his, her hands sliding into his hair, his jacket falling off her shoulders and landing in a heap on the ground.

He didn't care about the jacket or the rain. He just cared about this moment and this woman and making up for the three days they'd been apart.

He pulled Apricot closer, inhaling flowers and rain, his palms sliding up her narrow back.

His cell phone rang, and Apricot jumped back, her breath heaving from her lungs, her T-shirt and jeans clinging to her slender curves.

"The universe is conspiring to keep us apart." She laughed shakily, brushing wet strands of hair from her cheek.

"Not according to your mother." He dragged the phone from his pocket, glanced at the number.

"Daisy!" he muttered.

"She's got a sixth sense when it comes to the two of us."

"What she's got is the ability to piss me off faster than just about anyone I know," he ground out, hitting talk and pressing the phone to his ear. "If this is about Jet—"

"The girls aren't at school!" she wailed. "They're missing and it's all my fault!"

"What do you mean, they're not at school? Didn't they get on the bus?" He tried to stay calm, tried to tell himself that she was wrong.

"They did, but I forgot to give them lunch money. It was in my pocket when I got to work. I decided to bring it to them. When I got here, their teacher said they never showed up! The office was just getting ready to call home to see if they were sick," she managed to say through nearly hysterical sobs.

"Are you at the school now?" He needed to speak with someone who wasn't frantic.

"Yes," she sobbed.

"Let me talk to Principal Snyder."

"Okay."

There was a murmur of voices in the background, and he hoped to heaven it meant that Daisy was handing over the phone.

"Simon? Angie Snyder here." A crisp, clear voice carried through the phone. Angela had been principal at the Apple Valley Elementary School for two decades. She didn't panic. Didn't get overly excited. After so many years of dealing with kids and their parents, she had a steady calmness that Simon had always appreciated. Today, it was going to be invaluable.

"What's going on?" he asked, hoping that maybe Daisy had it wrong, that maybe the girls were sitting in their classroom working on math or reading or whatever they spent the first hour of the day doing.

"Good question, and it's one I'm trying to find an answer to."

That didn't sound good. As a matter of fact, it sounded pretty damn bad.

"If you can't answer that, maybe you can answer this. Where are my girls?"

"At this moment, I'm not sure."

"What do you mean, you're not sure?!" he nearly bellowed. "They were on the school bus. They've got to be at the school."

"They *were* at the school," she responded. "At some point, they must have left."

"With who?" He was gripping the phone so tightly, he thought the thing was going to explode, but he couldn't make himself loosen his hold.

Apricot grabbed his arm. "We need to get to the school," she whispered, scooping up his jacket, and dragging him through the orchard as Angie tried to explain that the bus driver had let the girls off at the school, that the hall monitor had seen the girls enter the building, that they'd never made it to their classroom.

What she was really explaining, what she should have just come out and said, was that the girls were gone. That somehow they'd gotten off the school bus and disappeared.

"Did you call the sheriff?" he asked as he and Apricot ran out from between apple trees and into Rose's backyard.

"My secretary just did. They're sending someone out."

"I'll be there in five." He disconnected and sprinted across the backyard and around the house, Apricot right beside him.

His phone rang again as he reached the SUV. He ignored it, knowing it was Emma, Cade or Max, wanting to touch base, come up with a plan, discuss options.

He didn't want to talk, didn't think he could. There was a cold, hard knot in his throat, a thousand-pound weight on his chest.

"I'm driving. I don't think you're in any shape to." Apricot snatched the keys from his hand and jumped into the SUV. She had the engine on before he opened the passenger's door, was pulling out as he slammed it shut.

She sped backward out of the driveway, tires squealing as she swung onto the road, gunned the engine, and raced toward the school.

Chapter Seventeen

Truth be told, Apricot didn't think she was in any better shape to be driving than Simon was. Her hands shook as she turned off the dirt road and onto the main thoroughfare that ran through town. The elementary school was less than two miles away. She saw the building every time she drove into town. If she hurried, they could make it there in two minutes flat.

"Slow down, Apricot," Simon said so quietly the words were just a soft suggestion at the back of her brain.

"Apricot, slow down!" he said a little more firmly.

"What?"

"If you get us killed, how am I going to find my girls?"

"Sorry." She eased off the accelerator. "I wanted to get you there as quickly as possible."

"I appreciate it, but I prefer to arrive in one piece," he said, a wry edge to his voice.

"Maybe the girls will already be there. Maybe they were just in the bathroom or library and got overlooked the first time those places were checked."

That's what she was hoping, that the girls were somewhere that hadn't been checked yet, bickering with each other about silly silence games or discussing childbirth and fake boobs.

"It's not that big of a school. They'd have been found if they were there."

"How long have they been missing?"

"The bus dropped them off forty minutes ago. They made it into the school. No one knows what happened to them after that."

"They're okay. I'm sure of it," she said more to herself than to him. Thank God they weren't in LA. Thank God Apple Valley was a small town filled with people who knew each other. Wherever they were, the girls were among friends.

Unless someone in Apple Valley wasn't a friend.

Big cities didn't corner the market on criminals, pedophiles, or lunatics.

She swallowed down the thought as she turned into the parking lot at the elementary school. Two squad cars were already there, and she pulled up behind them.

Simon was out of the SUV before it came to a complete stop, running to the building before Apricot managed to get her shaking hands to cooperate and open the door. By the time she was out of the vehicle, he'd disappeared from sight.

She jogged into the school's lobby, her clothes sticking to her skin, her hair plastered to her head. A couple of kids eyed her suspiciously as she followed the signs to the office.

Not that she needed signs.

She could hear someone wailing, the sound like the wild cry of an injured cat.

She opened the office door, stepped into noise and chaos like the kind she'd lived with every day of her life for most of her childhood.

Simon was in one corner, Cade and Max flanking him on either side, all of them listening to a trim, gray-haired woman who was trying to make herself heard over Daisy's cries. Behind a long counter, two receptionists were speaking on two different phones, both of them doing everything they could to make themselves heard. A man sat in a chair near the counter, arms dangling between his legs, a look of utter dejection on his face. A woman sat beside him, a hand on his arm as she spoke into his ear. If she had to guess, Apricot would say that they were the school bus driver and counselor.

If she had to make another guess, she'd say that Daisy's caterwauling wasn't bringing anyone any closer to finding the girls. As a matter of fact, she was pretty sure it was doing the exact opposite—keeping people from organizing the search in the most efficient way possible.

Since no one else seemed willing to deal with the problem, she decided she'd better.

"Daisy?" she said, keeping her voice at a normal range. Raising it would only escalate an already escalated situation. She'd learned that as a kid, and she'd used the skill often in her business dealings.

"Daisy?" she tried again. "You need to calm down. Would you like some water or tea?"

"How can I calm down when this is all my fault?" She yelled loud enough for everyone in the world to hear.

"You're going to have to try," Apricot said reasonably. "Being hysterical won't help anyone."

"This is my punishment from God. He's smiting me for what I did!" Daisy blubbered on, her nose running, her eyes weeping. "I lied. Liiiiiied!" she wailed. "Because I didn't want you to have Simon. I didn't want you to take my family from me."

Everyone in the room stopped talking and looked their way.

Daisy didn't look like she noticed; she was too busy raising her head to the heavens and begging for forgiveness.

"Daisy." Apricot touched her arm. "I really don't think anyone cares about that right now."

"And, then," Daisy continued as if she hadn't heard. "I did even worse. I hired poor Eliza Jane to help me prove the lie as truth. I see her at the library every Monday during story time, her little boy dressed in hand-me downs. Her parents barely help her with raising that child, and I knew she could use the money. I called her while Simon was gone, asked her to come over. Then, I held out five hundred dollars, just waved it under her nose and told her she could have that and five hundred more if she hid my things somewhere only you and Jet had access to." She sobbed, every word a little louder than the last.

"Daisy," Apricot interrupted. "You can confess it all to the sheriff once the girls are home. Right now, you just need to calm down so that we can figure out what's going on."

"I turned a hardworking young woman into a criminal!" she shrieked. "All because I fell. Fell and broke my phone. I felt like an idiot admitting it, because you were always around looking perfect and beautiful, and I knew that if I didn't do something, you'd steal my family from me. And then I took those kittens you gave the girls, and I left them outside because I wanted the girls to forget about you. And now God has taken the girls from me because of it. They'll haunt me forever. Their tiny dead bodies will be floating above my bed—"

Apricot slapped her.

The sound reverberated through the room.

When it faded, there was silence. Not a breath. Not a rustle of fabric.

"You hit me," Daisy whispered, touching the red mark on her cheek.

"You were hysterical."

"But . . . you hit me."

"Because I don't have time to brew you a cup of calming tea, and I'm not in the mood to listen to you talk about the girls as if they're already gone."

"They are. They're dead. I know it," Daisy intoned, but her voice never rose above a whisper.

"The girls—" Apricot responded, meeting Simon's eyes. He looked stricken, heartsick. "Are not dead."

"If they are, it will be because of me," Daisy said woefully.

"This isn't about you," Simon cut in. "It's about finding my kids."

"I know. It's just—"

Simon raised a hand, cutting off the words. "I don't have time to deal with your mental health problems or your guilt. Now that you've mentioned those cats, I think I know what's going on. The girls were really upset this morning. I bet they decided to leave school to search for the kittens. If I can figure out which direction they went, it shouldn't be too hard to find them. And when I do . . ." He shook his head.

"When you do," Max finished for him, "you'll

probably hug them close and hold on tight for the rest of your life."

"Probably," Simon admitted. "I just hope they stuck together. Evie will be fine on her own, but Rori will get scared pretty quickly."

Thinking about Rori wandering around alone made Apricot's stomach ache.

"We won't assume anything, but the girls are close, and I can't imagine them splitting up. Emma has already put out a call for volunteers. We should have a few dozen people out searching soon. In the meantime," Cade said, "maybe we can narrow the search down. Any idea what direction the girls might head? Do you think they'll head home or go somewhere else to look?"

"Good question." Simon raked his hand through his hair, paced to a window that looked out into the parking lot. "If I had to guess, I'd say that they'd head back home. That would be the direction Rori would want to go. Evie might—"

"The Shaffer house," Daisy said, so quietly Apricot barely heard her.

"Excuse me?" she said.

"Your place or your aunt's or whatever you want to call it. I bet the girls headed there. They were talking about it this morning, saying that you might have a special tea to attract lost cats."

"They did, and if I know Evie, that's exactly what she's going after," Simon said, already opening the office door. "And knowing Evie, she's making sure that she and Rori stay out of sight until they achieve their goal. I'll head in that direction while you coordinate the search, Cade."

He didn't wait for a response. Apricot didn't either.

She followed him back out into the rain, nearly running to try to keep up with him.

"Do you actually think they're heading to Rose's place?" she panted. She really needed to start working out, because she could barely keep up with him and he was only walking quickly.

"I don't know, but it's our best bet. If they *are* headed there, they'll stay close to the road. I hope. Take the SUV back to your place. If I find them, I'll call your cell phone, and you can come pick us up."

"I have a better idea. I'll come with you. Two sets of eyes are better than one, and if we find them, we can call Hubert. He'll come pick us up."

"Fine by me, but you'd better keep up."

With that, he took off, jogging through the parking lot and out onto the road.

She kept up with him for a mile, his easy loping pace not too bad. They split the road, Simon to the left and Apricot to the right, both of them calling for the girls as they scanned the farmland that stretched to either side.

At first, Apricot thought they'd been mistaken, that the girls hadn't come this way. Not with the rain pouring down and the wind blowing cold spray in their faces. She reached the mile-and-a-half mark before her lungs began to burn and her legs started to shake.

Up ahead, Simon was making quick progress, his voice ringing through the morning as he shouted the girls' names. Right where Apricot was, things were looking a little more grim. She was breathing so hard she couldn't utter a sound.

She slowed to a fast walk, taking a couple of deep breaths and finally managing to shout, "Girls!"

A piece of paper fluttered across the ground, skittering out from behind a tall spruce and landing a few feet in front of her. Apricot reached for it, but the wind picked it up, tossing it into a field of thigh-high grass.

"Son of a monkey's uncle!" she panted, darting after it.

The wind gusted again.

"Oh no, you don't!" she shouted, diving at the fluttering page and snatching it before the wind could carry it away. She landed on her stomach, her face in a puddle of water, holding the paper away from the ground.

She got to her knees, looked at the page. It was hard to read, but she could see the name scrawled across the top right corner, big and bold as life—Evangeline Baylor.

The girls had been there! It couldn't have been long ago. Otherwise, the page would have been too wet to flutter and float.

"Evie!" she screamed, jumping to her feet and scanning the field. "Evangeline Rose Baylor! You'd better come out here!"

Nothing.

She tried again. "I know you're out here. Everyone is worried sick about you. Come on out, and we'll go home and I'll make you both a nice cup of tea!"

Still nothing.

She didn't have her cell phone with her, and she had to make a choice—try to catch up to Simon or search the field herself. Since she didn't want the girls to get any farther away, she chose the second option, calling their names over and over again as she headed farther into the field.

In the distance, she could see Dusty's house, the chimney shooting white smoke into the air.

If *she* were an eight-year-old who'd run away from school, was soaked and tired and probably a little cold, that's the direction she'd have headed.

Which, of course, meant that that was the direction *she* had to go. She tucked the paper under her shirt, knowing it wasn't going to do one bit of good, but trying to protect it anyway.

She was halfway across the field when Simon shouted her name.

She stopped, waiting as he sprinted to her side.

Water streamed down his face, and his shirt clung to his muscular chest and thighs. It was his eyes that drew her attention, though, the anxiety in them spearing straight into her heart.

"What happened? I turned around and you were gone," he said, a frown furrowing his brow. "I was worried we were going to need two search parties. One for the girls and one for you."

"No." She shook her head, lifted the wet hem of her shirt and peeled the paper from her abdomen. "I found something. It's Evie's."

He took the page, squinted at the soggy sheet.

"Last night's homework," he finally said. "Where did you find it?"

"Near the spruce over by the road. It wasn't soaked through when I found it, so I don't think it had been there very long."

"They're close then. Of course, the grass in this field is so long, they could be a foot away and we might not see them." He shouted their names, shook his head when they didn't answer. "They're probably hiding somewhere. Scared to death they're going to get in trouble. Were you heading toward Dusty's?"

"It's the only building around. If I were eight, soaked to the skin and worried that my father was going to kill me, I'd probably try to find a house or a barn to hide in."

"I'm not going to kill them. I'm just going to ground them for life," he muttered.

"I'm sure that is their second option for punishment, and I'm sure they're not all that excited about that either."

"Then they shouldn't have left the school," he ground out. "Natural consequences suck, and the natural consequences of this stunt are going to be painful."

He trudged across the field, shouting the girls' names.

She followed, doing the same, the rain slowing a little as they cleared the field, stepped out onto Dusty's gravel driveway, and knocked on his front door.

He didn't answer, so they searched the yard, the back porch, the old tree house that someone had built in a giant birch tree. Every minute seemed longer than the next, every second that the girls were missing draining a little life from Simon's face.

Apricot watched it happen, her heart growing heavier and heavier. There was no tea that could fix this, no tincture that could make it better.

She took his hand, squeezed gently.

"We're going to find them," she said.

"I hope to God you're right," he murmured, the

words filled with a thousand fears she knew he would never speak.

"We are, and when we do, I'm going to make them both a nice cup of ginger tea. They can drink it while you lecture them on the foolhardiness of their actions and Lilac force-feeds them those cow tongue sandwiches she always . . ." Her voice trailed off, a spot of color near Dusty's barn catching her attention.

She sprinted forward, adrenaline rushing through her as she lifted the tiny pink bow triumphantly. Simon took it from her hand, pressed his finger to his lips, and gestured for her to follow him into the barn. It was dim and quiet there, the musty scent of wet wood and dry hay filling the air. True to Dusty's nature, the place was clean as a whistle, every tool hung from a hook on the wall, every stall mucked and empty.

Something rustled in the loft above their heads, tiny bits of hay sprinkling down on Apricot's shoulder. Simon brushed it off, his hand lingering, his palm warm against her cold skin.

"I don't know what we're going to do, Apricot," he said loudly. "If the girls don't return home, I may very well die of a broken heart."

He winked, and she smiled, because all the fear had drained from his face, all the worry had disappeared. He was himself again—the man who always seemed to be in control, who always seemed to know what to say and do, who could put up with his crazy sister-in-law and Apricot's crazy family, and even Apricot, because he was just that kind of guy.

"If you do," she said solemnly, "I will try to revive you with true love's kiss."

The thing in the loft shifted again, more hay spilling down.

Simon grinned, and Apricot's heart just kind of soared, her joy-meter just kind of filling up and spilling over.

"Only a princess can offer that," he said dramatically. "Are you a princess? Have you been hiding the truth from me? Do you have a kingdom where I can rest from my weary search?"

"As a matter of fact, I am, I have, I do. My orchard is my kingdom. The apple blossoms are my crown," she replied and was sure she heard a little girl giggle.

"I love apple blossoms," he replied with just the right touch of awe. "Decorate my coffin with them, okay? Because a father can't live without his daughters, even if he has a princess to love."

"Don't die on me, Simon!" Apricot cried, surprising a laugh out of him.

He covered it with a fit of fake coughing.

"I have to," he rasped. "I can't go on without my girls."

He dropped to his knees, fell to his back, lay there with his eyes closed.

"No!" Apricot shouted. "He's gone. His broken heart did him in." She knelt beside him. "What shall I ever do?!"

"You could try true love's kiss," he whispered, and she laughed, leaning over to do what he'd suggested, the sound of little girls scrambling down the ladder filling her ears as her lips touched his.

God, he tasted good! Like fall rain and promises.

"Daddy!" Rori cried. "Daddy, I'm sorry. I didn't mean to break your heart."

She rushed in, throwing herself on Simon's supine body, sobbing uncontrollably.

Evie hung back, her dress torn, one of her shoes missing, a look of abject misery on her face. "If you're really dead, Daddy, then my heart is going to be all broken up," she said, a silent tear sliding down her damp face. "And I really think that I might die too."

"Then I guess," Simon said, levering up onto his elbows, "it is really good that I'm not dead."

Evie squealed and jumped forward, wrapping her arms around his neck, telling him over and over again how sorry she was.

Somehow he managed to get to his feet, the girls clinging to him like monkeys, their loud apologies filling the barn.

He set them down, met Apricot's eyes. "Thanks."

"I didn't do anything."

"You led me right to my girls."

"You would have found them without me."

He shrugged, tucking a strand of wet hair behind her ears. "I learned something new about you today, Princess Apricot."

"What's that?"

"You're quite the actress. I especially liked the kiss."

She blushed. *Blushed!*

"Really? I thought it could use a little practice."

That made him smile.

"You know what? I'm thinking you might be right. But at this moment, I've got two girls who look like they could use a little warming up. How about we take them to Rose's place and do a little celebrating?" he suggested, pulling Apricot to his side. It felt right to be there. It felt good. It felt as if all the years she'd spent trying to be someone different than Apricot Sunshine from Happy Dale had been the lie and *this* was the truth.

"What did you have in mind?" she asked.

"Ginger tea and cow tongue?" he suggested.

"That sounds perfect!" She laughed, taking his hand and leading Simon and the girls home.

Chapter Eighteen

The girls didn't much care for cow tongue, but they gagged it down. Simon figured they were hoping the lack of complaints would reduce their sentence. Wasn't going to happen. Grounded for a month plus community service washing windows at the sheriff's department. He'd allowed Cade to come up with the last part of the punishment. The girls' offense had been serious and the consequences could have been too.

Thank God they'd been found safe.

"Well, I'm impressed," Lilac said, taking the girls' empty plates and setting them in Rose's sink. "Not even one protest. You're lovely girls, you know that? And that cow tongue is going to make you even lovelier. Now, my Apricot? She absolutely refuses to eat the stuff. That's why she's—"

Apricot sighed. "Lilac, the girls really aren't interested."

"Yes, we are," they said in unison, their heads just peeking out from the piles of blankets that Lilac and Rose had wrapped them in. They looked tiny, their hair still damp, their cheeks pink from the heat that Hubert had turned on high.

"She'll tell you all about it another day," Rose cut in. "Now, how about a nice cup of hot chocolate for both of you? Made from the finest cocoa in the world. I think you'll enjoy it a lot more than that god-awful sandwich my sister made you." She set mugs in front of both of them.

"Can we, Daddy?" Rori asked.

"I suppose that you can, but once you're finished, we need to go home. You're going to spend the rest of the day writing apology notes to the people at school."

"But, Daddy, we can't go home," Evie said, shoving away the hot chocolate.

"You can," he responded. "And you will."

"But we haven't found the kittens."

"Trying to find those kittens got you into this mess, and it seems to me you would be wise to not say another word about them."

"But they're babies," Evie cried. "And they're all alone out in the rain."

"They're not alone," he corrected. "They're together, and for all we know, they're already back at the house."

"Maybe you can call Aunt Daisy and ask?" Evie suggested.

No way was he going to tell the girls that their aunt had voluntarily signed herself into the psych ward at the hospital. Like the girls washing windows at the sheriff's department, that had been Cade's idea. Daisy needed help, not punishment, he'd said when he'd arrived to drop off Simon's SUV and check on the girls. He'd also said that he'd talked to Eliza Jane, who would have been down at the station being booked on tampering with evidence if not for Jet's unwillingness to press charges. Jet had told Cade that he wanted to forgive and forget and let the young mother learn from her mistakes. Cade had offered Eliza Jane a job cleaning his office twice a week. That, as far as Simon was concerned, was the best possible outcome. The girl had been desperate, and she'd done something stupid.

Daisy on the other hand . . .

Simon was still angry, still blaming her for the whole damn mess with the girls.

He raked his hand over still-wet hair, trying to hold on to his patience. He'd already meted out the girls' punishment, and he had no desire to be cruel, but the kittens . . .

Yeah. The kittens.

Despite what he'd said, he didn't think they were at the house. They were probably long gone, eaten by coyotes or snagged by a particularly vicious raccoon.

"Look, girls, I'll put up some fliers tomorrow and we'll see if anyone around town has seen your kittens, but for now, let's just drop the subject."

"It's very difficult to do that when your heart is invested," Lilac chided, handing Simon what looked like another one of her cow tongue sandwiches. "The girls love those kittens like you love them. Just as you wandered around for an hour in the pouring rain to find your daughters, the girls will be obligated to search for the kittens until they are safely home. After all, it's the way of life to want to be reunited with those we love."

"Lilac," Apricot said, taking the sandwich from Simon and setting it on a plate. "Drop it."

"Why should I?"

"Because it's not your business."

"The world is my business." Lilac gestured broadly, her bracelets jingling, the girls wide-eyed at the table watching her. "The children in it are my legacy."

Apricot sighed. "For crying out loud, Lilac, there's no need for all the drama."

"You asked a question. I'm answering it."

"You didn't answer anything. You gave me a run-down of your life philosophy. Now, seriously, drop the subject of the kittens. It is very hard to face reality when people are filling your head with dreams."

"What's that supposed to mean?" Lilac set her hands on her hips and glared at her daughter.

"Just that you should let Simon handle this." Apricot glanced at the girls, and he knew she was thinking exactly what he was. The kittens were gone. For good. And letting the girls think otherwise wasn't going to do them any good.

"Humph," Lilac responded. "You only say that because you don't know how much power a dream can have. The girls, on the other hand, they're still young enough to believe in fairy tales and happily-ever-afters."

"Like true love's kiss," Evie said. "I wish a kiss could bring our kittens back."

"Who says it can't?" Lilac asked.

"Can it?" Rori eyed Lilac over the edge of her hot chocolate mug.

"Only you can say for sure, and how will you know if you don't give it a try? My granny used to say that if you blew kisses into the wind, your true love would return to you."

"Lilac," Apricot warned, but the girls were already up and running toward the back door, their blankets left in a puddle on the floor.

Simon didn't even try to stop them.

What would be the use?

Trying to stop any of the women in his life was like trying to stop a tide from flowing in.

"Sorry about that," Apricot murmured as the girls and Lilac disappeared outside, Rose hot on their heels. Apparently, blowing kisses to the wind was a family affair.

"Why?" he asked, tugging her in close because that felt like the most perfect thing he could do.

"Because my mother is crazy? Because you don't need any more crazy in your life? Because the girls don't need their heads filled with a bunch of dreams? Because—"

He kissed her, because the true-love kiss hadn't been enough, and because he didn't need apologies or less crazy, or even fewer dreams. He needed her.

She moaned, her hands sliding under his shirt, trailing heat along his abdomen.

"You're going to be so sorry, Simon," she murmured against his lips.

"Because?" He nibbled his way along her jaw, his lips tracing a path across smooth, silky flesh.

"Do you even need to ask?" She sighed. "You just got rid of one crazy relative, and now you're taking on a dozen more."

"A dozen?"

The back door flew open and the girls raced in, followed by Rose.

"We did it, Daddy! We blew kisses to the wind! Now our kittens are going to come home to us, because Lilac says they're our true loves!"

"Told you," Apricot said, but she didn't step out of his arms.

"Told him what?" Lilac demanded as she reentered the kitchen, her gaze dropping to Apricot's hand, which was still, somehow, beneath Simon's shirt.

"That you," Apricot said, her hand slipping away, "are certifiable."

"Because I encourage children to dream?"

"Because you—"

The doorbell rang, cutting off what Simon figured was going to be a very long battle.

"Want me to get it?" he asked.

Apricot shook her head. "I will."

She flew out of the room and was back a minute later, a large picnic basket in her hands.

She looked . . . shell-shocked, alarmed, maybe a little scared.

"Everything okay?" he asked, taking the basket and setting it on the table.

"Dusty is here," she murmured as the gnarly old farmer walked into the room. "He found something in his barn."

"And if I find it in there again"—Dusty glanced at Rose, swallowed hard—"well, I guess I'll just have to come for another visit."

"What is it?" Simon asked, but he had a feeling he knew. Had a feeling, but told himself there was no way he could be right.

"Look for yourself," Apricot responded. "You won't believe me if I tell you."

He lifted the lid and something gray jumped out.

"Handsome!" the girls cried, giggling as the ugly kitten sped around the room, a big white feather in his mouth. They were so busy watching him, they didn't see two little black heads peering out of the basket.

Simon did.

He met Apricot's eyes.

She shrugged.

One of the kittens mewed pitifully, and the girls nearly fell all over themselves, grabbing the basket and taking their lost kittens out.

Darn it all to Grandma Sapphire's plantation and back! Apricot thought as she listened to the girls' excited squeals.

She was glad the kittens had been returned.

She was even happy that Handsome was clawing his way up her leg.

She was *not* happy that the basket of kittens had been delivered right after Lilac's silly ritual.

Handsome settled on her shoulder, dropping the feather as he perched there like an overgrown parakeet.

It floated to the table, as white and clean as it had been before the cat had dragged it out into the rain.

"It worked," Evie cried. "Daddy, it worked! Our kisses brought the kittens back!"

"Just as I said they would," Lilac proclaimed, smirking at Apricot.

"This has nothing to do with . . ."

Apricot was going to say it had nothing to do with kisses blown in the wind.

She *wanted* to say it.

But the girls were watching, their eyes big, their kittens clutched close to their chests.

She didn't have the heart to do it.

"Anything," she continued lamely.

"You just keep telling yourself that, dear," Lilac said, sweeping across the room, the floating edges of her muumuu catching Handsome's attention. The kitten jumped down and followed her to the food dish she was filling with kibble.

"There you are, my handsome boy," she crooned. "Girls, bring your babies here and let them eat. Dusty, how about you have a seat at the table? I'll make you a nice cow tongue sandwich. Hubert is out hunting mushrooms. If he finds some good ones, we'll send you home with a nice pot of fungus stew!"

"Sounds great!" Dusty took a seat, his eyes glued to Rose.

And Apricot had a sudden epiphany, a thought so terrifying that she wasn't sure what to do with it.

Kittens? Feathers? Noise? Chaos?

Good golly!

It was Happy Dale all over again.

"You look terrified," Simon whispered in her ear.

"I am," she muttered.

"I don't suppose you want to tell me why?" His hands settled on her waist, and he maneuvered her past the kittens and the girls, past her mother, past Rose and her besotted neighbor.

He walked her out onto the back stoop, and she collapsed on the top step because her legs just wouldn't hold her up.

Simon sat beside her, not saying a word.

The rain had stopped, the sun peeked out from behind the clouds, and the orchard glowed golden and beautiful. She could still hear the girls and Lilac, still hear Dusty's rumbling baritone and Rose's quiet laughter. A dozen yards out, Hubert picked his way along the edge of the yard, shoulders hunched as he looked for mushrooms. He glanced their way, raising a hand in a silent salute before he went back to his task.

Home, the world seemed to whisper.

Home, her heart seemed to respond.

She met Simon's eyes, and he smiled.

"Have you figured it out yet?" he asked.

She nodded, her heart too full, her throat too tight to speak.

"I thought so," he murmured. "Because you don't look scared anymore. You look like . . ." He cocked his head to the side, studying her intently.

"Like what?" she asked, her voice raspy and raw, because she'd thought she was running away from something, but really, she'd been running to it.

"Like you blew kisses to the wind and brought your true love home," he said.

"You know what?" she responded, taking his hand and holding it tightly. "I think that's exactly what I did."

Please turn the page for an exciting sneak peek of Shirlee McCoy's

SWEET HAVEN,

coming in March 2016!

The dress wouldn't zip.

Seeing as how the wedding was ten days away, that was going to be a problem. Adeline Lamont expelled all the air from her lungs and tried again. The zipper inched up her side, every slow, excruciating millimeter reminding her that she had a bigger problem than a butt-ugly, too-small, tangerine-colored bridesmaid's dress.

"Addie!" May Reynolds called from the other side of the bathroom door. "How's it going in there?"

"Peachy," Adeline hissed, the zipper finally finding its way home. She glanced in the mirror above the sink. Orange. Lots of it. Skin too. Shoulders. Arms. Chest. All of it pasty and white from too many days in Chocolate Haven's kitchen.

"Addie!" May knocked frantically. Probably with both her wrinkled fists. "Please tell me it fits! I don't have time to alter it. I barely had time to make it!"

"I wish you hadn't," Addie responded.

"What's that, dear?" May yelled, her voice edged

with panic. The poor woman would have heart failure if Addie didn't hurry herself up.

She glanced in the mirror one last time. Still hideous.

There was nothing she could do about that, so she yanked open the bathroom door and stepped into the narrow hall that led from the front of the shop to the kitchen.

It smelled like chocolate. Vanilla. Maybe a hint of the blood, sweat, and tears she'd been pouring into the place since Granddad had broken his hip and femur. She gagged, but managed to keep down the sixteen pounds of fudge she'd consumed while taste-testing batch after batch of Lamont family fudge.

God! If she ever ate another piece of fudge again, it would be way, *way* too soon!

May stood a few feet away, hands clasped together, her blue-white hair just a little wild. "Dear God in heaven," she breathed, her gaze dropping to Addie's chest. "You have breasts!"

Addie would have laughed if the dress hadn't squeezed all the air from her lungs.

"Most women do," she managed to say, her head swimming from lack of oxygen or, maybe, too much sugar and too little real food. When was the last time she'd eaten a meal? Two days ago? Three?

"Not Alice," May huffed. "Your grandmother was reed-slim. She wore clothes beautifully. Didn't matter what, she looked good in it."

"I am not my grandmother," Addie pointed out. *And even she wouldn't look good in this dress,* she nearly added.

"You're standing in for her at my wedding, dear,"

May responded, tugging at the bodice of the dress, trying desperately to get it to cover a little more flesh.

Wasn't going to happen, but Adeline let her try. Just like she'd let her insist that Addie be maid of honor at her wedding since Alice had passed away five years before the big day.

Sure Adeline would be the only under-thirty member of the wedding party, but she loved May. She'd loved Alice.

For them, she'd stand at the front of Benevolence Baptist Church wearing a skin-tight tangerine dress. She just hoped to God Randal Custard didn't decide to do a human interest story on the event. Sure it was cool that May had found true love at seventy-six years old. Sure it was wonderful that she was finally getting married after so many decades of longing for marital bliss.

What would *not* be cool or wonderful would be a picture of Addie plastered across the front page of *Benevolence Times*, her fudge-stuffed body encased in tangerine satin! Since she'd turned down Randal's dinner invitations seven times in the past month, it might just happen.

"May," she said, the thought of Randal and his camera and that picture souring her mood more than the last mediocre-tasting batch of family fudge had. "It's not going to cover any more than it does."

"But, I measured you," May responded, her voice wobbling. "And, I never measure wrong."

"I may have gained a pound or two since I took over the shop for Granddad." Or ten, but who was counting? "I'll lose it before the wedding."

"Promise?" May asked, gnawing on her lower lip as if that might solve the problem.

"Of course," Adeline assured her.

What else could she do?

"All right. I guess we'll just make it work," May said, probably channeling someone she'd seen on some sewing or fashion show. She'd been a home economics teacher at Benevolence High for nearly thirty years, had owned a fabric shop right next to Chocolate Haven up until a month ago. For as long as Adeline could remember, May had been obsessed with fashion.

Too bad that obsession had never translated into a good sense of style.

Unique was more the word for it.

Or atrocious, horrible, dated.

Adeline could think of a dozen other words, but it was late, she was tired, and the kitchen needed a thorough scrubbing before she left for the day.

"Of course we'll make it work," she responded, cupping May's elbow and urging her toward the front of the shop. "The wedding is going to be beautiful. Every last detail of it."

"How could it not be?" May raised her chin a half inch. "I've planned every last detail. Every flower, every bow, every song."

Every word that Jim and I shall speak during our vows. Every strain of music that shall play during the reception. Adeline added, mentally repeating the spiel she'd heard dozens and dozens of times.

Scrooge, her better-self whispered.

She was. She could admit that.

But . . . doggone it! She was an accountant. Not a chocolatier. Not a shopkeeper. Not a master creator of the coveted Lamont fudge. After nearly three weeks of trying and failing to be those things, she was getting grumpy.

The tangerine dress wasn't helping things.

Poor May wasn't either.

"I know you have," she soothed as she bypassed the glass display cases that had been in the shop since the doors opened in 1911.

"I can't have anything go wrong," May moaned, pressing a pretty pink handkerchief to the corner of her eye. "Not one thing." She reached out, tugged at the tangerine ruffle.

The dress still didn't budge.

"I'll jog every night from now until the wedding," Adeline assured her, reaching past her to open the shop door.

"You may need to run," May murmured. "Or sprint. That might work."

"Sure. Sprint. Sounds good." Adeline wasn't even sure she could manage a jog. She'd try, though. Because there was no way on God's green earth she was standing in front of five hundred of May and Jim's closest friends looking like an overstuffed orange sausage!

"Okay. Good." May offered a wane smile. "Now, I really have to get going. Doris Linder is creating a special updo for me and the wedding party. I'm going to have her do a trial style on me tonight."

"*Doris*?" Addie hoped she'd heard wrong. Doris had been doing hair in Benevolence, Washington, for longer than Addie had been alive. Maybe longer than *May* had been alive.

"Who else would I have chosen?" She patted her hair. "She does a wonderful beehive."

"Your hair is too short for a beehive."

"Have you never heard of extensions?" May stepped outside, cold February wind ruffling her short locks.

"I have."

"The other ladies and I will have them. Your hair is plenty long enough."

Thank God for that, Addie wanted to say.

She kept her scrooge-mouth shut.

May hiked her purse a little higher onto her shoulder and picked her way across the sidewalk that separated the shop from the street. She'd parked at the curb, her gold Cadillac gleaming beneath the streetlight.

"I'll call you tomorrow," she called as she climbed into the car. "To see how the weight loss is going."

"You do that," Addie said as she let the door swing closed, locked it and flicked off the light.

There.

Now maybe she'd be left alone. To get out of the dress. To clean the kitchen. To close out the register so that she could finally go home.

Poor Tiny.

He was probably miserable penned up in Nehemiah Shoemaker's back room. It had been sweet of her neighbor to offer to take care of the puppy while Addie helped her grandfather, but Nehemiah was nearly ninety and Tiny was too big for him to handle. The two of them spent most of their time in Nehemiah's family room, watching reruns of *Hogan's Heroes* and *I Love Lucy*. Nehemiah seemed to enjoy Tiny's company, but the poor puppy needed some time to play outside. If she'd known that Granddad was going to break his hip and femur . . .

But she hadn't, so she'd adopted a puppy because she'd been just a little lonely in her 1920s bungalow.

"It will be okay," she told herself. "Just make a list. Go through it one item at a time until you finish."

Get out of the dress.

Clean the kitchen.

Close out the register.

Retrieve Tiny.

Go for a jog.

She listed each item as she walked back into the hall, tugging halfheartedly at the zipper.

Then tugging a little more forcefully.

And a little more.

It didn't budge. She scowled, sucking in her gut and yanking the zipper with all her might.

Snap!

Something gave. She yanked the dress around so the zipper was in the front, eyeing the damage. The top part of the zipper held fast, but the middle section had opened to reveal an inch of pasty white skin.

Dear God in heaven, she'd busted the thing!

And now, she was stuck. An overstuffed sausage in synthetic orange casing. She'd have to cut herself out and replace the zipper.

She grabbed her faded blue jeans and soft gray T-shirt from the bathroom and walked into the kitchen. Several batches of discarded fudge sat on the counter. The last and final batch lay in the sink, the scissors she'd used to try and hack it from the pan discarded with it.

She didn't dare get within a foot of the mess. If

she got chocolate on the dress, May would never forgive her.

She bypassed the sink and walked out the back door. The stairs to Granddad's apartment were there, pressed up against the side of the brick building. An empty parking lot lay in front of her, separating the row of brownstones from a public green. Addie and her sisters had spent hours playing there when they were kids.

That had been before everything else.

Before Dad died.

Before Willow had gone quiet and secretive.

Before Brenna had decided Benevolence was the worst place in the world to grow up.

Before their family that had once been close and loving and wonderful had turned into four people going four separate ways.

She jogged up the stairs, metal clanging under her feet. She fished the spare key out from under the potted plant on the landing, had barely touched the knob when the door creaked open.

Surprised, she peered into the apartment, eyeing the shadowy furniture, the oversized TV they'd bought Granddad for Christmas. That would probably be the first thing a thief would go for. Not that there were many thieves in Benevolence.

She stepped into the silent apartment. Nothing had been moved. Not that she could see. She flicked on the light. Dust coated the floor and layered the coffee table. From her position, she could see into the galley kitchen and down the narrow hall that led to two bedrooms and tiny office.

"There's no one here," she said aloud.

A door slammed, the sound so jarring, she jumped

back, knocked into the doorjamb, her heart in her throat.

Someone *was* in the apartment.

She screamed—probably loud enough to wake the dead—and took off running.

Sinclair Jefferson had seen a lot of things in his thirty-four years of living, but he'd never seen anything quite like the woman who was barreling toward him. Body encased in a skin-tight orange *thing* that could have been a dress or a costume, she sprinted down exterior metal steps as if all the demons of hell were chasing her.

If she saw him, she didn't let on.

As a matter of fact, if she kept coming at the pace she was, she'd crash into him. He stepped to the side, pulling his real estate agent Janelle Lamont with him.

"Watch it," he said.

"How can I not? It's like a train wreck. I can't look away," she murmured, her attention focused on the orange-encased lunatic who skidded to a stop in front of them.

"Mom!" the lunatic yelled. "There's someone in Granddad's apartment."

Mom?

This had to be one of the Lamont sisters, then.

Not Willow. He'd gone to school with her. She'd been as polished as a brand-new penny, every bit of her perfect. Hair. Makeup. Clothes.

This Lamont wasn't polished or perfect.

As a matter of fact, it looked like she'd split the zipper of the ugly outfit she was wearing. He caught a glimpse of taut pale skin as she crossed her arms over her stomach and hid the gap in the fabric.

"What are you talking about, Adeline?" Janelle sighed.

Adeline.

The middle sister.

He had a few vague memories of a quirky-looking kid with wild red hair, but none of them quite matched the woman in front of him. Wide almond-shaped eyes, a curvy compact body, long braid of hair falling over her shoulder, she was almost pretty and almost not. Interesting was probably the word he was looking for.

"What I'm talking about," Adeline responded, enunciating every word, "is someone being in Grand-dad's apartment. I walked into the living room and heard a door slam."

"A vacuum effect from you opening the front door. There's no one in there." Janelle's gaze slid to Sinclair and she offered an apologetic smile. "This is a very safe town, Sinclair. Just like it was when you were a child."

"I'm sure it is," he responded, because, as far as he could tell, nothing much had changed in Benevolence since he'd left sixteen years ago. The streets were still clean, the houses and properties neat and tidy. Except for his brother's property. The one they'd both inherited from their grandfather. *It* was still a mess—old cars and trucks rotting on acres of riverfront property, weathered farmhouse filled to the brim with decades of junk.

Sinclair had come to town to take care of that. To turn the place into a home that his sister-in-law would be proud of. Gavin was supposed to be helping.

Maybe if he could stop whining about missing his wife long enough, he'd be able to.

"It's why so many people prefer Benevolence to the big city," Janelle said with a beatific smile. "Come on. Let's see if Byron's place will work for you. If not, I've got another in mind. On the opposite side of town as your brother's place, but it's quiet. Just like you want."

She started up the exterior staircase, and he followed, metal clanking under his feet. He wasn't all that concerned about the interior of the apartment. As long as it was cleaner than the last one they'd seen, quieter than the third and didn't smell like wet dog and cigarette smoke like the first, he'd take it. He had too much work to do to waste time looking for an apartment. Unfortunately, the closest hotel was thirty miles away. He could have continued staying with his brother Gavin, but Gavin had spent the last five days whining and moaning about the fact that his pregnant wife had walked out of their single-wide trailer and gone to live with her family.

Seeing as how the single-wide trailer was stuffed to the gills with stuff, Sinclair couldn't blame Lauren for walking out. He'd have done the same. He *was* doing the same. No way did he plan to spend another night in that hellhole. He'd sleep in his truck first.

"Here we are," Janelle called cheerfully as she stepped over what looked like jeans and a T-shirt and walked into the apartment. "Built in 1887 for railroad magnate Lincoln Bernard. His family lived here for nearly twenty years before they built that beautiful home on River Bluff. Grandview Manor?"

He nodded because he knew the place and because he thought that Janelle expected a response.

"My senior prom was there," he offered, stepping over the clothes and walking into the apartment behind her.

"My daughter Willow's, too. You graduated together," she reminded him. As if he could have forgotten. There'd been thirty-five kids in his graduating class. He'd known every one of them by name. They'd known him too.

That was the way things had been in Benevolence. Unless he missed his guess, it was the way things still were.

"I really don't think we should be in here," Adeline interrupted from the doorway.

"Of course we should," Janelle responded, flicking on a light in a small galley kitchen and motioning to the dinette set that sat in an alcove created by a window dormer. "What do you think, Sinclair? Perfect for a bachelor, yes?"

"Sure." He moved past the kitchen, peered down a dark hall. There was a window at the far end, moonlight filtering in through the glass and speckling the floor with gold.

"I'm telling you, someone is in here." Adeline pressed in beside him, the jeans and T-shirt Sinclair had stepped over clutched to her chest. "He's probably waiting in one of the rooms, hoping for a chance to attack."

"You've been watching too many horror movies, Adeline," Janelle said with a forced smile.

"I hate horror movies," Adeline replied.

"I hate standing around when I could be getting something done," Sinclair murmured, running his hand along the wall until he found a light switch. He

flicked it on. Nothing. Not a footprint on the dusty
floor. Two doors flanked each wall and a small cush-
ioned bench sat under the window.

He opened the closest door, peered into a tiny
office. No one there, but the room was clean and
didn't smell like dog.

His opinion of the place was definitely going up.

He opened the next door and the next. A bathroom. A nice-sized bedroom. No one in either. The
last door opened into the largest room. The master
bedroom, he'd guess, the furniture heavy nineteenth
century. There were two doors on the far wall. One
opened into a small closet filled with suits, dress shirts
and polished shoes. The other door was locked. He
turned the knob twice. Just to be sure.

"That goes into the building next door," Janelle
said as she swiped her hand over the antique dresser
and frowned at the layer of dust on her palm. "May
Reynolds had a fabric store there up until a month
ago. I'm sure you remember that."

Maybe. He hadn't spent much time in town when
he was a kid. He'd been too busy trying to keep the
farmhouse from falling down around his ears.

"Is it locked on the other side?" Not that it mattered. He'd done two tours in Iraq and one in
Afghanistan. He'd slept in dugouts and under the
stars. This place, locked door or not, was way safer
than those had been.

"Of course. Byron made sure of that when he
moved in. If I remember correctly, he installed a new
metal door. We can go over and take a look at it if you
want. The property is for sale, and I'm the Realtor."

"*I'd* like to take a look. If it's not, maybe that's the

door I heard slamming," Adeline said, reaching past him to turn the door handle. She smelled like chocolate and berries, and something that reminded him of home.

Or what he'd always imagined home should be like.

Home growing up had been a house filled with junk, a grandfather who drank himself into a stupor every night and cold soup served in chipped white mugs. Home now was his high-rise apartment overlooking Puget Sound. Clean lines. Modern. Dinner out most nights because he didn't like to cook.

"Adeline, really," Janelle sighed. "Let it go. No one is in the apartment. No one *was* in the apartment. The door on this side and the other both need keys. Byron and May are the only people who have them."

"I know that, and I also know what I heard." Adeline's hands settled on her hips, the clothes she'd picked up hanging limply, the gap in her dress revealing that sliver of creamy flesh again. His gaze dropped to the spot. How could it not? The woman had curves. Nice ones. And the kind of smooth, silky skin that begged to be touched.

"For God's sake, Adeline! Put your shirt on," Janelle snapped. That got Adeline moving.

She pulled the clothes back over her stomach, her entire face the color of overripe tomatoes.

She had freckles.

He hadn't noticed that before.

And eyes that might have been violet.

She left the room too quickly for him to see.

"I'm sorry about that, Sinclair. Adeline has always been very imaginative." Janelle ran a hand over her perfectly styled, perfectly highlighted hair. She had to be in her fifties. She looked a couple of decades younger.

He knew how much time and money it took to achieve that.

Kendra had been thirty and hell-bent on looking twenty-one. He'd put up with her obsession because she'd been smart and driven. They'd been a good match. Until they weren't.

Then they'd both walked away without a second glance.

Just the way he wanted it.

No months of back and forth sparring. No breaking up and getting back together. None of the overly emotional stuff Gavin was going through with his wife. Just—*this isn't working out anymore. It's time to move on.*

"How do you know she was imagining things?"

Janelle raised a razor-thin brow. "Sinclair, this is Benevolence, Washington. The crime rate is so low we barely need a sheriff's department."

That wasn't quite true, and they both knew it. There'd been a murder when Sinclair was a kid. Quite a few petty crimes. Vandalism. Drug use. Domestic violence. Those things existed in every town. Even ones that seemed as perfect as Benevolence.

He didn't bother correcting her. He wanted to sign the lease and get on with things. He had an overnight bag in his truck, a six-pack of Pepsi and enough paperwork to catch up on to keep him busy until dawn. "I'm not concerned about the crime rate. As long as I can have the place for the next couple of weeks, we're good."

"The lease is for a month," she reminded him as if they hadn't spent the better part of the afternoon hashing out the terms of his rental agreement. He'd pay for a full month. He had no intention of being there that long.

"With the option of extending for a second month," she continued. "You never know. You might decide Benevolence is the place for you. You won't believe how many people come here for a visit and end up staying."

He'd believe it.

The place had plenty of small-town charm, lots of interesting architecture and enough appeal to attract people from all over the country.

What it didn't have was enough appeal to keep him there for any longer than necessary. He'd seen the beauty of Benevolence when he was a kid. He'd seen the ugliness too. The gossip, the whispers. The pointed fingers. His family had always been on the wrong side of those fingers. He and his brother had been the topic of one too many whispered conversations, the focus of too many sad shakes of the head.

They'd grown up in the shadow of the tragedy that had taken their parents. Sinclair had no intention of living there again.

He followed Janelle into the living room.

Adeline was there, a gray T-shirt pulled over the dress, her long braid tucked into its collar.

She had freckles.

A lot of them.

And eyes that were such a deep blue they looked purple.

"I'm going to get the rental agreement. Why don't

you come with me, Adeline?" Janelle hooked her arm through her daughter's and tried to tug her to the door, but Adeline seemed as determined to stay as Janelle was to make her leave.

She pulled away, dropped down onto the plaid sofa. "I'll just look around. Make sure there's nothing here that Granddad might need."

"I already packed up most of Byron's things." Janelle frowned, glancing at her watch impatiently.

"All his old suits are hanging in the closet. His church clothes. Did you clean out the guest room? I bet there are a couple boxes' worth of stuff in there."

"I'm not worried about the clothes or the stuff," Sinclair cut in. He'd been in town nearly a week and hadn't completely unpacked his suitcase. That would feel too much like a long-term commitment. "I just need a place to sleep."

"You won't like it here, then. I'm running the chocolate shop for my grandfather while he recovers, and I work pretty late. I also make a lot of noise," Adeline said, pulling her braid out from the collar of her shirt and flicking it over her shoulder.

"Adeline!" Janelle nearly shouted. "Please, will you just leave well enough alone! Byron agreed that a short-term rental while he was recuperating was a good idea."

"He's on morphine, Mom. He'd agree to anything."

"For God sake! The man knows his own mind. No matter how much morphine he's been given. I'm getting the lease!" Janelle stalked from the apartment, her high-heeled boots clicking against the metal stairs.

"That went well," Adeline said, standing and stretching, the shiny orange fabric shimmying up her thighs.

"What? Pissing your mother off?" he responded, and she met his eyes, offered a smile that had him smiling in return.

He didn't know why.

There wasn't all that much to smile about.

He was in a hometown he hated, working to restore a house that should have been condemned years ago. He'd spent five days listening to his brother complaining while *he* hauled debris from the home they'd once shared with their grandfather.

"I do that without any effort at all," she replied. "What I was really trying to do was get her out of here so I could find some scissors and cut myself out of this," She plucked at the dress. "Thing."

"You don't want her to know you're stuck in it?" he asked, following her as she ran down the hall and into the office.

"I don't want her to know I'm taking scissors to it. If she finds out, she'll tell May. If she tells May, May could very well die of heart failure before the wedding."

"May?"

"The bride. She's seventy-six. Seventy-two if you ask her fiancé." She opened a drawer in a rolltop desk that sat against the wall, rifled through it and pulled out a pair of scissors. "Not that that will matter if she dies before her big day."

She hurried from the room, the scent of chocolate and berries filling the air as she moved.

And he realized he was smiling again.

He didn't want to be amused by her.

He didn't want to be amused by anything in Benevolence.

He'd spent most of his childhood planning his escape.

He'd wanted to put it all behind him—every moment of living in *that* house on *that* property in a town where perfection was the chosen sport and people competed for the honor of having the best garden, the best Christmas decorations, the most well-kept yard.

The only thing his family had ever competed for was the title of laziest homeowner.

They'd won hands-down every day of every year for as long as there'd been Jeffersons in Benevolence. That had been nearly as long as the town had been a town.

Not that that mattered to Sinclair. Not the way it had when he'd been the kid that teachers pitied, the one who received hand-me-down clothes from well-meaning church ladies every Christmas.

They hadn't understood the truth.

He hadn't wanted slightly used mittens, boots, coats. Hadn't really needed faded jeans and cotton T-shirts. Grandpa was pretty adept at picking those things out of trash cans and Dumpsters.

What he'd wanted, what he'd longed for, what he'd needed about as desperately as he'd needed air to breathe and water to drink, was a home. The kind that friends could visit. The kind that smelled like good food and furniture polish. The kind his friends lived in.

No church lady could have brought him that.

So, he hadn't really wanted anything at all.

Except to escape. Which he had. Thank you Uncle Sam and the good old Marine Corps! Seven years. Three tours. A bum knee and an honorable discharge, and he'd taken the money he'd saved, put it into restoring a row of painted ladies in San Francisco. He'd turned those around for a profit and continued on, building the kind of business his grandfather had always talked about having—using reclaimed materials from condemned buildings to bring at-risk properties back from the brink.

That was the difference between Sinclair and most of the men in his family. He didn't just dream. He did.

Maybe he could teach Gavin to do the same before he left Benevolence.

He doubted it, but he'd give it as good a try as he'd given his relationship with Kendra. He'd put his all in it. If it didn't work out, he'd walk away with a clear conscience and no regrets, go back to his life and his business and his clean, quiet apartment.

The empty one.

Which hadn't ever bothered him before.

The last couple of days, he'd been thinking about all those old childhood dreams. The ones where he'd come home and smell cookies in the oven- or fresh-baked bread. Where there was someone waiting for him with a smile and a "how was your day?"

Maybe it was coming back to Benevolence that had made him think about those youthful fantasies. Probably it was.

All the more reason to get out of Dodge as soon as humanly possible.

"Sinclair?!" Janelle called, her high heels tapping on the wood floor. "I've got the agreement."

Good. He was ready to sign it.

He might have to be in a town he hated, but he didn't have to spend his nights in a cluttered and dirty single-wide trailer listening to his brother complain.

That was the beauty of working hard.

It paid off. Gave a man the ability to do what he wanted when he wanted. Gave him the freedom to make decisions about where he wanted to be and when.

It couldn't warm his bed at night, couldn't fill a house with warmth and make it a home, but Sinclair would be happy for what he had.

That was part of his life plan. Contentment. Something his father hadn't had, his grandfather had never found, his brother longed for.

Elusive as mist on the water.

As difficult to find as water in the desert.

After Sinclair had nearly been blown to bits in Iraq, he'd realized that was all he really wanted. To be content with his life. He was, and when he wasn't, he found a way to make himself be.

Right now, that way was this apartment over a chocolate shop. Not one of the posh hotel suites he was used to staying in when clients flew him in to oversee restoration projects, but it was quiet, clean and close enough to the homestead to make for an easy commute.

"Good enough," he muttered as he walked out into the hall and went to sign the rental agreement.

Romantic Suspense from
Lisa Jackson

Available Wherever Books Are Sold!
Visit our website at **www.kensingtonbooks.com**

Books by Bestselling Author
Fern Michaels

___The Jury	0-8217-7878-1	$6.99US/$9.99CAN
___Sweet Revenge	0-8217-7879-X	$6.99US/$9.99CAN
___Lethal Justice	0-8217-7880-3	$6.99US/$9.99CAN
___Free Fall	0-8217-7881-1	$6.99US/$9.99CAN
___Fool Me Once	0-8217-8071-9	$7.99US/$10.99CAN
___Vegas Rich	0-8217-8112-X	$7.99US/$10.99CAN
___Hide and Seek	1-4201-0184-6	$6.99US/$9.99CAN
___Hokus Pokus	1-4201-0185-4	$6.99US/$9.99CAN
___Fast Track	1-4201-0186-2	$6.99US/$9.99CAN
___Collateral Damage	1-4201-0187-0	$6.99US/$9.99CAN
___Final Justice	1-4201-0188-9	$6.99US/$9.99CAN
___Up Close and Personal	0-8217-7956-7	$7.99US/$9.99CAN
___Under the Radar	1-4201-0683-X	$6.99US/$9.99CAN
___Razor Sharp	1-4201-0684-8	$7.99US/$10.99CAN
___Yesterday	1-4201-1494-8	$5.99US/$6.99CAN
___Vanishing Act	1-4201-0685-6	$7.99US/$10.99CAN
___Sara's Song	1-4201-1493-X	$5.99US/$6.99CAN
___Deadly Deals	1-4201-0686-4	$7.99US/$10.99CAN
___Game Over	1-4201-0687-2	$7.99US/$10.99CAN
___Sins of Omission	1-4201-1153-1	$7.99US/$10.99CAN
___Sins of the Flesh	1-4201-1154-X	$7.99US/$10.99CAN
___Cross Roads	1-4201-1192-2	$7.99US/$10.99CAN

Available Wherever Books Are Sold!
Check out our website at **www.kensingtonbooks.com**